DRAGONHEAD KEEP

A NOVEL

TITANHEART NOVELS BY ROSS D JENKINS

Dragonhead Keep

The Bear and the Thistle (Available January 2011)

Champion of the Faerie (Available Summer 2011)

For updated information regarding titles, availability and release dates, please visit www.titanheart.ca

Dragonhead Keep

A Titanheart Tale

By Ross D Jenkins

Titanheart Publications

This is a work of fiction. All the characters and events portrayed in this novel are purely fictitious.

DRAGONHEAD KEEP

By Ross D Jenkins

Published by Titanheart Publications (www.titanheart.ca)

ISBN: 978-0-9866877-0-9

Printed by Createspace.com

Cover Art by Brazen Edwards-Hager. For more information please visit www.brazendesignstudio.ca

To Joel and Lisa,

for listening

PREFACE

No matter how many times I hear it, I always find it hard to believe that my parents and their friends were ordinary people. To me, they will always be my heroes. I grew up hearing their stories and seeing them as all-knowing and all-powerful. It does not matter that I am an old man now, or that my own children and grandchildren view me as I viewed my own parents. In my mind's eye they continue to be the icons I strive to emulate and whose memories I seek to live up to.

It does not help that my parents and their Companions were the legendary Knights of Anduilon. Their actions reforged the High Kingdom and restored peace to the land. My 'uncle' was the High Wizard, my seneschal once slew an army, my 'aunt' was the first mayor of New Daranduil, and these are just the friends of my family. My parent's place in history is even more widely known.

Now that I am older and hear the legends that surround my own fame, I understand my parents more. I know why they would chuckle when they heard poems composed for them and grimace when the praise became especially purple. 'Real' history is both too exciting and too boring to be poetic. People do not want to hear that their heroes passed gas, experienced self-doubt or complained about mundane things such as over-salted stew.

Now that I have passed on the governance of the throne to my children (and I wish them well of it), I find myself comparing the 'official' histories of the events preceding the Crown Wars to the stories told to me by my mother and father and, of course, their friends. I am blessed, I see now, not only by my birthright and the crownmark I proudly bear, but by my unique position to have heard so much of how history really happened.

Will anyone read this? Undoubtedly. I am a High King of Anduilon. My place in history is fixed, and these works will no doubt be lauded about long after I have joined my ancestors in Zulanan. As people celebrate the pool where Illyria once bathed, or the tankard that my father once drank from, these writings will be treasured simply because a great figure of history wrote them.

But will they understand them? Will anyone take heed of my message and see the meaning within the stories I now commit to parchment? Of that I am less sure. It has been my experience that, from their heroes especially, people hear only what they wish to. They already know the messages that they want their idols to give them and will find them in their words, no matter how they have to be twisted.

Enough of this geriatric brooding; that is not why I write this document. I do this to record the events of my parents and their friends as they were recounted to me. I compile it from many sources, some contradictory, and give it now to you, the reader, and to history.

Everyone always asks 'when did it begin?' and 'how did it start?' but there is no simple answer. It can be said that there is no beginning save the Titan Wars that created the worlds we now live on. Everything since has merely been a reaction to a previous event. If I wished, I could trace the origin of this story to the Great War that shattered our land, or to any of the five centuries of darkness that followed.

Likewise, I will not begin this narrative with the emergence of Illyria, my foster mother, and Balien, who sired me, from the Ilthwood Forest. Their adventures in the kingdom of Nemora happen before the tale I now tell. They had made the company of Sephana and Theramus, but the characters of Eldoth, Myria, Odelmar, and the Free Mariner are still in their future.

Their story, as I see it, begins with the so-called 'Taking of Dragonhead Keep', when the future Knights of Anduilon first escorted Alwyn Longstrider, Prince of Derwyn, through the treacherous Karnem Mountains and into the neighbouring Kingdom of Karalon.

—Baldwin V, 112th High King of Anduilon

"And then did Emuranna, Goddess of Wisdom, divide the body of the Titan Anshar into five kingdoms to be ruled by the race of men and she name them Akkilon, Kalumfar, Karalon, Nemora and Tirim. 'Let the bravest and strongest of you come forth,' she said to her creations, 'and set yourselves against these great challenges that I have created. The mettle of your bodies and souls shall be tested, and those who succeed shall become kings. You will rule your kingdoms in my name and defend them against any who would take them from you.'

"Many brave and strong men rose and accepted their Maker's challenge. Some lost their lives and others their spirits, but in each kingdom one was found who was worthy and these men were proclaimed kings. Under their rulership did the people know peace and prosperity, and it was good.

"The bravest and strongest of these men was named Anduil, but he was not given a kingdom to rule. Emuranna spoke again. 'To you, Anduil, who have proven yourself to be the greatest of men, I give the highest honour. I name you High King of this world and all other kings shall serve you, but also will you serve them. To you, I give the power to summon the heart of the Titan Anshar. Only when the Five Kingdoms are united can you wield the Titan's Heart, and so does the task of fostering peace among the kingdoms of Men fall to you.'

"Anduil heeded Emuranna's words and ruled the Five Kingdoms well. Thus it was that for fifty centuries there was peace in the world of Man."

—Ancient Histories of the Middle Waters

CHAPTER ONE

The fort was old.

Alwyn ap Gwyn looked at the old, moss-covered stonework that surrounded him. Some was intact, but much was not. Ancient masons had shaped this rock centuries before he had been born and had shaped it into the walls and fortifications now in ruins around him. They had been Anduilmen—citizens of the High Kingdom of Anduilon—and had built this fort as a way-station for travellers in a time when people could wander safely between the five kingdoms. *That day is long over*, he thought sourly as he flicked an errant pebble off a crumbling wall. *Anduilon is five centuries gone, and all of us are just scavengers picking at her corpse.*

The man to Alwyn's left looked at him with sympathy. "Be patient." His voice was delicate, almost musical, with foreign, cultured tones that Alwyn had only heard from one other. "She'll be back soon and then we'll have word."

His name was Balien con-Exipiter, and he was an ambassador from the mysterious, secret city of Ilthanara. His features were honest, and his skin was clean and fair; unusual traits in an adult man. It was easy to mistake him for a youth, except for his eyes.

Alwyn scowled. "Shouldn't I be the one reassuring you? She's your sister. Aren't you worried?"

Balien shrugged, displaying a casual grace that Alwyn envied. "I trust her." He looked at Alwyn with knowing eyes. "I don't blame you for worrying. You bear a heavy load."

As if Alwyn needed reminding. He knew without looking that twenty wagons, sixty teamsters and fifty soldiers waited behind him. If any of the men or the goods they carried were lost, it was Alwyn who would have to explain why. It was a

3

daunting task, and one that would have been impossible without Balien and his sister. Although he was blood-heir to the kingdom of Derwyn, Alwyn, son of Gwyn, had never braved the Karnem Mountains. No sane man ever had, which meant it was entirely possible that Alwyn was mad.

Sane or crazy, he was here. For the first time in living memory, there was peace between the kingdoms of Nemora, and with peace came opportunity for those brave enough to grasp it. With the season's crops safe from plundering and enough men around to harvest them, a proper expedition through the forbidding southern peaks could finally be attempted. It was the first journey of its type in twenty generations and it was hoped even common Nemoran trade goods—cotton cloth and dyes—would be exotic to Karalon. A man who did such a thing would be lauded as hero in not just one but two lands, and, for Alwyn, such a reputation was worth more than gold.

Of course, to earn that reputation and collect that gold, he had to journey to Karalon and then return. One hundred men, fifty animals, and twenty tons of cargo all depended on one woman alone in the forest.

"Your elven customs remain a mystery to me, Balien," Alwyn said.

"Elves don't exist," Balien said. "They're a folk tale that everyone heard so many times that they began to think it was true. I may have been raised in a forest but I'm a Nemorman, just like you."

He had said some variation of this at least a dozen times over the last month. Alwyn refused to believe him. "So you say, but you and your sister are like no one I have ever seen. Your clothing, your weapons, the things you know…" He shook his head in disbelief. "If you were a Nemorman, just like me, then you would never allow your sister to go off and do something so dangerous, no matter how much older than you she is."

Balien gave a rare and brief smile. "I thought you knew her well enough to know that no one tells her what to do. Don't worry, Alwyn: there is no better tracker on this side of the Karnems. If she can't find a way past our problem, then it doesn't exist."

He hoped that Balien was right. He *had* to be right, or this entire expedition was doomed. If Alwyn succeeded, he would be heralded as a hero across all of Nemora but if he failed, his humiliation would be legend. Children yet unborn would laugh out loud when they heard the story of Alwyn the Idiot.

The expedition would never have happened without Balien and his sister. The pair of them had already explored the old Anduili roads that stretched between kingdoms and returned with tales of a land that hungered for northern goods. It had been Balien's sister—whose grace and beauty *were* superhuman, no matter what her brother said—who had convinced King Gwyn that a safe route through the Karnems existed, and that a treasure-laden caravan with Alwyn in charge could pass through it.

In charge. That was a laugh. Alwyn was in charge of his men, but there was no doubt about who led the caravan. Balien and his companions had scouted every step taken, hunted the game that the men ate, and chose the places they camped. They had also been the ones who had discovered the massive army of Nintaran beastmen barricading the road ahead of them.

They were almost free of the mountains. They had crossed the Urdom Pass four days ago and had been travelling steadily down hill since then. The last thing Alwyn wanted to do was turn everyone around and return the way he came, but he'd do that before he sent his meagre force to be slaughtered against an encampment of sharp-clawed, tawny-furred savages.

Alwyn the Mild: that was what people called him behind his back. Had he not been born a king's son it likely would have been worse, but the faint praise was damning enough. Not 'Alwyn the Courageous' or 'Alwyn Strong-arm,' or any number of given names that he could be proud of, but 'The Mild,' like he was a tasteless pot of stew.

No doubt someone named 'The Courageous' would have charged into battle and damned the casualties but Alwyn could not. His mission was to bring his men and his cargo to Karalon and back again. Yes, some casualties were expected, but these men represented the cream of Derwyn soldiery. He wasn't going to risk them needlessly.

"Someone's coming," Balien warned, pointing down into the forest.

Alwyn couldn't see anything. Despite Balien's statements to the contrary, mere Nemorman did not have senses so acute. "Is it her?" he asked eagerly. "Is it Illyria?"

Balien didn't answer.

Alwyn could see movement beyond, barely. There was indeed someone making their way towards them through the slender willows and tall grass, but instead of Illyria's golden hair, fine clothing, and regal bearing was a mishmashed collection of oversized men's clothes topped by a riotous burst of brown curls. It was Sephana, the servant girl. Alwyn knew next to nothing about her other than to say that she was not elvenkind. The men thought that she was an orphan of some sort, taken in out of pity.

"She's running faster than a quickling," he muttered aloud. "Do you think something happened?"

Balien just shrugged.

A minute later the girl was at their side, panting loudly as she drank down an entire water skin. Alwyn thought that she must have been burned as a child. There was no other reason for her to keep her sleeves lowered to her wrist or lace her shirt fully despite the heat of the day. He would never have paid her any mind if she hadn't been Illyria's companion, but at this moment she was the most important person in his world.

"Is Illyria all right?" Alwyn asked. "Does she need our help?"

Sephana shook her head and checked the ragged cloth that she always wore over her hair. "Sorry to disappoint you, but no. She's fine, and she has a message."

Alwyn smiled until he realized that the message was not for him.

"What is her message?" Balien asked.

"She says to be ready to go in twenty minutes. When she gives the signal you should press forward with everything have."

"Press forward?" Alwyn sputtered. "I have fifty men at arms. How can I be expected to press forward against an army?"

Balien didn't acknowledge him. "What is her signal going to be?"

She shrugged. "She said that you'd know."

Balien nodded and began checking his gear.

"Just like that?" Alwyn asked incredulously. "She says to charge into certain death without even telling you her plan, and you just agree to it?"

Balien stopped and pondered the question. "Yes." He laid a hand on Alwyn's shoulder. "Alwyn, I trust my sister with my life. You must remember that none of us would be here if it weren't for her. No one has seen where the beastmen are camped for her—"

"And me," Sephana interjected.

"—And Sephana," he amended smoothly. "If she thinks that there is a way through for us then we have to trust her."

Visions of shattered wagons and dead soldiers assaulted his mind's eye. "It's a big risk."

"All of life is a risk, Alwyn. Twenty minutes should be just enough time to get the caravan ready. If we are going to do this, we must do it now."

Alwyn opened his mouth but no sound emerged. "I..." He swallowed. "Give me a moment."

Balien nodded. "Illyria already risks her life for this. Remember that."

They left Alwyn to his brooding and walked down the trail. "Do you think he'll do it?" Sephana asked. She wished that she could loosen her shirt and feel the cool mountain air against her skin. It was way too warm for her to be running so hard with her clothes fully laced. *I may as well wish that I'm the high queen of Anduilon while I'm at it. The chances are about the same.*

"Yes," Balien answered after a moment. "I don't think his pride will allow him to retreat where a woman already shows courage."

"Two women!" she added crossly. *Honestly, it's like everyone forgets I'm here.* She expected it with jack-asses like Alwyn the Self-Important, but Balien's omission hurt. She'd been travelling with him for just over a year. Surely she must have made some impression by now…

He gave her a knowing glance. "I'm not belittling you, but you know that Alwyn is oblivious to everyone except my sister."

She snorted. "He's pretty stuck on her, all right." They arrived at the front of the line of wagons. A few men were gathered and talking quietly.

"Balien," the oldest one called out. "Is there word?"

He nodded. "Alwyn has yet to give the order, but we're advancing. You should expect fighting."

"I thought we might. Has the lass returned? Is she with Alwyn?"

Sephana frowned and bit her tongue. *I am invisible!*

"No," Balien answered. "She's still out there, planning something."

The older man smiled. "Ah, then it will be interesting if nothing else. Afon, Gwyl, come. We must make ready."

A shadow fell on Sephana and hands the size of shovels engulfed her shoulders. "Sephana," a deep, gentle voice intoned. "I am glad to see that you have returned. Are you well?"

She smiled and turned in the gentle grip. "Finally, someone asks! Yes, I'm fine." She faced a chest as wide as an oxcart and craned her head backward in a vain attempt to take in the face of the blue-skinned being that towered above her. "Thank you for asking, Theramus."

A blue thumb—light blue like on a robin's egg, not rich blue like the afternoon sky—stroked her cheek. The massive digit was the length of her hand. "I am always concerned for you, Sephana. These mountains are very dangerous, even for groups of people." Theramus was a Noss and spoke quietly but she could feel the rumble of his voice through her skin.

She punched him playfully. "You know I can take care of myself." If he had been a man it would have contacted his shoulder or upper arm. On Theramus, half again as tall as her, it was closer to his elbow.

He gave her a smile and gently tugged her hair. "Nonetheless, I worry." He glanced at Balien, who was securing his gear as well as his sisters. "Illyria is still afield? She is well?"

"As well as she can be surrounded by A'Cha." He frowned and looked at Sephana. "Did she say anything else when you were with her?"

"Nothing important."

She said it quite casually, but Balien must of heard something anyway, for he continued to look at her and she couldn't help but fidget under his gaze. His eyes could be very piercing when he wanted them to be. Finally, she looked away.

"What else did she say, Sephana?" he asked levelly. "What *didn't* she say?"

"She said not to tell you." She glanced at him briefly. "She said that if you knew you'd just get upset."

Irritation flared on his face, but he said nothing.

"Tell us what you saw," Theramus asked. "What do we face?"

"A'Cha, lots of them," she answered. "We counted about a hundred. The valley widens out ahead, and they're covering the whole thing, one end to the other."

He frowned. "It is unusual for them, both that they are gathering openly and doing so in such numbers. Were they being led by another being, perhaps of a different race?" Theramus knew everything. He was more than a hundred years old—literally—and had been everywhere.

Sephana snapped her fingers. "Yeah, there were these grey guys, about a dozen or so. Neither of us knew what they were."

"Did they have long hair and carry axes?"

"Yeah. What are they?"

"They are Vaulen: very strong warriors," Theramus said. "They often took control of A'Cha packs and combined them into large armies during the Great War. Of all the races, only the Djido were feared more."

"I've read tales about 'Grey Men' that live in the northern desert when I was in Ilthanara," Balien said. "Are these the same creatures?"

"Yes," Theramus agreed. "The Vaulen tribes were the ones who severed the line of kings in Kalumfar. It is strange for them to be so far south."

"Vaulen/Grey Men, A'Cha/Beastmen," Sephana muttered. "Why can't there just be one name for each kind of people? I always lose track of what I should be calling everything."

"Knowing who and what they are is far more important that what we call them," Theramus said. He looked at her. "Does it matter if you are called human rather than Reshai? No matter what label you go by, you are still Sephana."

Sephana glanced around her and checked that her head scarf was still where it was supposed to be. "Don't say that out loud," she hissed. "No one needs to know that about me. As far as everyone here is concerned, we're all just men—except you, I mean."

"I am sorry. I will of course keep your secret, though I still do not understand your fear. Your race should not cause you shame."

8

"I'm not ashamed; I'm afraid for my life. There's a difference." She checked to make sure that her shirt hadn't ridden up and that nothing was showing that wasn't supposed to. No one seemed to have heard or seen anything…this time.

Alwyn walked down from the fort ruins and stopped before them. "We should make ready," he said to Balien, not meeting his eyes. "We move out in a quarter hour."

Balien nodded. "You made the right choice, Alwyn."

Alwyn just nodded and made his way down the line of troops and wagons.

Theramus crawled up to the edge of the ridge. He kept his head low to the ground and moved up just far enough so that he could see the valley below. Balien moved similarly beside him but with much more grace. Alwyn, their commander in name, and Owain, senior-most of Alwyn's eorlmen, lay alongside him.

The valley was small by mountainous standards, perhaps a half mile across and ten long. Both the walls and floor of it were covered in a dark green blanket of conifers except for a gravelled floodplain a quarter mile across. The road they followed made its way down a steep, open hill to the floodplain, crossed over a small, arched bridge, and then climbed up the far side until it was swallowed by trees. The plain was clearly occupied. Crude wooden palisades stretched across it from east to west. Their length was interrupted intermittently by dirt mounds upon which rough box forts had been constructed. Tents and campfires were scattered about, around which were gathered—as Sephana had said—a great many A'Cha.

"They're facing the wrong direction," Balien said quietly to Theramus. "They're fortified, but not against us. We're behind them."

"Aye," Owain agreed. "That set-up is designed to stop people coming from the other way. From Karalon."

"There is more going on here than we have knowledge of," Theramus said. Balien nodded.

"We still can't fight that!" the 'prince', Alwyn, mewled. "There are too many. We'll be slaughtered."

Balien placed a calming hand on his arm. "We wait for Illyria's signal."

"Signal for what?" His voice was shrill. "What can one woman do to get us past all of that?"

Theramus had to look away lest his disapproval be seen. It saddened him to see how far some of the descendants of Anduilon had fallen.

Balien's jaw tightened momentarily. "We wait for her signal," he repeated.

"How do we even know what her signal is?"

A loud animal cry rang out from somewhere in the valley.

"What in the goddess's name was that?" asked Alwyn.

Balien rose to his knees. "It was our signal. We need to move."

Alwyn lay paralyzed. "What? That?"

Balien pointed into the valley. "Look down there." A'Cha were abandoning their posts to investigate the noise. "They're more worried about what made that sound than anything else. This is our chance!"

Alwyn was stunned. "I…uhh…"

"Alwyn, listen to me." Balien crouched down next to him. "This opportunity will not come again. My sister has spent the last hour finding whatever kind of monster that thing is, at great personal risk, to give us this opportunity." His voice became quieter. "If we do this, you'll be a hero. They'll sing your name through all of Nemora and Karalon."

There was a moment of silence. Panicked cries made their way up from the valley below. Another roar sounded, from closer this time.

"The lad's right, prince," Owain said. "This is our best chance."

"Yes." Alwyn nodded and got to his feet, his voice shaky. "Yes, we should do this. It's our best chance." He turned to Owain. "Ready the men. We move out on my order."

Balien stopped him. "Take your cavalry and attack the fort second from the end. Make noise and keep as many of them as occupied as you can. Owain and I will lead the infantry against the end fort and break through the wall there. All right?"

Alwyn nodded eagerly. "Yes, of course. We'll do it that way."

Balien looked at Owain, who met his eye and nodded.

"Let's go." He turned to Theramus. "Stay with the wagons. Don't let them stop for anything."

Theramus nodded. "It shall be so."

A third animal cry escaped the valley. It was much closer than the others and was followed by more yelling. The A'Cha were scattering in confusion. Something broke through the trees into the clearing, larger than anything Theramus had seen in one hundred years. It loomed larger than four carts put together and was covered in brown, shaggy fur. A slender, agile figure with blonde hair—seemingly no larger than a house-cat—darted around its feet.

Illyria.

"Then by acts of dark and mysterious magic did all the Gatestones open and the denizens of Nintara invade the High Kingdom of Anduilon. The Dakeen, 'ratmen', were the smallest and most abundant, but their lot was to suffer, not to fight. So great were their numbers that they swept across the kingdoms like a wave, falling upon towns like locusts and consuming or fouling everything in their path.

"They were followed by the savage A'Cha, the 'beastmen'. These creatures were swift and savage but disdained open battle. Instead they struck from darkness when men's backs were turned and soon every shadow was looked upon with fear.

"But by far the most dangerous of all Nintarans were the Vaulen: the Warmasters. In their own land they lived in large clans that were ever at war with each other. They ruled over Dakeen and A'Cha alike and used them like weapons but their warlike nature kept them forever at each other's throats. Indeed, the greatest weapon against the Vaulen were the Warmasters themselves."

—Introduction to The Nintaran Invasions, volume one. *Author Unknown*

CHAPTER TWO

"What in Gidim's Name is that?" Gharda, first of his band, favoured of his Lamm and faithful Vaulan of the Bekket-Ta, looked cautiously around the valley floor. He was an excellent specimen of a Vaul and a credit to his Olamm. His body was strong and muscular, his armour well tended, and his long, black hair hung in a braid down his back. His shield was slung over his shoulders and, like a good warrior, his blooding-axe was ready in his hand. Both shield and armour bore three black dots under a red half-circle: the crest of the Bekket-Ta.

If he had not been such an exemplary Vaulan he would not have been entrusted with this mission. Separated from the rest of the tribe in this wretched valley, Gharda had only himself, his band, and four packs of A'Cha dogs to enforce the will of his Olamm: Ta, the Strongest of the Strong. There were those who would see guarding a small, insignificant flank as an insult, but they would be fools for thinking so. It was a sign of trust and respect.

Respect aside, being stuck in this valley stank like horse dung.

Gharda held his axe at shoulder height while he scanned the endless tree-covered hills that surrounded them. The roar, impossibly loud, had definitely come from of an animal, but only the Eye knew what kind.

Navoi, band-mate of Olamm-Ta himself, stood next to Gharda and surveyed the clusters of A'Cha that surrounded them. A'Cha were strong, yes, and fast. Their claws could gut an unarmed man in one strike and their striped orange fur was warm and protected against some weapons, but, despite these gifts, they made poor warriors. They attacked from ambush or against weaker foes but had no spine for real battle. Given time and training, A'Cha *could* be effective if they were led by a strong handed Vaulan, but such work was an insult to one of the Warmasters. Given her way, Navoi would have let them flee back to their mountain caves, but her Olamm had commanded otherwise and thus Navoi obeyed. If her band-mate, dearer to her than any brother, wished for her to guard this remote pass with useless A'Cha dogs then she would do so, proudly and happily.

The A'Cha huddled together behind their fortifications. "Send word to rally the dogs," she ordered Gharda. "We cannot allow them to flee."

The creature, whatever it was, roared yet again. It definitely came from the east. Now that she knew roughly where to look, she could now see the tops of trees shaking and flights of birds erupting from the area. At the edge of the tree line, she could see a a pair of deer fleeing before it.

Another tree top jostled violently and Navoi swore. It was almost upon them.

She ran down her tower's rough wooden steps to the nearest group of A'Cha. They were hunched over with flattened ears and stank of fear. She slapped the flat of her axe across the back of the closest one. "Arm yourselves, damn you! Be worthy of your maker. You are warriors!" They stared at her with nervous, beady eyes before scrambling for their weapons.

She had just reached the second group of A'Cha when *it* came out of the trees. She cursed. It wasn't just some animal, but a nightmare from the age of legend. It was mostly bear, though at least three times as large. As if the idea of an impossibly huge bear was not frightening enough, this thing was also something...else. It was like a child playing with clay had taken two different shapes and mashed them together.

Feathers ran across its massive chest and down its forelimbs. Its skull was as thick and wide as a bears, but with a vicious curved beak instead of a muzzle. Beyond being some strange union of bear and bird, it was also misshapen. Its back bulged more on its left side than its right and, as it reared to an impossible height of at least three Vaulen lengths tall, she saw angry red blisters pockmarking its chest.

It gave a roar that would have quailed a lesser warrior. She saw now that it was wounded. Streaks of blood from several white-fletched arrows ran down its fur and feathers. Another arrow shaft appeared in its neck and it fell to all fours, swiping at something that Navoi hadn't noticed.

It was a human sow armed with a bow. It was scrawny, like all of its kind, and wore clothing that was too pretty to be armour. Its hair was yellow and wasn't secured in a warrior's braid. As Navoi watched it ducked the bear-giant's claw swipe and ran towards her.

She could give the foolish human no more of her attention. At the west end of the valley, where the ancient road descended from the north, a column of horse-riding humans were galloping down the hill with a group of infantry behind them. Navoi could only stare.

In front of her, the human female ran towards a group of A'Cha. They were staring flat-eared at the bear-thing and took no notice of her. She turned to the creature, drew an arrow to her cheek and loosed. It struck near the abomination's head, but did little more than annoy it. When the creature smashed bodily into the fort while trying to strike the sow, Navoi realized what the human was doing

"Ignore the creature!" Navoi commanded, gesturing towards the scrawny human sow. "Attack the female!"

Behind her, the line of human cavalry smashed into the largest A'Cha camp.

Theramus disliked battle. Though his stature was a great boon in matters of combat, he was not a warrior in his heart. He was no coward; he did not shirk from his duty when needed, but he knew that his strengths lay elsewhere. A warrior's greatest weapons were his mind and his heart. More battles throughout history had been won through bravery and canniness than strength of arms. There had been great Noss warriors, but most of his people were content to serve those who possessed those qualities in greater abundance. That was why he was happy to follow the directives of the young Nemorman, Balien, though he was only a fraction of Theramus' age.

Theramus jogged alongside the first of the wagons as Balien had bid him. These wagons held the future of Anduilon. Defeating the Vaulen-led army was meaningless if it cost them their precious cargo. There would never be alliance between Karalon and Nemora and the Dark Age that hung over all of Anshara would never end.

It was a great deal of importance to place in one caravan, but Theramus believed it to be so. It was his people's greatest strength: their belief in greater things. That same belief had led them away from their Maker and their native titan-world fifteen centuries past. It was why they had sworn loyalty to the High Kings of Anduilon and continued to search for hope, centuries after their adopted kingdom had collapsed under foreign invasion. The surviving humans had surrendered to despair and forgotten the greatness of their ancestors, but Theramus and his fellow Noss continued to remember and believe.

He had walked Anshara from shore to shore to shore, searching for hope but finding none. Others would have despaired, but in the third decade of his search he met a starving, freezing Reshai girl and nursed her back to health. A year later his path had merged with that of a Nemoran princess and her half-brother touring the lands outside their hidden forest kingdom, and he knew that he had found it again. In Sephana, Balien, and Illyria, Theramus had found hope, even if they themselves did not yet see it. Those two humans and one Reshai would make the world right again. He believed it and would give his last breath to make it so.

And, when they asked, he would fight for it.

The Derwyn prince, Alwyn, had taken his meagre cavalry and charged one of the wooden towers. The A'Cha fled before them. The bestial warriors were fast, strong, and savage but quailed before cavalry. Balien and the warriors he led were having a harder time of it, but he was a strong leader and deadly with his longsword. Under his command, they were clearing the wooden walls and an entire stretch had been stripped of defenders. It was an ideal location for the wagons to cross, except for one problem.

Sephana ran up to Theramus's side. The Reshai girl could run like the wind. "We can't get the wall down!" she panted. "We need your help."

He nodded. "It shall be so." Increasing his pace, he ran out in front of the wagons. The battle was making the oxen nervous and nervous oxen did not enjoy standing still. The wall had to come down before they either broke out of their traces, scattered themselves across the battlefield, or both.

The wooden wall stood before him. It was a battle fortification: crude, but strong. If Theramus had faced its front he would have had no choice other than smashing it into kindling, but it had been made to stop Karolmen from fleeing north. Its supports were exposed and because of it he could now able accomplish what would have been impossible otherwise.

Theramus hefted his hammer. It was designed for pounding in posts, not making war, and that suited him. The weapon struck the crossbeam where it met the top of the post and broke it in one hit. It struck again, this time at the bottom beam and it, too, was rent asunder. Theramus lay down his weapon, set both his hands against the edge of the wall and, with all the power in his eight foot, five hundred pound body, pushed.

The wood resisted his first attempt and only moved slightly. It weakened in the face of his second effort and surrendered completely against his third. On his final heave, the wall swung open for him as if it were a giant door. The first wagon passed through less than a minute later and did not even have to slow down. The human warriors cheered and Balien rallied them to protect the caravan's retreat.

With the wagons safely through, Theramus was free to focus on the well-being of his charges. He would not allow them to fall. Only Balien and Sephana were visible. There was a pained roar in the distance and Theramus ran towards it. Where there was danger, he knew, Illyria would not be far away.

Navoi cursed as another tower was smashed by the bear-creature and its defenders were hurled through the air. The yellow-haired sow had somehow continued to escape both the creature's might and her warriors' spears, and had lured the creature through the bulk of her forces while doing so. Half of the A'Cha and a third of her Vaulen had been killed by it, and only the Eye knew how many had fallen against the human warriors.

She heard the cheer and saw the cargo wagons passing through a breach in the wall. She had failed her Olamm. There was little else for her to do.

Navoi spun her axe high above her head and gave an ululating cry. "Leave the monster, let it kill the A'Cha!" she ordered the Vaulen that gathered around her. She turned to Gharda. "Olamm-Ta must know of what has happened here."

The band-leader frowned, then nodded and left. "The human footmen are vulnerable. Let us show them that we are not cowards. We will avenge our fallen comrades and wet the ground with the blood of their killers. For the Eye and Olamm-Ta, attack!"

They were ten Vaulen, but only fifteen humans in their rearguard. Perhaps Navoi would die and perhaps she wouldn't. Only the Eye knew. Blooding-axes raised high, she and her far-brothers attacked.

Sephana was busy doing what any sensible person did during a massive battle: staying out of it. It may not have been the brave thing to do but, for the smallest person on the field, it was the smart thing. She wasn't a total coward—she had a dagger and she knew how to use it—but that didn't mean that she was eager to charge down a group of angry A'Cha.

Off in the distance, Illyria was still playing tag with that disgusting owl...bear...*thing*. Having seen it up close, Sephana had no idea how Illyria was able to do it. Okay, sure: she was a skilled archer and carried a sword, but that giant bear was, well, *giant*. While Sephana didn't think that it could eat her in one bite, it probably wouldn't take more than three. Its beak was longer than her leg.

Someone—actually, a bunch of someones—gave fierce battle cries. Sephana turned in time to see group of those grey-skinned Nintarans raising their nasty looking axes and charging towards Balien and the group of Derwyn infantry. Balien shouted something and the men arranged themselves in a line, their shields forming a seamless wall that the Vaulen smashed into.

Theramus ran to her side. "Sephana, come. Illyria needs us."

She tore her eyes away from the battle between Balien's men and the grey-skinned Vaulen. He was facing off against the tallest of them, using his sword like a staff in that strange fencing style that only he used.

"What do mean, needs *us?*" she asked incredulously. "*I* can't fight that thing!"

"She is your friend and she is in danger. Come." He turned and ran towards the far end of the clearing. Cursing herself for an idiot, Sephana followed him.

"I don't think we're going to do much against it," she protested. "I mean, you're big but you're not *that* big."

"If not me then who?" he asked in a calm voice. "Illyria and the A'Cha have weakened it. Enraged as it is, I do not think it will stop until either it or Illyria are dead."

Sephana looked at the creature in question and gulped. Theramus was right. Theramus was *always* right (which never stopped being annoying), but that didn't make their task any easier. "Uhh, how?"

Theramus opened his mouth to answer, hesitated and then closed it again. "I am open to suggestions."

Alwyn reined in his horse. He was at the head of the caravan, half way up the hill on the other side of the valley. Behind him, dead bodies and shattered fortifications lay scattered across the floodplain. There were two pockets of fighting. One was on the far side where the bear creature was attacking and the other was below him where some of his warriors were engaged with a group of grey-skinned savages.

He didn't want to return. The path ahead of them needed to be scouted. It was a valid excuse to leave the battle to others. Balien had things in hand down below. The bear and the beastmen would surely kill each other off. Yes, he would stay. Good.

But…Illyria was down there as well. The bear creature was busy fighting *her*. She was forgiving: she'd surely accept his excuse of scouting the path ahead, but he wanted more than for her to merely *accept* him. The solution to his problem was obvious.

Not questioning his motives further, He waved his sword over his head. "Scout as far ahead as the top of the hill," he ordered half of his horsemen. "Gather the wagons there and wait for survivors." He turned to the rest of his men. There were only six of them. "The rest of you, follow me!" He led the charge down the hill, exultant that they had broken the line of beastmen. Finally, after everything that happened, he was doing something that felt *right*.

He and his men thundered towards the group of infantry and their grey-skinned opponents. About half of his men had fallen but there were only a few barbarians remaining. Balien was fighting with them, his long blade and deadly grace unique on the battlefield. His opponent was, to Alwyn's surprise, a female, but that made her no less deadly. Despite her feminine curves, her arms and shoulders were heavy with muscle and she wielded her axe with blinding speed.

Against Balien, it was not enough. There were three men, Alwyn saw, who no longer even fought and instead just watched the two battle. The female was taller and had a longer arm, but Balien's odd sword negated her reach. The two clashed and circled each other with grim faces in a vicious, deadly dance.

Alwyn came near the two fighters and reined in his horse, which neighed and squealed its displeasure. The female barbarian turned at the sound and her guard dropped for only a second but it was enough. Gripping his sword by the base of the blade, Balien stepped inside his opponent's guard and in a single motion disarmed her and struck her with the blade's pommel. When she staggered backward he swept the blade upward through her stomach and then down through her chest.

Glancing around and seeing the battle in hand, he nodded to Alwyn. "My thanks. Are the wagons safely through?"

"Thanks to your giant friend, yes. They wait for us up in the hills."

Balien nodded, but was distracted. He looked over at the far side of the floodplain where the bear-creature was still rampaging. His face was stone. "I need a horse. Now."

Alwyn nodded without thinking. "Sawyl, dismount."

Balien sat in Sawyl's saddle a moment later, controlling the horse like he had been doing it his entire life. "Illyria risked her life getting that bear to attack, and as long as it lives she remains in jeopardy." Every man listened to him raptly. "If you would repay that service then ride with me now." His horse reared with excitement but Balien kept his seat easily. He rode off without looking behind him.

For the first time since battle's beginning, Alwyn felt brave. He drew his sword without thinking. "For Derwyn!" he cried and followed. Behind him, his men did the same.

Theramus's blow to the bear's flank had little effect. The wooden hammer that had triumphed against wooden walls and A'Cha skulls met defeat on the bear's thick hide. He was fortunate that Illyria had sunk one of her arrows into its eye and made it clumsy. It spun and snapped at him with its beak, but Theramus was easily able to leap aside.

They were stalemated. While he, Sephana, and Illyria could continue to bait, harry and annoy the huge, wounded monster, its might was such that none of them could harm it. It was bleeding, yes, and obviously tired, but to deal with this creature as they were was to gamble with Zulum. One roll, sooner or later, would come up anchors.

The thunder of hooves announced the arrival of a group of Derwyn horsemen led by Balien. Theramus heartened at the sight.

"Sephana, lure it towards you!" Illyria called out. "Let the horsemen attack its blind side!"

She looked tired but still magnificent. He did not know how long had she been fighting the bear creature—far longer than the rest of them—but she still burned brighter and hotter than most men ever achieved. Her golden hair hung free and shone like a beacon, unaffected by the dirt and blood that covered her face and clothes. Her quiver was empty and her bow tossed aside but she held her sword—a curved elven slimblade slicked with blood—with the hand of a master.

The creature cried out with a sound that was impossibly deep and angry. He, Sephana, and Illyria were three points on a compass and the fourth point was charging towards them. If they had been true cavalrymen on massive destriers with metal-tipped lances, they could have slain the creature right there but they had none of those things. The unconditioned horses balked more than fifteen feet away and refused to advance. Balien, standing in his stirrups, was unhorsed by the sudden action and landed at the creature's feet.

The owl/bear turned to face its new foes and ignored Theramus and the others. Balien tried to scramble away but the creature reared back to strike.

Theramus, desperate to distract it, hurled his hammer at its head, but even has he did so Illyria leapt onto its back, raised her sword, and plunged it deeply into the creature's neck. The hammer struck the base of its beak. It cried out from both blows, rose onto its hind legs and clawed a feathered forelimb along its back. His hammer had pierced its beak and lodged inside its mouth. Illyria, somehow, remained in place on the thing's back and now hung more than fifteen feet off of the ground.

As Alwyn watched, Balien scrambled to his feet and slashed his sword into the thing's belly. "Attack!" he ordered. "Dismount and attack, while it's distracted!" This close to the stinking bear-creature which towered over them as high as the stone walls of Derwyn Keep, Alwyn could only stare. "Now, Alwyn!"

Stung into action, Alwyn dismounted his shying horse and his men followed. His broadsword looked tiny and ineffectual but he approached the monster—it was like a huge, fur covered wall—and sank his sword's tip into it. Its felt as effective as stabbing a stone, but he knew his blade drew at least some blood. Around him, the other men darted in and bloodied it with equal success.

The bear creature, choking on the hammer that the giant had hurled down its throat, took no notice of them. All of its focus was on Illyria who had either foolishly or bravely clambered onto its back and was driving her sword into it repeatedly.

The creature returned to all fours with ground-shaking force. Balien, standing before it, barely scrambled out of its way. The force of its landing lodged the hammer even deeper into its throat and the beast began to make deep, massive coughing noises. Balien, faster than a hawk, stepped in and slashed his longsword across its momentarily exposed throat. It cried out as blood gushed down the front of its dark shaggy chest.

Everyone cheered and attacked with renewed energy. Ignoring everyone like the fleas that they were, it stumbled forward and turned towards the forest's edge. It started strong but before it had even gone three of its huge body lengths—its trail soaked in its own blood—it had weakened considerably. Still clinging to its back, Illyria crawled up to its head and sank her blade into it up to the hilt. With a final cry of pain, it collapsed to the ground. With its eyes rolled up and its black bird-like tongue protruding, it gave a final shudder and died.

For a moment there was only silence. They were too far from the river to hear its gurgling and the woods had stilled once the battle had begun. None of the grey-skinned Nintarans remained standing and the only beastmen in sight were slain. Alwyn stared across the plain and at the carnage and destruction.

One of the men raised his sword triumphantly. "Victory!" he cried out. "For Derwyn and Emuranna!"

The other four horsemen raised their swords and repeated the cry. A few hundred yards away the remaining footmen cheered as well. Alwyn could not help but smile in relief. *There will be no stories of Alwyn the Idiot today. I will bring my king only tales of victory.*

Any such thoughts vanished when Illyria clambered off the creature's back, half sliding and half falling down its thick, shaggy hide. Alwyn rushed towards her but, in spite of his efforts, her brother arrived first to catch and steady her. She murmured something to him and he snorted before giving a reply. She laughed quietly before turning to Alwyn as he stumbled to a halt before her.

By the goddess, she was beautiful. Even covered in dirt and blood, her hair plastered against her head by sweat and grime, she remained the pinnacle of womanhood. How could he possibly have hesitated before coming to her aid? "Prince Alwyn, I am glad to see you are well." He let her voice, liquid and pure, flow over him. It was cultured and precise like her brothers, but sounded oh-so much more alluring from her lips. "My thanks to you and your men for coming to my aid." Her eyes took in the devastation along the floodplain. "I see that you managed to get the caravan across the barricade. Congratulations."

"I, umm, that is…thank you, my lady," he managed to utter, cursing himself for his inability to string together a full sentence. Her hand still rested against her brother's arm and Alwyn did his best to ignore the stab of jealousy that the sight inspired. *He's her brother. It means nothing.* Instead he stared into her eyes and found himself once again tongue-tied. They were a warm brown colour, flecked with violet. She met his gaze for a moment before turning to examine her sword.

He fled before he made a greater fool of himself.

Sephana watched Alwyn stammer something to Illyria which she replied to with a graciousness that Sephana could not have matched. It wasn't doing anyone any good for Illyria to put up with his clumsy attentions. If Sephana had been in her place, Alwyn would have been set straight weeks ago.

Balien put a hand on her shoulder. "Come on. We have to get back to the others." He stopped and gave her a quick, clinical once over. "Are you all right?"

"Better than him." Sephana kicked the paw/wing/forelimb of the dead bear. Its feathers were a deep gold colour and blended well with the rich brown of its fur pelt. Its blood was bright against the ground: a bright red brush stroke contrasting against the drab grey canvas of the plain.

"You know that he's going to get all the credit for this," she complained, pointing at Alwyn. "We did all the real work: Illyria brought the giant bear here, you killed it, and Theramus broke through the wall. It's not fair."

His eyes pierced her. "We don't do what we do for glory, but because it's right. Alwyn doesn't understand that, so what's the harm in giving it to him?"

Because he's a whiny boob! She wanted to say it aloud but didn't, though she was pretty sure he knew anyway. "Maybe not, but a little would be nice. It's not like we're getting paid for this."

Balien frowned. "Don't confuse glory with vanity. Emuranna knows what we've done, as do we, and Alwyn's men. If you're unhappy, Sephana, no one is forcing you to stay with us. You can leave whenever you wish."

She scowled. "You know why I'm here."

Illyria had to search for a few moments before she found her bow. Alwyn had finished fawning over her—thankfully—and was off dealing with his men. Her brother was talking to Sephana while strong, loyal Theramus struggled with the dead giant's beak in an attempt to retrieve his hammer.

Her bow, named 'Heartseeker', was Illyria's dearest possession. It was an ancient relic, a royal treasure, and had been given to her as a gift by her uncle, the King of Nemora. Made before the Great War, the secret of its construction had been lost long ago.

Her uncle, Kefeus Sheldrion, was the true king of Nemora and bore the Mark of the Hawk—bestowed on his bloodline by the goddess Emuranna—to prove it. Illyria had also been gifted with the 'x' shaped birthmark and, until her cousin's birth when she had been twelve, had stood a possibility of inheriting the crown along with the divine responsibilities it entailed. With the mark passed on to the next generation, she could no longer inherit but retained the ability of giving it to her children.

Children.

The thought disturbed her tranquillity like the now dead giant bear had shattered the serenity of the forest. It was not that she had any objection to continuing her family line…someday. It was the part that preceded it gave her pause.

Enough. There will be time to deal with that later, once Alwyn and his caravan make it through the mountains. There was no benefit to dwelling on tomorrow's problems when today's had yet to be resolved. Heart-Seeker was intact and they were exposed out on the narrow valley floor.

Balien caught her eye and understood, as he always did. Turning away from Theramus, who had succeeded in reclaiming his weapon, he went over to speak with Alwyn and his men. They shared a few words before the prince of Derwyn nodded and ordered everyone to move out.

Prince. He used the title in earnest and spoke of his father as a king, but Illyria cringed every time she heard him say the word. She had been six when she had learned that there was only one true king for each of the five kingdoms of Anshara. They bore unmistakable crownmarks, and their unions with the land was what ensured the prosperity of all who lived within. To refer to the men who claimed rulership across Nemora as kings was an insult, not just to her uncle but to every king who had ever honoured Emuranna's covenant. Her family called them 'Petty Kings' and they did so with a sneer.

Yet, despite her family's condescension, she could not blame the scattered kings of Nemora. The true royal family—her ancestors—had secreted themselves within the Ilthwood in the early days of the Great War. They had closed its borders to all and successfully defended it against the seemingly unstoppable forces of the Djido, but in doing so they had allowed their ancestral kingdom to be laid waste. When the snake-like Djido had finally been defeated and cast out a century later, the ravaged plains had been repopulated by refugees from across the world. These shattered survivors had no memory of the glory of High Kingdom and did not understand the privileges and responsibilities that came with the title of 'king'.

Her people, hidden within their secret city of Ilthanara, called themselves the 'true' Nemorans and looked at the world beyond their borders with horror and contempt. They did not forbid their own kind from contacting the outside barbarians, but none were allowed to enter. The few fleeting contacts between the reclusive Ilthanarans and the outside world became the stuff of legend. The Ilthanarans became known as 'elves' and all manner of magic and powers were attributed to them but, as Illyria and Balien had explained countless times, they were as mortal and mundane as anyone else. Few in the Petty Kingdoms wanted to believe them.

Illyria approached Balien and Theramus. The giant's massive beak—still impressive despite the hammer-sized hole punched into the side of it—lay next to Theramus's boot. She could not help but stare. Consumed by the heat of the moment, she had not allowed herself to dwell on the ramifications of dealing with a massive owl/bear. *I fought* that? *And won?*

She turned away with a shudder and glanced at her brother. Perceptive as always, he caught her brief stare and she could see his face beginning to darken. She looked away guiltily, knowing full well the conversation that was about to begin, and turned to Theramus. His still calmness, like a stone monolith in a forest before dawn, comforted her. "Was there any problem getting the caravan through?"

"No." He shook his head with the majesty of a stag shaking dew from his antlers. "Though we were greatly aided by the orientation of the fortifications. Had we been facing their front this battle would have had a different outcome. Would it not be so?"

She nodded, still avoiding her brother's gaze. "It would. Were there many casualties?"

"Ten."

"It could have been much worse." Finally, she looked over at Balien, whose expression could be likened to a thunder cloud. "We didn't see anything during our first crossing to indicate anything like this."

"This is not random, it was done deliberately by the Vaulen," Theramus told her. "It would only be done as part of a larger campaign. I fear that they have designs upon part, if not all, of Karalon."

She nodded, but her eyes didn't leave her brother's. She took two steps towards him and he quickly closed the distance until they stood face to face. His jaw was clenched and his eyes blazed with anger, but he said nothing. Illyria met his gaze unflinchingly and waited.

Seconds later his expression softened and shook his head ruefully. " 'Don't tell Balien, he'll just get upset?' "

Illyria smiled. "She wasn't supposed to tell you that." She opened her arms to him.

They embraced. "That was too close, Lyri. You could have been killed."

She shrugged. "I knew you'd save me."

"You said you'd stop taking foolish risks. You promised me."

"It wasn't stupid, it was necessary. Can you think of another way we could have gotten the caravan through with only ten casualties?"

"I...no." He released her. "I promised mother that I'd keep you safe."

"You did," Illyria insisted. "I promised her that I'd keep you safe, too, you know. I think we're both failing her."

They shared a smile, unified in their disdain of overprotective parents. She linked her arm into his and steered him towards where Alwyn and his men waited. "Come on. Let's help Alwyn make history. He's about to lead the first caravan across the Karnem Mountains in five hundred years."

" 'Thus do we, the Noss, pledge ourselves to the service of the High Kings of Anduilon. Long have we searched for one worthy of our service, and in you and this land we have found it. We will serve you loyally and with all of our blood, for as long as you are worthy and there is a land to serve. We recant the worship of Maskim, for he is petty and cruel, and give ourselves into the bosom of Emuranna, who is beautiful, wise, and kind. For all of our lives, for all of time, we are yours. So it is and so it will be, until WatersEnd.' "

—Pheldanus, First of the Noss

CHAPTER THREE

Sephana yawned and trudged towards the camp she shared with Balien, Illyria and Theramus. The pale yellow morning sun had finally cleared the dark lavender mountain tops. Finally, she could go to sleep.

Alwyn had ordered the last of the beer broken out so that the men could toast the memories of their fallen friends. Illyria had volunteered to cover the night's watches while the Nemormen mourned and celebrated. Sephana hadn't wanted any part of it, but Theramus had asked her with his puppy eyes and she hadn't been able to say no. She'd drawn last watch.

Around her, the caravan was slowly dragging itself to its feet. While they all moved slowly after last night's victory celebration, they were experienced caravaners by now. They'd be packed and ready to go within an hour.

She was greeted by the sound of steel on steel. Illyria and Balien, both looking disgustingly rested, were stripped down to their shirts and fencing with each other while Theramus watched. For a brother and sister, they fought completely differently. Illyria's blade was curved, shorter, and faster, with only small guard between blade and grip. Balien's weapon was almost a foot longer, as straight as an artist's brush, and had a wide crossguard. He made up for the loss of speed by laying one hand on the blade and using it as a guide and fulcrum.

She gave the two fighters plenty of room. Their tent, she noted, had already been packed up and lay in the cart that held their gear and belongings. *No nap for me.* She sat down next to Theramus, who wordlessly handed her a bowl of barley mush. "Who's winning?"

Balien reversed his blade and used the cross-guard to hook Illyria's ankle. She leapt over the attack—it was a common tactic for Balien to use—but was unable to resist his follow-up push and fell backward. He brought his blade down for a killing stroke against her neck but froze. Her own sword was raised against his stomach.

"Each has slain the other at least once," Theramus answered. "Your watch was quiet, I trust?" Beyond them, Balien held his hand out to his sister and pulled her to her feet.

Sephana snorted around her food. "There weren't signs of any A'Cha, or that one Vaulen who ran off, but I wouldn't call it *quiet*. Those idiots were up pretty late drinking."

"Be kind to them," he chided. "They lost friends yesterday."

"So?" Her hand tightened against her bowl. "There wasn't anyone watching over me when *my* friends died. Why should these guys have it any different?"

"Just because injustice was done to you in the past does not mean that you should wish it upon others." His voice was gentle. "Compassion is a virtue, is it not so?"

"No, it's a weakness." Scowling, she threw down her half eaten bowl. She wasn't hungry anymore. "Compassion gets you killed."

His face fell but she just glared at him. With a sigh, he looked away.

"Sephana, do you want to do some training with knives?" Balien called, holding out a wooden practice blade. "We still have some time before we leave."

"No I don't." she climbed into the bed of the wagon and began arranging gear. Pulling out a blanket, she lay down and pulled it over her head. "I'm going to sleep."

"She's tired," Theramus said and Illyria raised her eyebrows. She'd shared company with the Reshai girl for a year, (not that she was really a girl—she claimed to be twenty one) but Illyria could not claim to *know* Sephana. Perhaps Theramus could, but no one else.

She stepped into some trees for some privacy, stripped off her shirt and ran a damp cloth across her body. Acting as scouts and advisers for Alwyn was rewarding, but she missed the privacy and time required for a good bath. In Ilthanara, she'd bathed twice a day in heated tubs and had her choice of exotic oils and soaps. It was a luxury easily sacrificed, but she still missed it on occasion.

Her ranger's bath compete, Illyria dressed and returned to the camp. It felt like autumn instead of summer. It was easy to forget that Karalon, being farther to the south, was cooler than Nemora. She had been told that the snow remained on the ground for much of autumn and spring and all of winter in this kingdom. The temperatures stayed below freezing for months on end, which she had trouble believing.

She laced up her shirt, shrugged into her shorter, sleeveless tunic and covered both with her cloak. Both were from Ilthanara and, despite two years of wear, remained in flawless condition. During times when her home seemed very far away—like today— the soft, durable cloth and perfect fit were comforting reminders of her heritage.

Balien had done the exact opposite. Other than his cloak and sword he now dressed as any other Nemorman would. They had not spoken of it, but she thought that she understood. They had different relationships with their homeland, and different obligations, too. While duty demanded that she return home at the end of summer, Balien had no such restriction.

Illyria returned to the camp and began to comb her hair. Someone cleared their throat behind her. Turning, she saw it was Alwyn. "Good morning, your highness." He *was* a prince, despite his lack of proper bloodline, and she would address him as such. As a king's niece, she could do no less.

"Uhh, Good morning, Illyria." He was nervous.

Oh. It was going to be one of *those* conversations.

"Balien has just left to scout our path," she told him. She had wanted that job herself but her brother had beaten her two fencing matches out of three. (Their last match had ended in a tie, and hadn't been enough to overturn the decision) Travelling at the speed of ox-cart was frustrating and both of them vied for any chance to move about freely. "He'll leave the usual markers if there are any problems. We'll see him at lunch."

"That's, uhh, good. Thank you." He nodded and fixed his eyes on the cart wheel. Swallowing, he glanced at her quickly before once more looking away. "My lady, would you consider it bold if I asked you a personal question?"

"Not at all," she answered cautiously. She glanced at the wagon. Sephana was sleeping, and she didn't want to disturb her. Also, in the event that she wasn't asleep yet, she didn't think Alwyn would appreciate an audience. "I need to walk the camp's borders. Can we talk while I do so?"

His head bobbed. "Yes, of course."

Inwardly, Illyria sighed and waited patiently. She was fully aware of his infatuation with her and she knew, too, that she was what men called beautiful. She was not hypocritical enough to resent her appearance. She liked the attention it garnered her—usually—and she had learned long ago how to use a smile or a tilt of her head to help her get what she wanted. What did bother her was that many people seemed unable to look past her appearance. They were always surprised to find that she was intelligent, well-read, an accomplished tracker, and knew full well how to use the weapons she carried.

After a month in her company, she had hoped that Alwyn had learned to look past her more obvious features but, given how he was acting at the moment, she doubted it.

"You wished to ask me a personal question?" she prompted once they were away from the wagon.

"Uh, yes," he stammered. "I…well, that is…I do not understand why it is that you are aiding me. Forgive my bluntness, but I do not see what is in it for you."

She was surprised at his frankness but was reluctant to match his candour. "Your father asked me to." It was a safe, easy, diplomatic answer. "Consider it an act of cooperation between two kingdoms."

He frowned, unsatisfied. "As you have said before, and you will forgive me saying it, but what you are doing here goes far beyond diplomacy."

"It's important to me," she said simply. "Trade between Nemora and Karalon benefits everyone, the Ilthwood included."

"And will you be accompanying us back to Derwyn?" he asked after a few minutes of silent walking.

"Yes, of course. I have…" She didn't want to say it out loud. "…a family obligation that I must return for." She smiled, uncomfortable with his line of questioning. "And what will you do when you return to Derwyn a hero? Is there any great reward waiting for you?"

He stopped and looked her in the eye. "I was hoping to marry. There is a lady whose interest I am courting. I am hoping that my success will impress her enough to grant me her hand."

Emuranna's Strength. She dropped the pretence. "I'm sorry, Alwyn, but I can't marry you."

He stiffened. "May I ask why?"

"I'm…" The words stuck in her throat. "…already engaged." Jumping on top of the giant bear yesterday had been easier.

If possible, Alwyn stiffened even more. "Who is the lucky man?" His voice was like ice.

"One of my cousins, in Ilthanara. This has been arranged for a long time, Alwyn. I'm sorry." She wanted to apologize more but didn't think it would be well received.

He turned on his heel and walked away.

Sephana's head emerged shortly before noon. "It is good to see you awake," Theramus greeted her.

She blinked and looked around, hands automatically checking her head scarf. "I want to sleep in a real bed for once," she moaned. "I feel like I was lying on a pile of rocks."

"We will be resting in the city of Northhaven for two weeks while the trading and diplomacy occurs," he assured her. "You will have all of that time for proper rest."

"Didn't you say that Karalon was in great danger or something because of those Vaulen we fought?"

"I do not know how what we encountered yesterday will affect the trade mission," he admitted. Sephana said nothing, just blinked sleepily. "You do know that you can speak to me at any time, about anything?"

She shaded her eyes and looked at him. "What are you talking about?"

"What you said before, about compassion being a weakness. It troubles me to hear you say that."

She waved her hand dismissively. "Sorry. I was tired and grumpy. You should know better than to take me seriously at times like that."

"It is at such times that that we are closest to our true selves," he said quietly.

"Theramus…" She pulled herself to the edge of the wagon and swung her legs over the side. "Look, I'm not like you. I didn't grow up in some happy, pretty place surrounded by friends and family who hugged me all the time. I was a slave. It was awful and that was why I left. I'm sorry if doesn't makes me friendly enough for you."

"I have been to Akkilon and I have seen how the slave-caste live. The Reshai there have a very strong sense of community. Did you not have that comfort when you were a child?"

Her eyes flared. "Don't tell me about my own people. You think you know everything because you're a million years old and have been everywhere, but you don't know me. I'm sorry that I don't fit your recipe of what a perfect person should be. I'm not a saint and I never will be. I've…done things." She scowled and looked away. "So just leave me alone, all right?"

She vaulted off the wagon and stalked off.

Theramus sighed. She would return. She would mutter an apology and pretend it had never happened and all would be well. He regretted that he had pushed her, but the world would need her soon and she had to be ready.

There was a warning shout from the front of the caravan. Sephana ran alongside the rapidly halting train of wagons to where Illyria and Alwyn stood. Wary soldiers formed ranks and readied weapons.

Fifty yards ahead, just before a turn in the road, stood four horsemen. They were armed with shields and spears and wore steel armour under black and yellow surcoats. As she watched, a second person climbed down from the lead horse and spread his arms widely.

"It's Balien," Illyria announced. "Lower your weapons. It's my brother and riders from Karalon. We've made it!"

The men cheered. Balien and the four horsemen approached and were met by Alwyn.

The lead man dismounted and held his hand out in greeting. He was good looking, in Sephana's opinion, with broad shoulders, a strong, clean shaven jaw and a nice smile. His armour was of the Karalinian style and made of countless interwoven metal links.

"On behalf of my liege, Willem Jannery, Lord of the Northern Marches, greetings. I am Sir Gennald Hanley. Welcome, your highness, to Karalon." He spoke with a high, clipped, accent.

Alwyn smiled and took his hand. "I am Alwyn, son of Gwyn, Prince of Derwyn. I greet you this day in the name of peace and future prosperity. My sincerest thanks to you and your men."

Sephana would have been more impressed if she hadn't listened to Illyria and Balien coach Alwyn to say those exact words every night for all of the last week.

Gennald motioned for his men to dismount. He looked at the long line of animals, wagons and men in wonder. "Your man Balien told me, but I didn't believe it. Your whole caravan made it through."

Alwyn glowed with pride. "It wasn't easy, I assure you, but my men are brave and dedicated."

"His *men*," Sephana muttered. "He didn't think Illyria was a man this morning when he was drooling over her."

Theramus shushed her.

Illyria stepped between the two men. "Excuse me, my lords, but I must warn you, Sir Gennald: we encountered a large force of Nintaran warriors not ten miles back. We slew most but there were survivors and they may return with reinforcements. It would be best if we were to keep moving."

Gennald's eyes lit up. "You must be Illyria, the elven princess. My lord spoke of your beauty, but I see that he understated himself." He bowed with his head and shoulders. "It is my distinct pleasure to meet you." Illyria smiled more brightly at the handsome knight then she ever had at with Alwyn. Unseen by both, the prince of Derwyn scowled fiercely.

"You speak truly." Gennald straightened. "My scouts reported an armed encampment of dogmen in the Marchel Valley last week. I mean no disrespect to you or your men, Prince Alwyn, but we expected to only find a few survivors. How did you possibly get your entire caravan past them?"

Alwyn, distinctly *not* looking at Illyria, coloured slightly. "It was difficult, but we managed. I'll tell you more about it later. Perhaps when we're finally free of these mountains?"

Gennald nodded. "Yes, of course. We should be off. These hills aren't safe." He remounted his horse. "When the road passes beyond these trees in four miles, we will be in the Northmarch proper. I have twenty more men waiting there to escort you to Northhaven. Whenever you are ready, my lord."

Alwyn nodded and gave the order to move out. Within five minutes, twenty wagons hauled by forty oxen, one hundred men and eighteen horses were making their way down the ancient, overgrown road.

To everyone's relief, the steep downward slope lessened, but the endless forest of pine continued on. The open plains and waiting escort of men were less than a mile away, but, with their rate of travel restricted to that of the slowest ox, it remained more than an hour away.

Illyria and Balien moved in advance of the caravan, accompanied by Sir Gennald, who walked along side them leading his horse. Alwyn had made some excuse to be elsewhere.

"The dogmen have always lived in these mountains," the knight explained to Illyria, smiling. It was a nice smile and she could not help but return it. "Believe me, we've been trying to chase them out since before my grandfather's time, but they're impossible to root out. They're too good at hiding and setting ambushes, and they breed like rabbits." He shrugged. "If they stayed there and didn't bother us it would be fine but they're always sending out raiding parties. The only edge we have over them is cavalry."

"But you've never seen any of the Vaulen?" Balien asked.

"You mean the Grey Men? We started seeing them last year. They come with the dogmen on their raids, but they don't usually attack. They just…watch. They'll fight if you corner them and they're deadly with those axes they carry. Horses don't scare them."

"Theramus says that they have a history of commanding the A'Cha into battle," Balien said. "He says that they can gather them into armies of thousands."

"Emuranna help us if that ever happens," Gennald said grimly. "I don't think I've ever seen a group larger than fifty." He glanced over at Theramus' distinctive outline. "That giant, blue man: he's yours?"

"He is our friend and he travels with us," Balien corrected. "No one owns him."

Gennald looked at Balien oddly. " 'Own him?' Forgive me: that was not what I meant. In Karalon, when we say someone is yours or belongs to you what we mean is that he is your vassal. It is the same way that I am my liege's man; as his knight I swore an oath to serve him, and so he too takes care of me and my family. It is our way here."

Balien frowned. "Oaths should not be required to ensure what decency should provide. Theramus is not sworn to us, or we to him."

"And the girl with the curly hair? She is not yours either?"

Illyria smiled. "Graveyards could be filled by those who would tell Sephana she owed them anything."

Gennald frowned. His eyes lingered on hers and she made no move to look away. "You and your companions are a strange group: elves, girls, and giants, with no one serving anyone. How do you get anything done if none of you are lord?"

"Why would a title be needed when what is right is always so plainly before us?" Balien asked

Gennald's brow wrinkled in confusion. "It is not that way in Karalon. Everyone must serve someone."

"Excuse me, Sir Gennald?"

He looked over at Illyria and smiled. "Yes, beautiful elven princess?"

She smiled widely. If anyone else had said that to her she would have immediately corrected them but from Sir Gennald it sounded...nice. She tried to calm her features and recall her question. "You have used this term several times: knight. I thought it was your name for a horse-warrior, but I think now that it is more than that."

"Yes and no." His cheeked dimpled nicely when he smiled. "Not all knights are horsemen and not all horsemen are knights. Out in the Northmarch," he waved his hand generally in front of him, "where cavalry are our best weapon against the dogmen, those of us who serve our lords do so best from horseback, but any man who vows to defend his lord and follow the Code is granted the title of knight. It is the greatest honour that can be given."

" 'The Code?' "

"The Code of Chivalry. We swear to serve our lords in Emuranna's name and our behaviour must always be worthy of her at all times. We swear not only to service but to be honourable, courteous, brave, obedient, and respectful at all times. We must always behave in accordance of the Code, or we lose her grace."

"You swear to absolute obedience?" Balien asked.

Gennald's voice hardened. "Of course. A vassal serves his lord absolutely, or not at all."

Illyria stepped between the two men, smiling broadly. "Thank you, Sir Gennald. That was most enlightening."

"My pleasure, princess." Once again their eyes met and held.

Illyria could feel cheeks warming and forced herself to look away. "Call me Illyria, please."

"Only if you will call me Gennald."

"Of course...Gennald." Behind her, Balien fell away. "However, you are incorrect with your title. I am not a princess."

His brows lowered in confusion. "I'm sorry, I don't understand. Are you not niece of your land's king?"

Her eyes met his briefly before looking away. "Yes, I am, but only those whose crownmarks are active bear that title. I cannot no longer inherit the throne."

His eyes widened. "You have a crownmark? Truly? And you come here?"

"Yes."

He paused for a moment. "What is your title, then?"

She wrinkled her nose. "Among my people, we are called 'Children of the Mark'."

"Then your proper title would be 'Child Illyria'?" Gennald laughed loudly and she found herself laughing along with him.

"Please never say that again."

He continued to chuckle. "I will call you 'Lady Illyria' then." His eyes met hers and darkened. "That you are a lady, I have no doubt."

Her laugh died stillborn in her throat. *This is going too far.* She schooled her expression until it was as cool and still as a pond at dawn. "You are very kind, Sir Gennald."

He calmed himself and straightened. "If you will excuse me, I must see to my men." His tone was formal but his eyes danced merrily. "Lady." He climbed fluidly into his saddle and rode off towards the rear of the column."

She could hear Balien coming closer. "We were just talking, that's all," she protested before he could speak. She couldn't meet his eyes.

"I'm not judging you, Lyri," he said mildly. "He seems like a good man."

She leaned against her brother's side and he wrapped his arm around her shoulder. "He is," she murmured, taking comfort in his strength. "That's the problem."

Theramus looked across the bare, windswept hills and smiled. His ancestors had lived in mountains and he always felt that ancient affinity when near them, but his own experience had taught him to distrust them. They were wild and dangerous and he was glad to be free of them.

Before the Great War, all of Anshara had been ruled by men but, when the Nintaran Invasions had begun, sovereignty over all of the land became impossible. The fracturing of the High Kingdom had begun then, though it had taken the arrival of the Djido and their endless slave armies to fully rend the land asunder. If the last High King had not created the Shieldstone, then even the small, scattered entities that now called themselves 'kingdoms' would not exist. All would be under control of the dreaded snakemen.

The caravan and its Karalinian escort moved in a slow curving line in front of him. They were making good time, but the battle two days ago still made him nervous. There was more to that situation then they knew, and many questions remained unanswered. *Balien and Illyria will determine what this mystery is and do whatever is needed to solve it. It will be so.* With his help, of course, and Sephana's. That, too, would be so.

One of Gennald's fellow knights galloped towards the caravan and spoke to the senior knight. His news must not have been good, for within a minute Gennald was riding off in the direction from which the other knight had come. Balien, sharing a horse with Illyria, followed and Alwyn rode abreast of them.

"Balien, Illyria, do you need me?" Theramus called.

Illyria shook her head. "Stay with the caravan and keep them on guard. Don't let them stop for anything until you hear from us."

They soon passed out of sight. Theramus nodded his assent before turning back to the latest group of men to be placed under his protection.

"It will be so."

"What in Emuranna's name is *that*?" Sir Gennald whispered. Illyria wished that she had an answer for him.

She, along with Balien, Alwyn, and Sir Gennald, all lay on the crest of a rolling hill. The knight who had led them here remained with their horses, safely out of sight in a hollow behind them. There was a steep, scrub filled ravine in front of them, but it was not the ravine that inspired Gennald's question, rather what was in front of it.

'It' was in fact two beings: a large, lizard-like creature half again the size of a horse and the A'Cha that rode on top of it. The mount bore a crude saddle without stirrups and a sort of bridle around its head. The A'Cha looked stiff and awkward on its perch. Its ears flicked back and forth on the sides of its head, a sign of nervousness.

"Is that a dragon?" Alwyn asked in a whisper, looking at her.

Illyria understood Alwyn's confusion. She wished that Theramus was with her. Surely he would know what this strange, unknown, but definitely dangerous creature was. She had never seen a dragon in the flesh, but this creature shared many qualities to the drawings that she had seen.

Every inch of it was covered in thick, dark green scales except for its chest and underbelly, which were more of a pale yellow. (If Sephana were here she could surely tell everyone what the colours were called). It was shaped like a dragon, mostly. It had a long tail about as long as its torso, a powerful, sinuous body, and a large, triangular head. Its head was dominated by a huge mouth filled with sharp, vicious-looking teeth and two small, malevolent eyes. Unlike a dragon it had no wings and its forelimbs—while clawed and deadly—were too small to bear its weight. This creature, whatever it was, walked solely on its huge hind legs.

Alwyn was still looking at her, as were Balien and Gennald. Balien met her gaze and shrugged minutely. "I don't think so," she whispered. "It's a giant lizard of some kind."

"What is a giant dragon-lizard doing here in the Northmarch?" Gennald whispered, "And how did that dogman manage to catch it for riding?"

Dragon-lizard. It was as good a name as any. "I'm sorry, I don't know."

"There's more than one of them. Look." Balien pointed across the ravine.

They followed his finger to another A'Cha mounted on a dragon-lizard in the distance. Both lizards stopped frequently to sniff at the ground.

"They're searching for something in the ravine," Illyria realized. "Look at where the A'Cha—"Gennald gave her a blank look, "—*dogmen*," she amended, "are looking."

"What do we do now?" Alwyn asked.

Before Illyria could answer, the knight behind them pulled on Gennald's boot. "Sir Gennald, you need to see this," he whispered. "I found it under a rock."

He was holding a ripped and bloody piece of cloth whose original colour was indeterminable. Gennald took it and fingered some gold coloured embroidery. His face was ashen. "This is my father's. This symbol—" he fingered a stylized flower stitched in gold thread, "—is from our family crest."

The wind changed. Before Illyria could drop the stained piece of cloth the scent of blood travelled down the hill towards the nearest dragon-lizard. Its wedge-shaped head turned towards them and gave a low, dangerous growl.

"Hide!" Balien ducked his head down below the grass but it was too late. The A'Cha made some sort of a growling call in its native speech and snapped its reins. The dragon-lizard and its rider rushed up the hill with frightening speed. All she could see was a wide mouth full of teeth and two grasping claws below it.

The creature thundered straight towards Illyria and she scrambled to get out of its way. *Those teeth could sever my leg in one bite!* Midway up the slope, before Illyria could even get her feet under her, the A'Cha yelled something and yanked the creature's reins hard to the left. The dragon-lizard snarled and turned towards Gennald but had its head jerked back to Illyria. Mount and rider stopped three yards short, both emitting loud, frustrated vocalizations, before the lizard resumed its toothy charge at Illyria.

Their short argument (for that was the only way she could describe their interaction) gave her a chance to get to her feet and draw an arrow. Even as she pulled back on her priceless heirloom bow she was sighting down the arrow's length and seeking a target.

Illyria had learned early in her life that she had a special affinity with the bow and arrow. When she had left Ilthanara she had been the best archer under the age of forty. Using Heartseeker, which drew as easily as a child's practice bow but hurled arrows harder and farther than even the strongest man, she was unsurpassed.

Assuming that she was allowed to fire. Gennald stepped in front of her and spoiled her shot. "My lady, get behind me!"

She cursed, sidestepped the interfering but well intentioned knight, and loosed her arrow hastily. She missed her mark—inside its huge mouth—but her steel tipped arrow glanced off the scales on the side of its scaled head. The deflected arrow passed near enough to the A'Cha rider that it flinched away and jerked its reins accordingly. The massive dragon-lizard stumbled and jerked, missing both Illyria and Gennald.

Gennald's sword bit into its side. The dragon-lizard turned towards the Karalinian knight and lunged with its snapping teeth. Stepping backwards and drawing again, Illyria loosed and struck the A'Cha high in its chest. It clutched at its wound, screaming, and dropped its reins. Balien, on its other flank, stepped in to attack but was struck by the spinning beast's large tail and was sent sprawling.

It was all that Alwyn could do not to piss in his armour. Nothing in his life, not even the massive bear monster two days before, had frightened him as much as this giant lizard creature did now. He heard Illyria scream out for her brother and saw the elven prince roll to avoid massive claws. Somehow the sound of her anguished voice spurred him into action when his own fear did not.

The furred beastman rider, while wounded, remained in its saddle. *Stop the horse, stop its rider* he heard his old arms master say to him. Managing to avoid the same tail that had knocked over Balien, he stepped to the monster's side. His sword was still jammed in its scabbard—*oh, be honest man: your hands were shaking too much to get it out*—so he grabbed the beastman's arm with both hands and pulled. Without stirrups or a grip on its reins it was unable to resist as Alwyn dragged it to the ground.

Alwyn knew nothing more of what happened to the others. The beastman, while injured, was far from dead and was not without its own claws. It outweighed him by thirty pounds at least and had six inches of reach. If it were not for Alwyn's leather armour, it would have gutted him in the first few seconds. All he could do was wrestle with it and fight for his life.

The dragon-lizard reared and back stepped as Alwyn pulled the rider off of it. Illyria buried a feathered shaft deep into the creature's neck while Sir Gennald grabbed Balien's hand and pulled him free.

"Illyria, behind you!" Balien yelled. Illyria drew an arrow to her cheek as she turned. The other dragon-lizard, running faster than any horse, was almost upon them. Her arrow struck near its knee, causing it to stumble. The A'Cha on its back squawked in surprise as it was jarred and fell completely off the beast, dropping its reins as it did so. As Illyria nocked another shaft, the dragon-lizard roared in anger but, instead of continuing its charge, turned and buried its teeth into the neck of the A'Cha now lying in front of it.

The poor—*poor?*—A'Cha gave out a terrified scream and beat ineffectually at the scaled face and neck of its former mount. The dragon-lizard shook its orange furred prey with bone-snapping force. It only took two shakes before the A'Cha hung limply and the dragon-lizard wandered away.

Illyria shook her head in disbelief and turned back to more immediate battle. The dragon-lizard lay on its side and was screaming, a massive wound opened in the side of its neck. Balien, covered in gore, raised his sword above his head and brought it down into the open wound hard enough to sever its head completely. As she watched, Gennald attacked the A'Cha grappling with Alwyn and impaled it through its chest.

Alwyn felt the beastman stiffen and, a moment later, go limp. He pushed the now dead body off of him and accepted Sir Gennald's offered hand. "My thanks," he said grudgingly. Balien knelt beside the severed dragon-lizard head. "Balien, are you well?"

He nodded wordlessly and pushed himself to his feet by the blade of his sword. He turned to where Illyria, bow drawn, was looking towards the ravine.

Alwyn looked where her arrow pointed but saw nothing. "Where is the other one?"

She lowered her bow and shook her head, bemused. "It killed its rider and then ran off with the body. I hit it once, but not fatally."

"It is fortunate for us that the A'Cha don't make very good beast-riders," Balien commented. "At least one of us would have died if they hadn't been fighting with each other."

Alwyn agreed and turned to Gennald. "What was it that you found just before we were attacked? A cloth?"

Sir Gennald nodded glumly. "It belonged to my father. I can only conclude that these either these dogmen or those lizard-things killed him."

"If I may ask," Illyria said softly, "why would your father be out here?"

Gennald threw up his hands. "I have no idea. He rules Durnshold, more than fifteen leagues from here." He looked around him. "There's no reason for anyone to be out here. We don't allow any settlements this close to the mountains. It's too dangerous."

Illyria turned to the ravine. "Something's out there," she warned and drew back an arrow.

Alwyn looked but saw nothing. "Is it the lizard creature? Has it come back?"

"I don't think so." She shook her head while her pale blue eyes scanned the horizon.

"I hear it, too," Balien said. "I think it's a voice."

Alwyn tilted his head to the side, straining with his mortal ears to hear whatever phantom sound it was that only elves could perceive.

Something moved at the edge of the ravine. It was a man, crawling on all fours and wearing a crimson surcoat. Finally Alwyn was able to make out what he was saying.

"Gennald," the thin reedy voice whispered from the base of the hill. "Son."

Gennald gaped. "Father?"

" 'In all of the titan-world there are no creatures more powerful than the inhabitants of Deremsar, the get of Melal: dragons. There are none mightier, none greedier, none more vain, and none less inclined to compromise. To be a dragon is to be a king of all you survey. Dragons do not subserve. Of all the beings on all of the worlds, only dragons have the ability to travel between them at will. As the dragons continue to grow, however, so does their need for territory. Soon, not all of the lands of the Middle Waters will be enough to hold them, and on that day the entire cosmos will tremble.' "

—*Rytonis the Just*

CHAPTER FOUR

His bed-name was Tarim, but those unworthy of such familiarity called him Ta. He was the Olamm of his people, mightiest in his chiefdom and had earned the right to lead through honourable combat. Olamm-Ta stood on the small hill and surveyed the army that lay below him. It was mostly made up of cowardly A'Cha, a fact he did not like, but had found no way around that. His clan of loyal Vaulen—deadly warriors all—were simply too few to conquer the ice kingdom of Karalon without aid.

He shivered but resisted the urge to put on his cloak. This land, with its endless seas of green forests, was too damn cold. The A'Cha assured him that this was a perfect example of a summer day but Ta remained chilled. He, like the rest of his far-brothers, came from warmer lands.

This entire Kingdom was hideous, but he would rule here before he ever served in the glorious desolation of his former home. The Khalamm had given him a choice: serve him and adopt his heretical ways, resist him and face certain destruction, or leave Kalumfar entirely. Ta would die before he accepted the new ways, but he was not eager to run headlong to his death; not while there were other options.

He was a Vaul and his Maker, Gidim, had created his people to rule. He would not skulk in caves like so many of his brethren. If this cold, green land was all there was then he would claim it. If that meant using the A'Cha as weapons then he would do so. He would use any tool within reach if it gave him his kingdom.

"Olamm-Ta, my axe is yours." A lone Vaulan knelt before him. He had been there for the last quarter hour, axe held across his palms, waiting for Ta to recognize him. Ta took the offered weapon and gestured for its owner to rise.

"You are Gharda, are you not? First Axe of the White-Knife band?"

The disarmed Vaulan rose to his knees. As was customary, his armour had been removed and his chest was exposed. "Yes, Olamm. I serve with your band-mate, Navoi, at the far pass."

Olamm-Ta's eyes narrowed. "You would not be here if the news was not dire. Report."

Gharda met Ta's eyes. "Olamm, your near-sister is dead, and the outpost she commanded destroyed."

Ta hid the pain that lanced through him. Navoi had been closer to him than any other. It had pained him to banish her to the remote pass, but the mission had been an important one and there were none that he had trusted more. "Did she die well?"

Gharda hesitated. "She…died in battle, Olamm, but her slayer survives her."

Ta held the handle of Gharda's axe with whitened knuckles. "Tell me."

Gharda recounted his tale. When he had finished he straightened his shoulders and looked Ta squarely in the face. There was no fear in his eyes. Having told of his failure he was ready to die.

"Who is this human boar that slew my band-mate?" Ta growled.

"He is young, Olamm. Barely an adult, with long dark hair worn freely. He is slight of frame and wears no armour. His weapon is like no other in this land. It is a sword, but its blade is long and thin. He uses it both one handed and two with equal skill."

"I will have my revenge upon this human," Ta swore. "I shall feast upon his heart, if the Eye wills it."

"If the Eye wills it," Gharda repeated. He remained bare-chested on his knees. Ta hesitated.

"I know you stand ready to die, Gharda, and it speaks well of you, but I need every axe." He reversed the weapon he held and offered it back to the kneeling warrior. "These A'Cha prove difficult to train. Seek out Aerun, one of my band-mates. He will find a use for you."

Gharda paused before accepting the offered weapon. "Yes, Olamm." He rose to his feet and trotted down the hill to the army below.

"You are unnecessarily weak, Olamm," spoke a hissing, reedy voice from behind him.

Ta turned and glared at the diminutive, green-scaled being standing behind him. "I accept your aid and your council because we are of use to each other, but do not tell me how to rule my people." He smiled and raised his axe. "You are fast with your magic, I will grant you, but I am swift as well. Do you wish to test which of us is quicker?"

It hesitated before bowing deeply. "Forgive me, Olamm. I spoke out of place."

Ta lowered his axe. "It is forgotten. Now tell me more about these riding lizards you have conjured up." He would use any weapon to win himself a kingdom, even ally himself with a Djido.

Sir Gennald's father, Harrin, lay fevered and sweating. "His wound is infected, he's malnourished and exhausted, but none of it is fatal." Balien told everyone. Illyria wasn't ashamed to admit that her brother's skill in the healing arts surpassed her own. "He should recover if we can get him to Northhaven tomorrow."

"He will," Sir Gennald swore. "I will take him to the healer's door myself."

"You will not," his father ordered weakly from the cot where he lay. His face was pale and sweat dotted his brow as he fought to remain conscious. "Let these good people do that. You must focus on retaking Durnshold. That is all that is important."

"I'm sorry, but I don't understand." Alwyn said. He had donated his tent and bed to the ailing man. "I thought we were going to Northhaven. Where's Durnshold?"

"We are going to Northhaven," Gennald told him impatiently. "It is the seat my liege, March-lord Hanley, and he must know of what has happened. Durnshold is a keep, the most important in all of Karalon. It guards the only bridge across the Lyssal River." His face was grim in the flickering torchlight. "If someone has taken control of it, then the whole kingdom is vulnerable."

"Why did you travel this way?" Illyria asked the fevered man gently. "Why didn't you make your way to Northhaven?"

"And how was the keep taken, father?" Gennald added.

"Stop, all of you." Harrin raised a shaking hand. His voice, while weak, still rang with authority. "I only have the strength to tell this once, so heed my words." Everyone quieted. "The reason I came this way, young lady, is that the road to Northhaven is blocked by more of those lizard creatures. I knew that my son was waiting at the Urdom road for all of you and decided you were my best chance." His face clouded. "I almost made it, but those lizard things track better than bloodhounds. They killed my horse and I barely managed to escape into that ravine." His voice faltered.

Gennald knelt and took his father's hand. "You did make it, father. You have warned us. Now what happened at the keep?"

"There was magic, that much I do know," he spat. "My men would never have betrayed me otherwise."

Gennald cursed. "Magic? Truly?"

"My own personal guard held me at sword point while my seneschal opened the gate and let those lizard things and two dozen dogmen into the keep."

"How do you know they weren't just bribed?" Alwyn asked. "I'm sorry," he said to Gennald's shocked look, "but it's easier for me to accept that you were betrayed than that a wizard has somehow appeared. The wizards died out with the High Kingdom."

"I saw him control them!" the older man yelled before breaking into a fit of coughing. He waved away his son's offer of water. "I saw my men's faces. They were ensorcelled. I'd stake my life on it. They didn't answer to their own names and only obeyed the wizard's instructions. All of them did, even the dogmen."

"The wizard, was he human?" Balien asked.

"Yes. I'd strangle him myself if I could. I can't believe any man would betray his own kind, and to dogmen at that!"

"How did you escape, my lord?" Illyria asked.

Harrin grinned weakly. "I know my keep better than any traitorous magic user. I played at being weak and the wizard reduced the number of guards on me. When they weren't looking, I snuck out a hidden passage and went down to the stable." He scowled. "They control the whole town. I didn't know who I could trust, so I grabbed the nearest horse I could and ran. When I saw that the road to Northhaven was blocked, I made my way here, and the rest you know."

"You did very well, my lord," Illyria assured him. "You have passed on your message and should rest." She looked pointedly at the others.

"Rest well, father," Gennald said gently. "I will restore our honour, I swear it by Emuranna. I will retake Durnshold keep."

Lying on the pallet, Harrin smiled weakly. "I know you will, son."

"I have journeyed to every corner of Anshara, and I have never seen the like of this." Theramus declared after examining the severed head.

"It's not any kind of dragon?" Alwyn asked.

"It is definitely not so. No dragon would subject itself to being ridden by another creature, especially something as lowly as an A'Cha. Perhaps it was altered by the Djido, like the creature we fought earlier, or it is an Interloper from another Titan-World." He fervently hoped that the latter was not the case.

They were all silent.

Sephana examined the head. "There's something between its eyes."

"It's a mark of some kind, almost like a brand." Balien drew his knife and cut it free from the creature's skull. "Do you recognize it, Theramus?"

The square patch of thick green scales framed a raised circle the size of an Anduili gold sovereign. A symbol lay inside it. "I do not. It is not a letter or number from any alphabet I recognize"

Sephana pulled on Theramus' upraised hand and held it close to her face. "I know what that is." She looked up at him and then out to Illyria and Balien, jaw knotted and eyes bright with anger. "I saw it all the time in Akkilon. It means 'slave.' "

It took half an hour to persuade Sir Gennald not to ride to Northhaven until morning. If it hadn't clouded over and started to rain just before sunset, he would likely never have been convinced. He chose to leave at first light instead and reach Northhaven before noon. The rest of the caravan would press hard and arrive hopefully by nightfall.

Alwyn had no idea what would happen when they arrived.

His hood up because of the rain, Alwyn was walking back to his tent when he saw Illyria sitting in the lee of a wagon tarp and staring into a dying cook-fire. Emotions warred in his heart. His love for her remained undiminished. He saw her golden hair in his dreams at night, heard her laughter, and the felt her hand in his. However powerful his love, it had been rivalled this morning by bitter disappointment when she had told him of her engagement. A small, rational part of Alwyn's mind chided him for being so foolish. She was beautiful, intelligent, of age and, above all, royal. Her marriage had likely been arranged since she had been a child.

That whisper of common sense had been drowned out by the scream of jealous anger when he had seen her not just talking but laughing and flirting with Sir Gennald. The flame of anger continued to burn as he walked to Illyria.

"Will you see him off?" he asked without preamble.

She looked up, confused. Her face was lost in shadow. "I'm sorry?"

"Sir Gennald." It was hard to say his name without snarling. "Will you be seeing him off in the morning?"

"I may. I haven't really thought about it." She looked at him warily. "Why do you ask, your highness?"

He paced like a caged dog. "I see how the two of you look at each other."

"I don't know what you mean."

"You stare at each other when the other isn't looking," he accused. "I can see it. Everyone can see it."

"Does he really?" She smiled briefly, then regarded him through narrowed eyes. "I don't know what you want me so say, Alwyn."

"Have you told him that you're engaged?" he growled through clenched teeth.

"I have not, not that it's any of your concern."

"Will you do so before you bed him or after?" Even as he said the words he knew that he had gone too far.

She rose to her feet slowly and precisely. Her face was a mask. "It has been an eventful day and you are tired, your highness." Her voice was chilling. "We shall speak again in the morning."

His anger fled and was replaced with panic. "Illyria, wait. I'm sorry." He stepped in front of her. "I spoke without thinking. Forgive me, please."

Her eyes blazed with barely contained anger, yet her words remained cold. "There has been nothing unseemly in my dealings with Sir Gennald, your highness, nor in my dealings with you. If you were led to believe anything regarding my affections, I apologize. My relationship with you has always been and will remain that of allies striving towards a common goal." She stepped around him. "Good night."

"Wait, please. I'm an ass, and I'm sorry. I'm…" He stopped and tried again. "You are…" No, that wasn't it either. He cleared his throat. "None of that matters right now. May I ask your intentions in regards to these Vaulen, and this whole business with the dragon-lizards and Durnshold Keep?"

She regarded him in icy silence for what felt like an eternity. "I don't know." Her tone wasn't warm, but it also wasn't quite as chilly as before. "I will give what aid I can, certainly, and ensure that Lord Harrin survives his journey to Northhaven." She tilted her head. "What are your intentions, your highness?"

She's still talking to me! "I cannot get involved in a foreign war. I am sorry if this seems cowardly to you, but I must represent the interests of Derwyn."

"There is nothing to apologize for. It is a sensible position."

He licked his lips. "It is my thinking that that this land will erupt in war within a week, and I mean to beyond its borders when that happens. Will you come with me?" he asked. "The force that we fought in the mountains could not possibly have been reinforced yet. If we leave Northhaven quickly we can be over the Urdom pass before anyone knows that we've even left." He met her eyes. "I would see you safe, my lady, even if you are promised to another."

She gave him the faintest of smiles and his heart soared. "Kind words, your highness. I…" she hesitated. "I am sorry that I did not tell you about my engagement. It was not my intention to cause you pain."

"Will you come with me?" he asked her again. "Your arrangement with my father involved escorting us both to Karalon and back."

She was silent a moment. "I will of course honour my agreement with your father. My companions and I will see you safely back across the mountains. If you will excuse me?"

Alwyn stepped aside. "Of course. Have a good night, my lady. Sleep well." He knew that he certainly wouldn't.

Illyria slept fitfully and was awake in plenty of time to see Sir Gennald off. The rain had tapered off an hour before and the morning, while still cool and damp, was clear.

Alwyn's accusations still rang in her ears. While she disliked the idea that she was the cause of the hurtful anger in his voice she refused to feel guilty. *I never gave him any false indications. I never said anything that wasn't truthful.* If he had imagined something from his interactions with her, then it was his error and not hers. She would not be held responsible for something she had not done.

'I see how the two of you look at each other.' While some of his words had been jealous bile, that one held merit. She had shared several warm looks with the handsome Karalinian knight, and some of them had lingered more than was appropriate.

'Have you told him that you're engaged?' No, she hadn't. There was even less reason to do so with Gennald then there had been with Alwyn. She wouldn't be in Karalon long enough for anything to happen—if she was inclined to let anything happen, which she was not—and he was likely to be engaged in military action anyway.

She would remain civil and polite with him. She didn't want to give him the wrong impression. Also, she hadn't forgiven him yet for spoiling her shot against the dragon-lizard.

The lamp of Nuran was just cresting the hills when she saw Sir Gennald leading his horse to the edge of the camp. "Sir," she said, smiling.

"Lady." His stern features broke into momentary smile. "My men will see you safely to Northhaven," His gold and black surcoat was resplendent in the morning sun. "Take care of my father."

"I will." He was close enough to touch, but she refrained. "Ride well." His eyes locked with hers. She thought he would reach his hand out but instead only nodded before vaulting into his saddle and galloping off. There was just enough light for him to see. She slowly made her way back to the tent she shared with the others.

He hadn't said anything, or even touched her. She tried to ignore her pang of disappointment. It was just as well. Alwyn's caravan would be back in the mountains in less than a week and would emerge in Nemora three weeks after that. SummersEnd—the date she had promised to return home by—was less than a month later. It was the minimum amount of time needed to properly plan a royal wedding on Autumn's Heart.

A wedding. *Marriage.*

Her mother, Kyria, had not wanted Illyria to leave Ilthanara but had ultimately supported her daughter's decision. She had been the one who had championed Illyria against the wishes of her eldest brother, the king. King Kefeus had agreed in the end but had insisted on the addition of a caveat: a fixed wedding date as a guarantee of Illyria's return. He had made her swear on her father's grave that she would do so. Many things about Illyria's upbringing had been unconventional but on this matter he had had been adamant: as a damsel and Child of the Mark she was required by custom to wed and produce an heir. To not do her part to continue the royal bloodline—even if her children never received the crown—would be a betrayal of her people. Balien, being only her half brother, was exempt.

Illyria's father had died before she could form any memories of him. He had been a proper crownmarked prince and, like all men of the Ilthwood, had done his part to safeguard its borders. He had encountered a man being chased by a group of others during one of his patrols. For reasons known only to Emuranna he had defied custom to aid the single man though it cost him his life. Her father had taught the stranger the phrase of hospitality with his dying breath which could not be denied. An exile from his own people, the stranger had been grudgingly accepted into Ilthanara and allowed to stay in the residence of his saviour's widow.

Kyria had never loved her husband—it was not required in royal unions—and in the stranger, Britheon, she had discovered a joy seldom found among Ilthanaran nobility. When they had asked the king for permission to marry after the year of mourning he had not objected. Illyria and her younger half-brother had been raised in a house of love, but it was also a house that defied Ilthanaran custom. Illyria had worshipped her adopted father and wanted to be like him in all ways. There was no law forbidding him from teaching her the use of bow and sword, despite modern custom, and so she had learned those skills alongside her brother from her father's hand.

Her uncle had allowed it, with the proviso that she also be instructed in the decorum required of a princess, and that she fulfilled her obligation of marriage. Illyria had agreed blithely; to a ten year old such an time seemed a lifetime away. It was only as she approached adulthood that the restrictions of her promise begin to weigh on her like shackles.

Britheon had died much as her birth father had. She and Balien had been patrolling with him when they had been beset by attackers. It was Illyria's first life or death battle and she had frozen in fear. Her adopted father had died protecting her, though he had insisted with his final words to her that she not blame herself. He had private words with Balien, the child of his blood, before expiring. He had been buried as a citizen of Ilthanara with full royal honours.

Illyria and Balien had left for their tour of the petty kingdoms within a year of their father's death. She had found them shockingly primitive compared to the sheltered kingdom where she had been raised. They barely communicated with each other and, given Illyria's court training, negotiating peace and then trade was, while not easy, natural and satisfying.

The greatest of the so-called 'petty kingdoms' was called Derwyn and its ruler, King Gwyn, had eyes that were quick to see opportunity. At peace with all of his neighbours for the first time in generations, he cast his eyes across the seemingly impenetrable Karnem Mountains. Illyria had thrilled at the idea of exploring another kingdom and volunteered (along with Theramus and Sephana) to journey there as his representative. Their current mission was the end result of that exploration and while her deadline drew ever nearer, she still had time to escort and advise Alwyn on this first, most important, trade mission. She was coming very close to the time limit imposed by her king, but with her timely retreat across the mountains she would return home with weeks to spare.

All was as well as it could be. Why did it feel so *wrong?*

" 'There are six colleges of magic and in each college five rings of mastery. Only one who masters the fourth ring will be given the title of Wizard, and only a wizard of all colleges can withstand the ordeal needed to become an Archmage. Only then does a wizard's true education begin.' "

—The words of Renthalin

CHAPTER FIVE

"No, no, that won't do at all!" Eldoth glowered at the large, tattooed lizardman that had been given to him by his Djido master. "I told you to clear everything out of this room, not just move it to one side. Get everything out of here now." He rolled his eyes. "I was told that you were an *intelligent* creature and capable of following instructions. Apparently that is not the case."

The creature was a muscular biped covered with dappled yellow scales. Its name was Draxul and it growled at Eldoth angrily. As further indicators of its mood, its large amber eyes were narrowed to slits and its long fingered hands clenched and released at random intervals. If it wanted to kill him, it could do so easily with any of the above mentioned limbs or the two strange, hooked swords strapped to its back and Eldoth would have very little to say about it.

Fortunately for him, it could not. Obedience to its Djido master forbade such an act, just as it required Eldoth to aid him. Baiting the moronic creature was perhaps unwise, but it was entertaining, and being the lord and master of this dead, empty castle held few other distractions. There were only ten books in its 'library'. Three were ledgers, two were volumes filled with insipid poetry, one was a largely embellished history of the local nobility and rest fanciful mythological tales. It was useless rubbish, all of it.

"Take too long," protested the lizard-thing with its limited vocabulary. "Be late. Not finish." Its lizard mouth spoke the human tongue with difficulty and its voice reminded Eldoth of a quacking duck, an angry, weapon festooned duck covered in mystical tattoos, but a duck nonetheless.

"Then take some of those furred dolts off of guard duty and have them gather people from the town," Eldoth instructed. "They're stupid peasants who probably can't even spell their own names, but they are surely capable of this simple task."

The lizard-thing just stood there.

"Well, what are you waiting for?" He waved it away with his hand. "Go."

It gave him a final, impotent glare, turned, and left the room. Once he was sure that it was gone, Eldoth locked the door. Certain that no one was watching, he crossed to the closest chair, sat down, and dropped his face into his hands.

"What am I going to do?" he moaned.

He was the prisoner of a Djido. A Djido! There weren't supposed to be any left. The histories said that they had all either been killed or cast out centuries before.

Their cruelties, both magical and mundane, had been so excessive that even the kingdom they had claimed for their own, Akkilon, had overthrown them. Their names were still whispered with fear twenty generations later and images of their scaly faces—part human, part snake—were spat upon by all free men.

Now, not only was there a Djido sorcerer free in Karalon, but Eldoth was his prisoner and, worse, was barred from using his own wizarding powers. He fingered the leather, rune-scribed headband adhered to his forehead. If he had his stele he could remove it and fight his way free of this infernal place, but Draxul kept the magical device on its person at all times. There was no way he could overpower the imposing creature without it. It was his jailor as much as his minion.

"I'm doomed."

This particular task was only going to occupy it for two or three hours. Hopefully Eldoth could conjure up another hollow excuse for why he could not yet begin the duty assigned to him. He was sure he could delay the inevitable by perhaps a day, but what then?

Perhaps the old man had escaped. Eldoth had received no reports from the cavalry that he had sent out in pursuit. There was no way that one man could defeat two thunder lizards. They were as fast as horses and incredibly vicious, but those assets were offset by their riders' tremendous stupidity. The old man might have outwitted them. Maybe he had been able to reach a city and summon help. Maybe…

Maybe what? The keep was impenetrable. Ten men on top of its walls could hold off an army. Whoever held the keep controlled the bridge, and whoever controlled the bridge held the fate of the Karalon in their hands.

Heavy footsteps sounded in the corridor and he rushed to the door, unlocking it and settling his sneer in place. The lizardman opened the door and glared at Eldoth suspiciously.

"Well?"

"Slaves come," it quacked. "Sun end, room clear. Then you search."

Not if I can't think of something else to delay you. "Yes, then I search," he answered contemptuously. "Don't worry your tiny little mind. I will unlock this castle's secret for our master."

It hissed at him and left.

The city of Northhaven was crude and ugly but impressive nonetheless. The walls were merely functional with no thought put into ornamentation. What stonework there was beyond its faded grey palisades was blocky and dull, and Sephana knew from her previous trip that there wasn't even one tiny statue inside. Even these dull structures, however, could not diminish the dramatic silhouette the city cast against the setting sun. It hung blazing red above the tallest building, casting its orange-tinged light across the steep hill and river valley that it overlooked. Rocky cliffs formed three of the city's borders and the fourth—criss-crossed by a steep switchback path—was only marginally shallower.

"Are the oxen going to make it up to the gate?" she asked Balien doubtfully. The two had been walking together and idly chatting since their hasty dinner break. "They're getting pretty tired."

He shaded his eyes and examined the steep grade ahead. She couldn't see his eyes in the dark shadow. "They're going to have to. It's too dangerous to stay outside."

They passed into the long shadow cast by the hill. "I'm trying to figure out if sleeping in a real bed for the first time in a month is going to be worth climbing that hill." She eyed the road critically. "It looks even steeper than it did the last time we were here."

"It might be the only night you have to sleep in one," he warned. "If Alwyn has his way we could be off again as early as tomorrow."

"I know," she sighed, "but even a single night is better than nothing." She'd slept in few enough actual beds that even one night would be noteworthy. She scratched her head through her head scarf and let herself imagine how good it would feel to let the breeze flow through her hair. She glanced up at Balien. "So we're really heading back out so quickly? We're not staying here at all?"

His lips tightened minutely. "Alwyn wants to get back across the pass before the mountain road gets any more dangerous. He's willing to abandon the wagons if he has to."

"I hope Sir Gennald is all right fighting those lizard things." Her concern was more for Illyria than the knight.

He didn't reply, but she could see his jaw tighten.

They walked in silence for a while. Balien got dark and quiet like this sometimes, usually after arguing with his sister. They tried to keep their disagreements private but it was impossible to hide things in such a small group. Sephana didn't really get what he had to be broody about. Unlike her, he had a home, a family, and a future ahead of him. When he was finished playing caravan guard with Illyria he could go right back to his hidden city and be welcomed with open arms. If anyone had an excuse to be broody, it was his sister.

"Is she really going to do it?" Sephana asked when it became too quiet. "Marry her cousin?"

"It's what she agreed to." He noticed her scowl. "I know Turius. He's a good man."

Sephana snorted. "Sure, as long as she produces an heir for him and serves him politely."

He gave her an odd look. "She'll be married. Marriages are about children." He paused. "Not all of them are bad, you know."

She couldn't help the disbelieving snort that came out of her mouth. It was easy to forget that Balien hailed from a hidden forest paradise and had grown up insulated from the real world. He meant well, but sometimes he really didn't know what he was talking about.

A pair of horsemen waited at the base of the hill. Alwyn rode up to the head of the column to meet them and offered no objections when Illyria accompanied him. They had said little to each other during the day, which was perhaps just as well.

The two men were obviously nobles. Both horses were...*clothed*...in black and yellow cloth that covered their bodies but left their necks and tails free. Alwyn had never seen anything like it. It was odd and without a doubt expensive, but very striking. He liked it. Something like it would look handsome on his own horse when he returned home victoriously. Perhaps it would ease his father's unhappiness when he learned that his son came back without an elven bride.

The elder man had to be the lord of the city, Willem Jannery, though his dress was rather plain. Next to him was a youth, somewhere in that frustrating place between boy and man, who was dressed much better.

Alwyn stopped a horse length away. "Lord Jannery, I am Alwyn ap Gwyn, Prince of Derwyn." He nodded to the older man deferentially. "I greet you this day in the name of peace and future prosperity." It was easier to say this time.

The man shuffled uncomfortably and would not meet Alwyn's eye. Beside him, the youth reddened. "I am Davin Jannery, acting March-lord of Northhaven," he said stiffly. "On behalf of my father, greetings and welcome to Northhaven."

He sends a boy to greet me? Alwyn kept his irritation hidden. He needed to compress two weeks of negotiating and bartering into two short days. There was no need to antagonize his host. "My apologies, lord Davin. I meant no insult. The letter from your father indicated that he would be meeting me."

"My father—that is, Lord Jannery—was regretfully called away on the command of King Lionar," the boy, Davin, said with an air of reciting a line much practised. Alwyn could relate. "He extends his deepest apologies and offers you his every hospitality in his absence."

Alwyn nodded. "My thanks." He looked behind him. "It has been a dangerous journey. I would like to see my men and cargo into the city before nightfall."

"Of course. My man, Addison, will see to their needs." Davin nodded to the older man. "If you will come with me, Prince Alwyn, dinner has been prepared for you and your knights in my father's manor."

Alwyn nodded. As much as he wanted to get down to business, he was not fool enough to turn down hot food and, presumably, a down-turned bed.

Illyria stepped forward. "Excuse me, my lord?"

Davin turned at the sound of her voice. Alwyn could see his eyes widen as he took her in. Elvish princesses were obviously unheard of here.

"I, umm, yes?"

She bowed smoothly. "I am Illyria of Ilthanara, Companion to Alwyn ap Gwyn. If I may ask: when your father left on the king's business, was it before or after Sir Gennald returned?" The boy just stared at her. "Sir Gennald did return, did he not? He should have arrived here by noon today."

Davin and the older man, Addison, exchanged a look. The boy looked away first. "Yes, Sir Gennald returned today, but my father left two days ago. They did not meet."

Illyria's eyes narrowed. "Is he well? I'd like to see him."

The boy stared at his pommel. "He took sick. I don't think he can have visitors."

It was a bald lie, even to Alwyn's ears, but Illyria seemed to take no notice. "I see. Thank you, my lord." She turned to Alwyn. "Enjoy your dinner, your highness. I will see to your men and the cargo." Her eyes, a dark shade of blue, met his sharply for a moment longer than they needed to. Alwyn understood her message, or at least he thought he did: *be careful.*

He held her gaze and nodded, hoping that she received his own non-verbal confirmation. "Then I leave the matter in your hands, lady." He spurred his horse forward. "My lord?"

The boy nodded, relieved, and led Alwyn up the steep path.

"Is there anything else you require, err, *miss*, or shall I escort you to my lord's manor now?" asked Addison, the march-lord's seneschal.

Illyria paused. Getting the train of tired oxen into the city had been a long and unpleasant task, and Nuran had fully set by the time the last wagon trundled through the city gate. A large portion of the city's population had come out to greet the foreign visitors and cheer their arrival, despite the late hour. Space had been cleared for them in the city's marshalling yard. Most of the men had to make do with the same tents and blankets that they had slept in for the entire journey, but hot food and cold beer had been waiting for the road-weary Nemormen. It went far to improving their mood.

With the camp laid out, animals tended, men fed, and cargo secured for the night, Illyria was finally able to continue with her business. "Everything is perfect, thank you, but rather than go to the manor I was hoping to see Sir Gennald."

"S-sir Gennald?" he stammered. "He-he's, umm, ill." His throat bobbed like the pigeon's head.

She smiled sweetly. "So I was told, but I'd like to see him anyway. He was only with us for a day, but we got along well. I am concerned for him."

Addison grew nervous. "The knight is…well, he fell into a fever. He is raving and disconsolate."

Illyria met the factor's eyes squarely. "My lord, please, let us stop lying to each other. I saw him this morning and he was hale as an ox. I would ask you to please let me see him, even if he lies on Zulum's gate."

He grimaced. "My lord—that is, lord Jannery the younger—gave strict orders that sir Gennald was not to be seen by anyone."

"And why is that? Did you not hear his news about his father and the fall of Durnshold keep?"

"Lower your voice, woman!" He stepped in close. "That is not to be spoken of, by order of my lord!"

She stared, ignoring for the moment how she had been addressed. "Why did he command that? He should be rousing every man within these walls for a counterattack."

He looked away. "Whether I agree with you or not, I cannot contradict my lord or disobey a direct order."

"Isn't your lord Davin's father?"

"Before he left, Lord Willem said that young Davin spoke for him 'in all things.'" He shook his head sadly. "The rules of fealty are clear. Until my lord Willem returns or we receive word of his passing, his son is my liege and I cannot disobey him. To do so would be my death."

She rubbed her brow. "Davin is not *my* liege and I am under no compulsion to obey his orders. If you cannot take me to sir Gennald, then would it be against your honour to at least tell me where he is?"

Addison smiled with relief. "Gladly."

Theramus sat cross-legged on the floor and reflected upon the many hindrances of being a Noss living in the world of men. He was accustomed to doorways being too small for him and having to walk sideways through narrow hallways. Their furniture could not accommodate him, their dishes didn't fit his hands, and even the largest men eyed him with trepidation

There was also the hindrance of age. His kind took long journeys on their life-roads while the paths taken by men seemed to grow shorter and shorter. In the forty years of journeying across Anshara, two entire generations of men had been born and a third was within sight. Men could do great things—he believed this to be so—but only after learning years of hard-won wisdom. They had to survive the trials of adolescence with its accompanied flares of passion and apathy first. Youths loved with greater intensity, embraced causes with greater passion and hated with hotter fire.

They could also be incredibly petulant and stubborn—as young Davin was being right now—and Theramus was growing weary of it. Even the most insufferable of children could become the wisest of men, and it was possible that young Davin might someday become a champion of his people. That was dependant, however, on Theramus not throttling him first.

They were in their second hour of their celebratory dinner and the boy continued to prattle on about the labyrinth of petty lies and promises that made up Karalinian court life. Any attempts to speak on other subjects lasted only a few minutes before Davin again wrestled the topic back where he wanted it to be. Life in Nemora, the perils of crossing the Karnem Mountains, the pitched battle waged in the Marchel valley: none of it was more important than listing the names and positions of the Golden Bears and the Anderites.

"The grain harvest has been diminishing for two years running?" Balien asked with genuine concern. He had been raised in a royal court and had a greater tolerance for such things. "This is worrisome."

"I know!" Davin nodded, his face aflame with a fanatic's zeal. "It's just more proof that the Bears don't have a foot to stand on. They're hypocrites, all of them."

"My concern is more farmers and those dependant on the food they provide," Balien chided. "Famine always hits the poor hardest. Surely that must be the greatest concern of both parties."

"Of course, of course." Davin waved his hand dismissively. "But that is just my point. The Golden Bears aren't doing anything, just hoping that things magically get better. Prince Ander isn't going to stand around in his garden. He's going to take action!"

Theramus forced back a sigh. Beside him, Sephana shifted restlessly in her seat and played with her cutlery while Alwyn drank down yet another goblet of wine. Dinner's final course had just been taken away. The repast had been excellent and a welcome change from camp food. Theramus, like the others, had been willing to humour their young host during their meal, but that humour was quickly fading and the lad was too oblivious to notice.

A human girl entered the room. By her dress, Theramus guessed that she was noble as well. "Davin, are you *still* talking about politics?"

Davin flushed and stared into his wine cup. "I'm entertaining, Elorin," he said evenly. "This is not a place for women."

Theramus placed a warning hand on Sephana's leg even as, on her other side, Balien did the same. She glared at both of them, but kept her silence.

"Don't be silly. There's already a woman at the table." She curtsied. "Forgive my brother's manners. I am Elorin Hanley. I take it that you are the delegation from Nemora?"

Alwyn bolted to his feet. "It is a pleasure, my lady. I am Alwyn ap Gwyn, Prince of Derwyn." He gestured to Theramus and the others. "This is Balien, Theramus and Sephana, my…men."

Balien stood. "A star shines upon our meeting, my lady. It is my honour to meet you."

Her cheeks reddened. "You are too kind, Sir Balien."

"Why are you here, Elorin?" Davin growled.

She turned to her brother. "I came to meet our important guests, since you didn't bother to introduce us. Also, to suggest if maybe you shouldn't retire for the evening. It is late, and your guests have had very a long day."

The boy flushed, embarrassed. "I was going to introduce you tomorrow."

"It has been a long day," Balien suggested. "If you would excuse me, my lord?"

The boy blinked. "Uh, yes. Of course."

Everyone quickly echoed him. Elorin curtsied again. "May I escort you to your rooms?"

"That would be most kind." Alwyn nodded to Davin. "Good night, my lord. We will discuss business in the morning."

They fled the room as quickly as propriety would allow.

Illyria waited impatiently in the dark solarium. She did not want to be alone with her thoughts but was unable to escape them. She had met with Sir Gennald (who *had not* been inflicted with a fever) and he did not like what he had told her. She had almost stormed into the dining room to have words with young Davin but had not trusted herself to remain civil. Instead, she had met his older sister, Elorin, who volunteered to pass a message to her companions. All she could do was wait until they arrived, but she didn't know what she was going to say to them. She didn't know anything anymore.

Finally, she heard voices approaching. "This isn't the way to our rooms, my lady," Balien said.

"I'm sorry, it isn't my intention to deceive you," the maiden replied. "I bear a message from your sister."

"Is Illyria all right?"

She smiled at her brother's concerned tone. His devotion to her was a greater comfort than even the warmest blanket. She considered Theramus her friend and, to a lesser degree, Sephana, but her love for her brother was absolute.

"I'm fine, Balien," she said as they entered the room. "Thank you for bringing them here, Elorin."

She curtsied. "It was my pleasure, my lady."

Balien looked at her curiously. "Why are we here, Illyria?"

She took a deep, shaky breath. "Thank you for coming. There has been an unfortunate development." Her voice hardened. "Sir Gennald has been imprisoned by orders of lord Davin. All men sworn to him have been recalled for the defence of the city. There is no action being taken to recapture Durnshold."

There was a moment of silence. "Why would he do such a thing?" Theramus asked.

Alwyn snorted. "Because he's a stupid brat who doesn't know what he's doing."

Elorin glared at him frostily. "Mind your words, sir. He is my brother and the current lord of this city."

He scrambled to correct his blunder. "Your pardon, my lady. I spoke hastily, but I stand behind my words. He is a boy and is ill prepared for this task."

"Lady Elorin, would I be correct in assuming that Sir Gennald is a Golden Bear?" Balien asked.

Elorin nodded.

Illyria frowned. "Sir Gennald mentioned that term as well, but I didn't understand what he meant."

"A Golden Bear is someone who remains loyal to the king," Balien told her. "There are a group of nobles who feel that the king is weakening. The last two harvests have been low and they think he's lost his connection to the land."

Illyria's breath caught. Only an accusation of treason was more dire. "That could lead to civil war."

"My father and his men all support the king, everyone except Davin." Elorin explained. "He has friends that he corresponds with and they have convinced him to support Prince Ander. My father forbade him to speak on the subject, but with him gone and Davin acting as lord…" She shrugged helplessly.

"Where is your father, my lady?" Balien asked. "Does his leaving have anything to do with this?"

She nodded. "King Lionar called for an emergency council. My father left within an hour of getting the letter."

"The kingdom has been invaded by foreign attackers," Theramus protested. He was standing in the room's centre like an oak surrounded by shrubs. "This has nothing to do with internal politics. Why would Davin imprison his strongest warrior?"

"Because he doesn't believe it," Balien answered. "Wizards, magic spells and dragon-lizards? It too far-fetched. Davin thinks it's an excuse to strip him of his power." He turned to Elorin. "Am I correct? He thinks that Gennald is attempting to subvert him?"

"I believe so, yes. They used to be friends. Davin worshipped Gennald before all of this, but now he hates him."

"He feels betrayed by his former mentor," Theramus murmured. "From what you say, I think that hatred will cloud his reason."

Sephana had to speak up. "Excuse me. I don't mean to sound insensitive, but why do we care about any of this?" Everyone turned to look at her and she fidgeted under their combined scrutiny. "I mean, aren't we going back across the mountains right away? None of this is our problem…is it?"

Balien filled the uncomfortable silence. "She does have a point, Lyri. Why are you so concerned about this?"

Sephana had never seen Illyria look so hesitant. Her normally bright eyes were the dull grey of wash water.

"I don't know," Illyria admitted quietly. "You're right, Sephana: this has nothing to do with us." She met Sephana's eye briefly before glancing at Alwyn. "We've made promises and have responsibilities. Getting involved here would jeopardize all of that. I've been telling myself this over and over." She turned to her brother, her expression asking for help. "It doesn't make sense," she continued. "It's just that…"

Balien finally spoke. "It's just what?"

Her face hardened. "Doesn't it bother you?" Her tone was indignant. "People are danger and we're in a position to help them, but we're choosing not to. Don't you find that…offensive?"

"It's better than getting eaten by a dragon-lizard," Sephana blurted and everyone's eyes fixed on her again. She flushed and was happy for once to be Reshai: no one could see her embarrassment. "Seriously, I don't want to fight those things. Let's just go back…" she looked away. She had been about to say 'home'.

"What do you want to do, Illyria?" Balien asked bluntly. "Say it. You know I'll support you no matter what you decide."

"What can we do?" Sephana asked loudly. "There's only four of us."

Elorin's face clouded in confusion. "But you have over fifty soldiers."

"Forgive me, my lady, but she does not," Alwyn told her. "Those men belong to the kingdom of Derwyn and are tasked with the protection of the trade caravan. I'm sorry, but I cannot put them at unnecessary risk."

Theramus glared at Alwyn. "There is an entire kingdom of people at risk. Thousands will be killed if an army crosses into the Karalinian heartland. If it is in your power to prevent that then you must do so."

Alwyn's face hardened with resolve. "What you say may be true, but my duty lies with my kingdom and this trade mission. My men must stay with the caravan." He turned to look at both Elorin and Illyria. "I'm sorry."

Theramus made no effort to hide his contempt.

"Illyria, what do you want to do?" Balien asked. "You have my support."

"Mine as well," Theramus declared.

They looked at Sephana, who blanched. "What?" she squeaked. "I don't want to do this. Why can't we stay here?"

He could forgive her for not having courage now. She would later, when it counted. "I will protect you with my life, Sephana. I swear it will be so."

"I…" She sighed and rolled her eyes. "OK, fine." Theramus hid his smile.

Balien looked at his sister. "Illyria?"

She glowed with confidence, completely ignorant of how she commanded the room's attention. "Alwyn, how long will it take you to complete the trade, re-provision, and be ready to go?"

"No more than two days, if I can help it."

"If you leave on the dawn of the third day that leaves us two days and three nights." She turned to Elorin. "Can we get to Durnshold and back by then?"

"You should." The girl's face was aglow. "I can give you a map."

"We can't retake a keep in two days with just four people," Balien warned.

"No, but we can scout it, find out what their numbers are and bring that information back here." She said. "Elorin, would your brother change his mind if we gave him proof that this isn't some hoax to discredit him?"

"I think so, yes."

"My lady, please do not do this," Alwyn pleaded. "Saying nothing of your promise to aid me and my father, this is reckless." He lowered his voice. "I do not wish to see you hurt. Please."

"Thank you for your concern, your highness," she said politely. "I will return in time to honour my obligations." She shared a look with Balien. "All of them."

"So we're really doing this?" Sephana asked, resigned.

"I don't know," Balien gazed levelly at his sister. "She hasn't asked us yet."

Illyria took a deep breath. "Balien, Sephana, Theramus, will you please help me in this?" Her voice softened. "Helping these people, it feels *right*. More right than anything I've ever done before. I don't know why."

Theramus did.

"Because it is noble and right. Because all men on Anshara are united, no matter what kingdom they belong to." He laid his words of comfort over her like a blanket on a winter's day. "Because it is the duty of those with power to protect those without it for the benefit of all and because to see evil done and do nothing is to be party to it. I will proudly serve you in this endeavour, Illyria, and beyond."

"I…thank you, Theramus." She blinked away tears, her eyes turning a warm brown. "That was very well said."

"You have my support, Illyria. Always." Balien said.

Sephana just shrugged. "I already said I would, but I'm not going to make a speech about it or anything."

Illyria smiled. "Thank you, all of you," She turned to Lady Elorin. "My lady if I could get that map? And trouble you for some supplies?"

Elorin rose. "You shall have anything you require." The two of them left the room, discussing logistics

"I'm not going to get to sleep in that bed tonight, am I?" Sephana moaned.

Theramus put on his most sympathetic expression. "No, I am afraid not."

Alwyn departed alone, his face stormy.

" 'There are too many!' wailed the soldier to his lord. 'The Nintarans flow from the mountains like waves from the sea!'

" 'Remove this coward from my sight,' snarled the lord in disgust. 'Karalon still stands.' The lord turned to the wizard. 'Aid me in stemming this tide. We can no longer hold the marchlands, but the heart of our kingdom can be defended if we stop the beastmen here.'

" 'As you command, so I obey, lord of Karalon,' said the wizard. 'On this river I shall build you a mighty fort, and this fort shall sit over a bridge that only the righteous can cross. In the name of Anduilon and the High King we both serve, I swear that it will be done.'

"The fort was built and so too the bridge. Many armies did assail it, and against its might did they break themselves. Though kingdoms fell and names were forgotten, never did the fort fall, nor were the heartlands of Karalon ravaged."

—Karalon and the Great War, *Author Unknown*

CHAPTER SIX

Olamm-Ta watched as a pack of thirty A'Cha made their way across the training plain. They were mounted on the terrifying riding lizards that the Djido sorcerer, Veeshar, had brought with him when he entered Ta's service. The A'Cha had no mounted tradition. The orange-furred beastmen hated horses as much as horses hated them. That fear and their inability to organize had doomed the otherwise formidable race to eternal servitude.

He did not have the time to teach them fully. Like dogs, A'Cha were best if trained from cubs. Left to their instincts, they used teeth and claws as their weapons. It made them deadly to peasants and conscript armies, but useless against trained, armoured soldiers. If he had ten years he would have taken the next generation of cubs and drilled them with spear and shield until using them was as natural as breathing. Such an army would make even the Khalamm quake in fear, but Ta could not wait that long. He had made an oath and he would not renege.

The A'Cha he had were all adults. His Vaulen drilled them in the use of weapons, but they handled them awkwardly and would no doubt drop them it their first real fight. Even with his soldiers leading them, they were only fractions of the warriors they could be.

The A'Cha were stiff on their new mounts as they floundered through a series of adapted cavalry drills. The Vaul had spent many lifetimes perfecting mounted combat and Ta hated that they had been forced to abandon their horses in Kalumfar. He and his far-brothers would have made better riders than the A'Cha, but there had been too many 'training accidents' and his Vaulen were too precious to him. Better to let the A'Cha perform the unenviable task.

"These thunder lizards will be the superior of any human cavalry they face, Olamm," Veeshar rasped. Ta disliked the brown scaled sorcerer with its condescending, obsequious manner, but he was not so foolish as to refuse the aid it offered. The creature had a secret agenda, of that he had no doubt. The histories of his people were rife with tales of Djido trickery, but Ta was confident in his ability to keep it at bay. Yes, the creature had a body-guard—a sharp-eyed lizardman covered with tattoos, but it would not be able to save it if Ta brought the full might of his clan against it. Even wizards could bleed if you struck them hard enough.

"Yes, I believe that they will," Ta answered. "I would have liked another month to train them, but they will do." He watched as the 'thunder lizards' and their riders ran across the field in an approximation of a formation. "My soldiers are getting restless. If they do not see action soon they will begin fighting one another." Another hazard of dealing with A'Cha. "When will you control the river fortress? I cannot move until then."

"We occupy the keep even now, Great Olamm," it hissed. "It was done two days ago."

"Occupation is not enough," Ta growled. "You promised me control. It has great magics that you said you could give to me. You said that you had a servant unlocking its secrets for you and that it would be done by now. Yet we are still standing here, hiding in the hills like cowards."

"It will be soon, Great Olamm, soon," it assured him. "A day. Two at the most, I swear it."

"I don't want your oath." Ta trusted the Djido's god less than he trusted it. "Just do it. You have two days. We march on the third."

"Of course, Great Olamm."

Ta walked back to his tent. Navoi's killer still walked free. Ta did not care if it was served hot, cold, or tepid: he wanted his revenge, and he could not get it while he remained in these mountains.

Northhaven was a just a receding silhouette—an inky black shadow floating in a pool of midnight blue sky—when Sephana finally took off her head scarf. At last, after a month, it was safe. She combed her fingers through her long, curly hair, shook it free, and gave a contented sigh. She hated hiding who she was. In a perfect world, she would be able to walk through a crowded square with her hair free and her arms bare while wearing a comfortable dress. It wouldn't matter what people saw when they looked at her. It was her favourite dream but also one that would never come true.

She knew what people would do if they saw her like she was now: they'd hunt her down and kill her. Maybe she'd be stoned to death, or perhaps they would burn her at the stake if she wasn't just ripped apart by an angry mob. It was a small comfort that she'd be spared the fate that befell many young women in captivity. Men weren't attracted to snakes. They'd see the lines of scales on her brow, arms and back and, worse, her tail and the words 'Djido-spawn' hissed into her ear pits would be the last ones she heard.

The word 'Reshai' came from the Djido language. It meant 'by-blow'. The hated snakemen had occupied most of Anshara during the Great War, but the centre of their power had been the jungle kingdom of Akkilon. They had ruled there for centuries before the war turned against them and their oppressed citizenry cast them out. For one hundred and fifty years the women of Akkilon had been forced to endure the depravations of their cruel overlords. The first few 'by-blows' had been drowned at birth or left to die of exposure, but eventually their numbers became too large to ignore. Not recognized by their snakemen fathers and shunned by the humans around them, the Reshai became an entire race and culture of slaves

It had been a wretched life, and Sephana had hated it. When the opportunity had come for her to escape Akkilon, she had not hesitated. She wasn't proud of how she had achieved her freedom, but she refused to apologize for surviving and living free.

Well, more free. She still had to hide her true nature from almost everyone, but she wasn't forced to live in slave-towns like in Akkilon, or be tolerated in ghettos like her people were in the other kingdoms. She still had to cover her forehead and hide her ear pits as well as endure wearing long sleeved shirts no matter how hot the weather was, but it was still better than the alternative.

At least she could be herself around her friends.

Theramus, bless his big, blue heart, had never looked down at her. Well, he did—he was eight feet tall—but he had never treated her as anything less than an equal. He didn't fully understand the danger of her position, but he respected it like he respected her. Illyria and Balien also treated her like an equal, but those two were as out of place in this world as she was. It was funny sometimes the things they just didn't 'get' about the world outside their precious Ilthwood.

Sephana shucked her outer shirt and revelled in the feel of cool air against her bare arms and midriff. The brown and yellow stripes of her scales travelled up the outside of her arms and along the length of her spine. Next, she undid the button on the back of her loose, baggy pants and let her tail slither free. Like the rest of her, it was covered with dark brown scales with rings of pale yellow. It was a hand-span wide where it separated from her back and slowly tapered to a point just above her ankles. Flexing and extending it, she swung it around in a wide circle behind her and sighed.

Balien, his face grey in the faint moonlight, glanced over at her. "Feel better?"

She stopped and twisted her back and tail in one direction and then the other before rejoining him. "It was really cramped. Hiding it like I have this last month has been hard."

"We'll be near Durnshold Keep around noon," he warned. "You'll have to hide everything again by then."

"I know, but even a few hours will be worth it." She had learned long ago not to take even a moment of freedom for granted.

They made good time. Unleashed like dogs on the hunt, the four of them had travelled steadily through the night and morning. They followed a narrow footman's path instead of the wider, flatter road. It was harder to walk but more direct and allowed them to avoid meeting with any dragon-lizards.

The golden globe of Nuran—created by Anur to bring heat and light to all of the titan-worlds—hung high in the sky. Illyria and her three companions knelt behind a small rise on the path as they surveyed the hill-top fortress of Durnshold.

"Why is it green?" Sephana asked.

The walls and tower within were made of a milky green stone completely unlike the grey rock most other stone buildings were constructed from. The bridge that the castle overlooked was made from the same substance.

"It is made of heartstone," Theramus replied. Sephana's hair hung free and Illyria could see the line of brown and yellow scales through her cloud of chestnut curls. The scale patterns were quite pretty and it saddened her that Sephana had to hide them so often.

"What's that?"

"It is a magically created stone that is indestructible. The High Wizards used in important constructions before the fall of Anduilon." Theramus's low, bassy voice rumbled like a far-off waterfall. "The art of its construction was lost when the High Kingdom fell. That castle and the bridge it guards were likely made during the Nintaran Invasions."

Balien studied the terrain surrounding the keep. "With the ravine surrounding it you have to use that one path to get in, and the ramp up to the gate has no cover. It would take army months to take it."

"I can see why the Karalmen have staked so much of their security on it," Illyria agreed. "That bridge really is the only place to cross the river."

"So how are we going to do this?" Sephana asked.

Illyria evaluated the milky green fortress, the bridge it guarded, and the steep, foreboding chasm that it spanned. "The gates of the keep are still open." She pointed to the wide, wooden gate set in the wall's centre. "There are people crossing the bridge, too. They're probably from Durnston, the town of on the other side of the river."

"Do you think they control the town, too?" Balien asked.

"Probably. Look." Sephana pointed to the bridge. In addition to people making their way across it, Illyria saw a dragon-lizard and A'Cha rider walking casually along its length. They shied away from the creature but did not flee from it.

"I wonder if the town's people are being controlled by the wizard, like Lord Hanley spoke of, or are just under threat by their weapons," Illyria mused.

"We cannot tell that from this distance," Theramus said. "We will have to get closer to the town."

"We have to cross the river and approach the town from the other side," Illyria announced. "I don't see another way around it. Either that or we circle around to the north and try to scale the castle wall."

"We'd never make it during the day time," Sephana warned her. "We'd be spotted for sure."

"Crossing the river is going to be dangerous," Balien said. "Both sides are sheer cliff for miles, but I saw a place we can try upstream."

Illyria trusted her brother's judgement. "Any other suggestions?" she asked. No one said anything. "Then we should go. Balien, lead the way."

The four of them made their way upstream along the rocks.

"What in Emuranna's name?" Sephana was two thirds down the cliff, being lowered by a rope tied around her waist. With a gravel bar at the base, a large rock mid-stream, and a seam on the opposite cliff, it was the best place to cross that they had found, but that wasn't saying too much. Fed by ice-fields high in the mountains, the Lyssal River was wide, violent, and fast. She didn't think that a 'good' place to cross it existed.

The path below her wasn't supposed to exist, either. Certainly a wide, flat walkway running along the length of the cliff hadn't been visible from the top. She swung herself away from the cliff face and then towards it. The cliff overhung the river where they were, so that while she was being lowered straight down, she had been unable to touch the stone since the beginning of her descent. It took a few more swings but she was able to grab an outcropping of stone and then lower herself onto the path.

It was real. She jumped up and down on it a few times before leaning out and looking down to the river below her. There may have been a sound from above her but the roaring water, amplified by the cliffs, made hearing anything impossible. She looked up and saw three heads leaning over the cliff edge. She heard another cry—Theramus?—and then suddenly the rope around her waist was jerked up and she found herself hanging in the air.

Anxious arms hauled her over the cliff edge and to her feet. "Where were you? What happened?" Theramus asked with obvious concern. "Did you catch an edge? Did you fall?"

She explained about the path she had found, and they told her how, after swinging out from the side and then in again, she had simply…vanished.

She leaned over the edge of the cliff and looked as hard as she could. There was definitely nothing there. "So it's invisible, and anyone on it is also invisible," she mused. "I wonder where it goes."

"We don't have time to explore it," Illyria said. "We need to cross the river."

Sephana nodded reluctantly.

Theramus disliked swimming. Part of that, he had to admit, was because he tended to (as Sephana phrased it) 'sink like a giant blue anvil'. In this instance his anvil-like qualities had been a benefit and allowed him to resist the Lyssal's efforts to wrest him in its powerful current. Instead, he had sunk up to his chest before finding footing on the submerged rocks.

Lowering themselves to the bank of the river had been difficult and dangerous. They had secured ropes across the rushing white water and the others crossed successfully. Sephana particularly had displayed a nimble agility that he envied. The ropes had tried their best to keep him aloft, but his weight had overcome their strength halfway across.

'Hang on, Big Blue!" Sephana called from the far bank. The river's roar almost defeated her voice. She draped the heavier of the two ropes across her chest and leapt nimbly onto the higher guide rope. Suspended by her arms, legs, and tail, she quickly shimmied along it until she hung above him. She released her arms and hung above him with casual grace. Stretched out to her full length, her explosion of hair surrounding her face like a halo, she lowered the rope down into Theramus's reaching hands.

"Loop it around your chest and use it to haul yourself to shore!"

She had returned to shore and was already combing her hair before he made two steps. Theramus secured and held the rope tightly, knowing that the river's strength dwarfed his own. He lost his footing once and managed to regain it, but the second time that the current grabbed him, he could do nothing as it hurled him like a toy. The shore's edge struck him with crushing force. He felt like an insect on the edge of a willow switch and held the rope desperately with both hands. Slowly, stubbornly, he drew himself upwards while the river beat him mercilessly.

It dragged him under with a grip of iron and forbade him air. He pulled himself up one hand length, and then another. His head broke the surface and he gasped in a breath, but it was more water than air. He coughed and felt his grip weaken. Watery hands pulled his fingers free and oblivion called to him. *I will not let my journey end like this!*

The river seemed to have different intentions.

Illyria, Balien and Sephana strained to pull the rope towards them. The 'bank' only met the shore for a short distance. Eight feet. They only had to pull him eight feet and he would be close enough to pull free of the water. Illyria cursed the mysterious wizard whose actions had begun all of this and then lord Davin, his father (for leaving his son in charge of the Northmarch), and her uncle (for issuing his ridiculous ultimatum) and Gennald (for not saying anything before riding off yesterday).

They continued to pull. Slowly, arm-length by arm-length, they hauled upward until finally Theramus's thick blue wrist came into view. Behind her, Sephana secured the rope slack. When there was no way for him to slide back downstream, she and Balien ran to the shore's edge. With Balien's hand firmly upon his wrist and Illyria and Sephana grabbing whatever was close enough, they finally managed to pull him up onto shore.

His normally blue/grey skin was just grey and, worse, he was not breathing. "Get him on his side, let the water out," Illyria ordered. It took all three of them to roll him over. His hand still clutched the rope in a death grip.

Sephana was in tears. "Wake up, you big blue idiot. We didn't fish you out of that damned river just to have you die on us." The ashen Noss made no response. "Open your mouth. Breathe!" She brought both of her fists down upon his side and, to Illyria's surprise, he began coughing out what seemed to be gallons of river.

Illyria, kneeling by his head, was drenched in the spit up but didn't care. Rubbing Theramus's back and assuring him quietly, she watched over him as he recovered. Across from her, Sephana burst into uncontrollable tears. Leaving Theramus to Balien's ministrations, Illyria took the trembling Reshai into her arms.

"Shh. It's all right. He's alive. We saved him. Emuranna was with us." Sephana continued to shake in her arms. Her own eyes were damp and she knew it wasn't just from the river. It was, Illyria realized, the closest she had ever been to Sephana

When she turned, Theramus was sitting up and looking at the two women. She didn't know how a person with no body hair could manage to look so bedraggled but he had found a way. She smoothed down a handful of curly brown hair. "Are you all right?" she mouthed at him over Sephana's shoulder.

He nodded and got unsteadily to his feet. He placed giant hands on both Sephana's and Illyria's shoulders and slid Sephana against him. "I am very proud of you." His voice rumbled as he spoke, like the purring of a giant cat. "Thank you for saving me. I will always be in your debt."

"What the hell is wrong with you?" Sephana snarled, pushing out of Theramus' embrace. Her eyes, red and puffy from crying, blazed with anger. "Don't you know how to swim? Didn't you learn how to do that in the million years you've been alive? Can't you even pull yourself up a stupid rope?" She pushed herself away from him violently. "Don't you dare do that to me again! Do you understand, you big blue idiot? Never again!" She stormed off without waiting for a reply and began coiling rope in furious jerks.

The climb out of the river chasm was good in that there was no way to talk to anyone, leaving Sephana free to take out her frustration against the cliff-face. She was the natural choice to find the best path up the cliff and ensure that the safety rope was secure in case anyone fell.

By the time the others made their way up the narrow, vegetation filled crack in the cliff wall, her anger was mostly spent. She watched silently as Balien, aided by his sister's hand, pulled himself up to ground level. She wordlessly handed him a full water skin and somewhat fresh oatcake. He accepted both with a silent nod.

While Illyria surveyed the surrounding terrain, Sephana wandered over to Theramus who, while looking better than when they had fished him out of the river, was still about as bad as she had ever seen him. He smiled at her as she approached.

"Still coughing up water?"

He chuckled. "Thankfully, no. All is well with you? It is so?"

"Oh yeah, sure." She examined her boot-tip. "Uh, sorry about before. I shouldn't have yelled."

She quickly turned to go but had forgotten just how long his reach was. In the afternoon sun, the hand holding her wrist reminded her of marble. "There is no need for you to apologize. I took it only as a sign that you care, and I am honoured that you choose to bestow such feelings upon me. Thank you for that gift, Sephana, as well as for saving my life."

If she had been human her cheeks would have been flaming. When she finally squirmed free she headed as far away from him as possible.

Balien knew when not to say anything and the two travelled in comfortable silence as they cautiously approached the town of Durnston. When Illyria gestured for them to circle around the south end of the town and observe until evening, he nodded and motioned for Sephana to follow him. They crept around the border of the town until they found a shaded observation spot opposite Illyria and Theramus.

Unlike the ancient keep across the river, Durnston was as drab and colourless as any other Karalinian town. The houses were wood and stone, lined both sides of the main road, and were centred around a market square. Most of the residents were gathered in the middle of the square being guarded by a dozen spear bearing A'Cha.

A pair of mounted A'Cha patrolled its perimeter. Groups of soldiers in mail manned improvised barricades at both ends the main road.

"At least they aren't dead," Sephana said quietly, the first words either had spoken in more than an hour.

"Yet," he whispered in reply.

They sat and observed mostly in silence, speaking only to confirm numbers of the enemy. The sun slowly made its way across the sky.

"Find now," Draxul quacked. "No more play."

"I'm not playing," Eldoth replied irritably. The emotion was not feigned; he had been unable sleep for more than a few hours. The continuous demands for progress from his impatient jailor combined with the stomach-churning anxiety of lying to it did not make for sound rest. "The chamber is proving harder to find than I anticipated. I will discover its location. Soon."

"Find now," it repeated angrily. Powerful muscles tensed in its thick neck as it clenched its jaw and bared its teeth at him. It stepped closer until its fetid breath washed over him. "Find now or I pain you, monkey."

Eldoth could not help but cower before the creature's vulgar and primitive threat—its horrible command of the Anduili language not withstanding. Such displays of physical thuggery were feeble attempts at control by the unintelligent and ignorant, and Eldoth was decidedly neither. It was unfortunate that at this particular moment, he was unable to use either his massive intellect or broad education to aid him. Even worse, his greatest weapon: his mastery of the magical arts, was currently denied to him.

It jabbed a sharpened claw into his chest, making him yelp with pain. "Find now!"

Eldoth rubbed at his chest and glared. "Or you'll 'pain' me, again. Yes, I understand." Despite its limited vocabulary it always found a way to make its intentions known. "Brainless ruffian."

It stepped close, raising claws the size of daggers. "Where?"

"All right, all right!" he yelled, disliking how shrill his voice sounded. "I'll find." He waved his hands across the room. "It's not in here. We'll have to try another room."

It narrowed its eyes. "You said here. You said behind wood."

Yes, he had said that, and the delay caused by that lie had given him twelve hours of respite. He had directed the angry townspeople to move all of the furniture in this dining hall first to one side, then another and finally outside into the courtyard before banishing everyone from the room—including Draxul the pea-brain—so that he could 'search in private.' The fabrication had given him a few blessed hours of peace.

It needs me, I cannot forget that. "Well, obviously I was wrong. The symbols are very old, you know, and written in a language that I can barely read." He gave the creature a smug smile that he did not feel. "I would welcome another interpretation, if you would care to translate." Its mouth tightened but it said nothing. "Oh, wait: you can't translate for me, because you spent so much time learning to hit people with sharp sticks to that you *never learned to read!"*

It snarled and raised a clawed hand. It took all of Eldoth's will not to flinch as it stopped just short of his cheek. "Where you find?" Its breath reeked of rotting meat.

Eldoth let out a shaky breath. "I was wrong in my translation. It's not on this floor, but the hall below us. You'll have to clear it out, by which I mean all of the furniture, carpets and wall hangings. The mark could be anywhere."

It quacked to itself it its own language, showering Eldoth in flecks of stinking saliva. "Room below huge."

Yes, it was. It was the castle's great hall and it would take hours upon hours to clear out and 'search'. Eldoth shrugged. "Then you had better get some monkeys together and start, hadn't you?"

It placed the four claws of its left hand against his chest and pushed gently. Any harder, both knew, and it would draw blood. "You find, or beating heart I eat." It turned to leave and Eldoth was struck by its tail, staggering him.

Eldoth waited until he was alone before vomiting into the corner.

" '...the worlds in the Middle Waters, Titan-worlds and Fragment-Worlds all, lie upon the endless ocean that is the Maelstrom, but do not think that they float and drift freely. All worlds are connected to one another and to Heaven's Anchor by unbreakable 'ropes' of pure magic, what some mortals call "etheric cables" or "ley lines."

" 'These "ropes" do more than bind the worlds to one another, they also act as gateways. When the ropes are "straight", for lack of a better word, a connection forms between one world and another. Depending on the distance between worlds, the time of year, and the condition of the Maelstrom, these 'gates' may stay open for a minute, an hour or a day. Magic, also, can open, close, or extend a gate's natural duration.

" 'When a gate is open, any being from either side can wander freely between worlds. Some cross out of curiosity, others out of avarice. Animals, in particular, seem drawn to them and, often, they are trapped on the other side when the gate closes. Here in Anshara, we call these cross-world intruders "Interlopers".

" 'If there are no other questions, we will continue. Next...' "

—*Anonymous lesson excerpt, recovered from the ruins of Old Aukaster, Karalon*

CHAPTER SEVEN

"What is that?" Illyria asked. She and Theramus had been watching the town for about three hours. Other than keeping the townsmen imprisoned in the market square, nothing had happened, until now.

She pointed to the bridge where a group of three crossed from the keep to the town. Two were A'Cha, but the third was of no race she'd seen before. She couldn't make out any details, but it wasn't a man, A'Cha or Vaulen. It had yellowish skin, a large head, and a line of spikes that ran down the length of its back to the end of its large tail.

"Is it another kind of dragon-lizard?" she asked.

"I hope that it is," Theramus replied. "I hope that both it and the other lizards are merely Interlopers that wandered onto Anshara, like in the ancient tales."

She turned and stared. "Why do you wish that? That would mean that Shieldstone has failed."

"Yes." His broad face was creased in a massive frown.

"I still don't understand."

"An intrusion into Anshara by Interlopers would be bad," he said gravely, "but it is not the worst thing that could happen."

"Then what is?"

Theramus pointed to the yellow lizard now nearing the edge of the town. "Because if that creature is not a dragon-lizard than it can only be one of the Hrallar, lizardman soldiers from Idjisar." His face was stony. "And if that is one of the Hrallar, it can only mean that the Djido have returned."

Balien nudged Sephana awake. She sat up, blinked sleep out of her eyes, and examined the sky. She'd only been asleep for an hour. Considering that all of yesterday, most of last night, and the first half of today had been spent either walking or climbing, an hour of sleep wasn't much at all.

"What's going on?" She looked across the town and the bridge and keep that lay beyond it but, more asleep than awake, couldn't focus on any one part of it.

He pointed between the town's edge and the bridge. "Another kind of creature, some kind of lizardman. They're gathering people up for some reason."

"Oh, good. Something else whose name we don't know."

They watched in silence as the lizardman—its skin was the colour of old mustard, mottled with black spots—directed the two A'Cha in the gathering of twenty-odd men and women.

"You don't think that they're going to…*eat* them, do you?" she asked reluctantly.

"I don't think so." He sounded confident and she chose to believe him. It was better than the alternative.

The shuffling, reluctant group of humans made their way down to the bridge. "They're going back to the keep." She examined the path, the speed of the group and the number of guards. The lizardman and the two A'Cha were at the head of the group and a single dragon-lizard and rider were at its tail. An idea formed and she blurted it out before her common sense could get in the way. "I think we could sneak our way in."

"What do you mean?"

She was already tying her head scarf around her head and tucking away her tail. "They're not watching the middle of the group. If we can get down to that rock," she pointed with one hand to a large, steep rock near the end of the bridge, "then I think we can just walk out and join the group without being noticed."

Balien thought a moment, nodded, and then began shucking his sword and travelling garb. His dark eyes examined her. "Are you sure you want to come? It's going to be dangerous."

Sephana didn't answer. Just started making her way down towards the road. "I know. Let's just go before I wake up and to come to my senses."

"What are they doing?" Theramus demanded of everyone and no one. He and Illyria could see Sephana and Balien clambering down the hill opposite them. "They would not be so foolish as to attempt a rescue. It is not so." He gathered up his mallet and planned the most direct route to the bridge.

"No, wait." Illyria laid her hand atop his. "Balien isn't even armed. I think that they're just joining the group."

They looked so small from this distance. "This is not a safe course of action."

"Balien wouldn't do it if he didn't think he had a chance," she assured him. "But it's not Balien that you're worried about, is it?"

She had the truth of it but he was not in a mood to discuss it. "I have worry enough for both."

As they watched, first Balien and then Sephana stepped into the group of peasants crossing the bridge. Neither the A'Cha or the Hrallar seemed to take any notice. Theramus wanted to crush something but could do nothing as the cavernous gate of the green-walled keep engulfed them. He released his hammer from aching knuckles. "What happens to them now is beyond our control."

"They'll be fine. I trust them both." Illyria smiled, but the bright blue of her eyes betrayed her true feelings.

"Find now?"

Had Draxul said something? Eldoth didn't hear it. He stared instead into the group of peasants labouring in the large hall.

I'm going mad.

It was the only explanation. Starvation had combined with stress and lack of rest to cause him to lose his mind. How else could he explain what he now saw?

He saw it again: a flash of teak coloured hair, curled like cinnamon bark. He hadn't seen hair quite like that—outside his dreams, anyways—in several years. It was tied under a dirty brown cloth, but he knew that hair…or at least he had, once. He couldn't quite tell: the woman's back was turned to him as she carried a sack out of the hall, but her height and gate were frighteningly similar.

It can't be her.

He watched as the woman—she had to be a peasant from the town—walked to the door. She'd have to turn to pass through it and then he'd know. He would only be able to see her in profile, but it would be enough. She was nearing the corner and preparing to turn. Eldoth held his breath.

A scaly hand spun him around. "Find yet?"

Eldoth looked up and found himself staring at Draxul's angry eyes. "What?"

It hissed something unintelligible. "You play much. No do." It pushed him with one hand, rocking him back on his heels. "Find!"

Eldoth didn't answer. He leaned around Draxul, trying to spot a glimpse of teak coloured hair, but it was too late. She had gone. Draxul pushed him again, with both hands this time, and Eldoth almost fell.

He snapped. "I am not playing! I am *waiting*, you incompetent, foul smelling, walnut-brained *imbecile*." All of the rage, stress, and uncertainty of the last two days combined to snap his last thread of patience. "I cannot search and examine the room while all of this furniture is here. The runes could be anywhere; on the floor, the walls or the ceiling. They are invisible to the naked eye." He was shouting now. "When will it finally sink into your thick, scale covered skull that I cannot do what you ask until all of this is gone and you leave! Me! Alone!!!"

There was complete silence. Eldoth bent over gasping, leaning his hands against his knees and looking up at the imposing lizard man.

"No play. Find." it quacked and then left the room.

Sephana froze outside the great hall. She knew that voice. Even without the lengthy tirade of insults, she could never forget that tone of exasperation.

Balien came up to her, dressed in his black hose, boots, and a loose, crimson shirt. "What is it?"

She pulled him into an alcove. "I know him. The wizard, I mean, the one who's supposed to be in charge of everything. I know him." She frowned. "There's been a mistake because he can't be a wizard. He's really arrogant, but he can't do actual magic."

Balien placed his hand over her mouth. "Sephana. Stop." She stopped. "You said you know him." She nodded. "How?"

She pulled his hand away and took a deep breath. "He's..." It was too embarrassing to say out loud. "He's my husband."

She peeked up at Balien in the alcove's shadow. His face was blank and he blinked twice, slowly.

"I'm sure there's much more to this story, but it will have to wait. Are you sure he's your husband?"

She nodded. "His name is Eldoth. He's from Akkilon. We...separated...before I left."

"I won't be able to show him mercy just because you know him," he warned. "If he's involved in this, he's going to get the same punishment as anyone else."

"But he's not, don't you see?" she asked. "He's being controlled somehow. Even if I hadn't just heard him now, I know him. He's...well, he's a jerk. He's smug and annoying and thinks he knows everything but he's not evil. He'd never get involved in something like this willingly. You have to believe me."

Balien frowned. "Even if that is true, then what do we do about it? All we have are daggers."

He was right, but still... "I don't know, but we can talk to him at least, right?"

"Yes, we can do that." He held up a finger in warning. "Be careful."

When Eldoth looked up again, she was there. "Sephana?" He winced at his unimaginative word choice. *After all this woman did to you, all you can say is her name?* He *was* losing his mind.

"Hello, Eldoth." She quirked her lips into what might have either been a grimace or a smile. "What kind of a mess have you gotten yourself into?"

He'd always loved her smile.

Her voice was just as he remembered: a clear soprano filled with humour, impatience and just a touch of sadness. He glanced around nervously. Draxul was elsewhere, Emuranna's Grace, and the few peasants nearby gathered furniture nervously and ignored them. Draxul had threatened to kill anyone who spoke.

It was the threat of death that returned him to his senses. "Are you some illusion being used to trick me? Tell me something that only you and I would know." He had to be sure. If this was some sort of dream, she would not have been wearing those ill-fitting men's clothes, or look as if she hadn't bathed in a week. In his imagination she always wore...less.

The roll of her eyes was enough to convince him but her words confirmed it. "We were married in the overseer's office because the Elders wouldn't let us use the gathering hall. His name was Torvis, he stank of radishes, and he tried to grope me during his Blessing. I had to threaten to stick a knife in his crotch." She raised her eyebrows. "Is that enough?"

It was. "What are you doing here?" he hissed. "How did you get in? The entire town is guarded."

She smirked. "Just because people can't get out doesn't mean that they can't get in. I'm here with some friends and we wanted to know what's going on. I didn't expect to find you here."

He let out a short laugh and it felt good. How long had it been since he'd last done that? "You are the last person I expected as well, believe me. As for what is happening: this fortress is being held in preparation for an invasion, and I am being held against my will."

"We know about the invasion, but what's all this talk about a wizard? Are they talking about you?"

Eldoth drew himself to his full height. "Of course they are."

"But you're an accountant!" she protested.

Her words struck like daggers. "And you were a midden slave," he said acidly, knowing the barb would hurt and happy for it.

Her eyes blazed. "I couldn't have been that low: I got you to marry me."

"So you admit it finally." He had forgotten where they were and what circumstances they were in. She did that to him. "Our marriage was just a ploy to you. You were using me the whole time."

Her eyes flashed. "Of course I was using you! I used you to get out of the middens and the crone's tent and you used me for cooking and sex. That's what marriages are!"

"Sephana!" a voice hissed. Eldoth blinked and remembered where he was. A dark haired man in a red shirt was glaring at both of them angrily. He realized just how loud he had been. By the embarrassed look on Sephana's face he knew that she'd come to a similar conclusion.

There was an angry roar from the doorway and Draxul stormed in. "No play, no talk!" It advanced towards them and grabbed Sephana by one arm. "I tell you, talk to monkey, monkey die." It pushed her against the wall with one clawed hand and raised its free hand to her throat. She looked very small in his grip.

Sephana couldn't believe she had been so stupid. (No, wait: yes, she could.) Why had she thought that she could enter into a conversation with Eldoth and not have it turn into an argument? Her mistake was likely to cost her life.

"No!" Eldoth shouted. She pulled against the lizardman's grip. It lashed at her throat but she ducked her head. A claw still caught her high on her cheek but not deeply.

Her head scarf caught in its claw and it flicked it aside impatiently before raising its hand for another strike. It stopped mid-swing and cocked its head in confusion.

"What you?" it asked in very rough Anduili, its voice high and raspy. It was looking at her forehead.

"She's an ally," Eldoth told it, gripping its wrist with both hands. "Look, she bears the mark of our master." He reached in with a shaking hand and pushed her hair aside. He was showing it her headscales, she realized, and her earpits. "She is no danger. She is here to help me." His eyes met hers. *Play along*, they said.

"I am," she said in a voice shakier than she would have liked. "I serve our, uhh, master." Behind Eldoth, she caught sight of Balien approaching with some sort of cudgel. She shook her head minutely and tried to remember what Eldoth had been yelling about earlier. "I'm helping Eldoth find the runes you're looking for."

The lizardman broke Eldoth's grip easily and released her. It made some combination of hissing and throat clearing sounds at her.

"She's not from Idjisar," Eldoth told it. "She doesn't know your language."

"How you here?"

"My master sent me here," She said quickly, examining its face for any sign of whether it believed them. It could be frowning or smiling and she wouldn't know. "It...*he*..." she amended at Eldoth's wordless correction, "knew that you were having troubles finding...it."

It thought for a moment. "Why no tell me?"

"Veeshar doesn't answer to you," Eldoth said in that condescending way that he was so good at. "He doesn't have to tell you what his plans are. You, like me, simply have to obey."

The tattooed lizard paused then threw Sephana towards Eldoth. She stopped herself with her hands on his shoulders and felt his arms close around her. "Both you find," it ordered. "I watch."

Sephana tried to pull out of Eldoth's arms but he held her firmly in his embrace. She stiffened when he lowered his mouth to her ear. "I need my stele," he whispered when his lips were hidden in her hair. "It's in that pouch on his hip."

She dropped her forehead to his shoulder. "What's a stele?"

"It's a kind of stylus used for doing magic. I can free us if I can get it."

She looked up at him, startled. He eyes were only inches from hers. "You can really do magic?"

"Yes! I already told you." he growled indignantly. "Can you get it? You always were fast with your hands."

The lizardman stepped in and pushed the two of them apart. "No play! Find!" She wasn't about to let such an opportunity pass by. Faking a stumble, she fell against its hip and slipped one narrow hand into the pouch Eldoth had indicated. There was indeed a thin rod slightly longer than her hand within. She concealed it in her palm as she fell away.

Hah! I still have it! She'd been a filcher her entire life. Growing up as the lowest of the low in an Akkilinian slave town, if she hadn't learned to steal she would have starved to death. There had been fewer reasons for her to practice in recent years but apparently her hard-won childhood survival skill hadn't degraded.

The lizardman's hand snapped out and grabbed her wrist. "You die now."

Okay, maybe I don't have it.

Everything happened quickly. One moment Eldoth was whispering to Sephana while he embraced her—the happy warmth of which he did not have time to think about—and the next Draxul was quacking death threats and trying to disembowel her.

He had just made the decision to come to her aid when she transferred something from one hand to the other and threw it. The object bounced off of his chest and almost fell to the floor before he realized what it was—his stele!—and scrambled to catch it. At the same time, the other man—the one in the red shirt wielding a cudgel—leapt at the lizard.

By the time Eldoth retrieved his stele and tried to use it the melee had evolved. Sephana was free and holding the cudgel while the man held one of Draxul's swords.

Eldoth felt along the leather headband around his forehead and tried to find the runes that trapped his power. He had felt them before, during stolen moments alone. He knew the spell they scribed and what marks he had to make in order to disable them, but in his fear everything felt the same.

"Come on!" Sephana yelled, trying to use her club against the lizardman. "You've got your magic pen. Get us out of here!"

"It doesn't work like that," he replied testily and threw down his hands. Removing the headband in these conditions was impossible. "Quickly, we must escape while it's distracted!" He ran to the exit but she didn't follow. "Sephana! Come on!"

"I can't leave Balien!" She said incredulously.

"Yes you can," the dark haired man grunted—Balien, obviously—as he traded blows with Draxul. "Get him out of here and find Illyria. She'll know what to do."

Eldoth had no idea who Illyria was, but the idea met with his approval. "Yes, yes. We must go. Come on. I know a secret way out."

"I'm not leaving him!"

"You're just getting in his way," Eldoth insisted and she shot him an angry look. "He's a strong warrior. He'll be fine."

"I'll be right behind you," Balien assured her. At that moment Draxul entangled Balien's sword with its own and pulled it from the man's hands. Balien ran towards the door. "We're outmatched here. Flee!"

Eldoth still stood in the door, startled by the speed of events. Balien pushed him out the door in front of him. Sephana was right behind him and Draxul was only steps behind them both. "Come on, Eldoth, run!"

Eldoth ran.

For all of Eldoth's faults—had he really just said 'you're just getting in his way'?—he knew the layout of the keep very well. Once committed to a plan of action, he pursued it quickly and efficiently. That had always been one of his strengths and she was glad that he was the one they were following.

Balien had grabbed a spear off the wall, but Sephana hadn't been so lucky. She could have gotten her own spear, but, given how heavy it was and the width of the corridors, she knew she would have been more hindrance than benefit. She *would* have gotten in his way (and she would take the fact that Eldoth was right in this situation to her grave).

The lizardman, Draxul, was frighteningly good with his strange, hooked weapons. Its swords weren't really swords in that they didn't have blades. Basically they were just metal sticks with hooks on the end. There were spikes on the hand-guards and pommels, but that was it. Balien had been at a disadvantage the moment he had grabbed it and had been disarmed in seconds. Now that Draxul had both of his weapons they were in even bigger trouble.

Oh, and its tail had a studded steel weight on the end. That couldn't be good, either.

"Where are we going?" she asked the back of Eldoth's head. Draxul had had been joined a group of A'Cha.

"A study on the second floor. There is a secret passage there," Behind them, Balien used his spear to keep their enemies at bay. The A'Cha bayed in excitement.

They went up a flight of stairs and turned left. "If you knew there was a secret passage why didn't you use if before?"

"Because I could never have made it out of the keep by myself." He passed through an archway into some kind of meeting room and went to an alcove. Sephana followed close behind him and almost ran into his back when he stopped. He was staring at the wall intently.

"So where is it?"

"It's on this wall somewhere," he muttered, pointing in front of him.

"You don't *know*?" Sephana groaned. "How do you know that it's here if you haven't actually found it?"

"Because the former lord used it to escape through," Eldoth replied testily. "There's nowhere else it could be."

"Find it quickly!" Balien called from behind them. He lunged forward and caught Draxul high on its leg with his spear. The lizardman snarled in pain and retreated, motioning to the three A'Cha behind it to advance. "I can't keep this up for long!"

Former lord? "Oh, you mean lord Harrin."

Eldoth looked at her briefly before returning to his examination of the wall. "You've met him? He escaped? He did get word out?"

"Of course," she answered. "Why do you think we're here?"

"Then where's the army? Why aren't a hundred knights charging down the hill to our aid?"

"No army," she said with the cheeriest voice she could muster, just because she knew it would annoy him. "Just us."

He looked at her, horrified. "Just you? They sent a midden-slave and a single warrior to liberate an entire keep?"

"Former midden-slave," she corrected with a scowl. "And I wouldn't be so quick with the insults. Where's all this magic you're supposed to be able to cast?"

"I can't cast spells with this headband," he snapped, "and I can't remove it while I'm in mortal peril!"

"What exactly are we looking for?" Sephana asked in desperation.

"Some sort of concealed triggering mechanism," Eldoth replied. "The door itself is magical. I can see its outlines clearly." He pointed to a clear section of wall. "I had hoped that the trigger would be in proximity to it, but it's not." He looked around him. "It has to be near here. The lord triggered it so it must be mechanical. It will slide, or press, or pull out."

Sephana closed her eyes and let out a shuddering breath. She looked over at her former husband gravely. "I'm betting my life on your really being a wizard, Eldoth."

He stopped and turned to her, his expression sincere. "I was never the one who lied in our relationship, Sephana."

I'm not sorry for what I did. It was the only way to escape my life. I swear that it was. She could see no duplicity in Eldoth's earthy brown eyes no matter how hard she looked.

"All right." She bent to her task, looking for any crack, indentation, or deformity in the walls or floor. She could hear the sounds of battle as Balien risked his life to defend hers but banished it in the same way as her guilt. There would be time for that later. Right now, two lives depended upon her and thousands more would later.

She knew stonework. She'd scrubbed enough of it on her hands and knees, and emptied more than her share of stinking pits of human waste before managing to seduce and marry an arrogant, sarcastic tally clerk and escape it. She cast experienced eyes and fingers along the walls, seeking anything out of the ordinary. On the far wall, near the floor in a gap between two bricks she found something: an oblong protrusion half of a finger length in.

"I think I have it!" She tried pressing down on it, then sliding it both side to side and up and down. She pulled it towards her with her fingertips and felt it move. There was a 'click' in the wall behind her.

"Yes, that's it!" Eldoth called. She turned to see and saw a dark rectangle where plain stone had been only moments before. He was already stepping through.

"Balien! Come on! We have it!" He nodded wordlessly and began to retreat towards her, the tip of his spear preventing anyone from following. One furry A'Cha lay dying on the floor while the others remained at bay.

The lizardman rushed forward with blinding speed, its hook swords extended. Balien tried to pull his spear out of its reach but it caught the head between both hooks and then lashed out with its tail. The steel-shod tip came down upon the wooden shaft and shattered it. Balien took a quick glance at the short pole in his hands, hurled it at the lizardman, then darted towards the door.

Sephana could see Eldoth holding the stylus she had stolen for him—his stele, he had called it—against the wall. Once Balien was through the door he scribed a curved line against the wall. The doorway began to shrink as green stone grew out of the wall on each side. Less than a second later there was a deep 'thump' as the two halves joined and the door shut. Darkness enveloped them.

The only sound was Balien's hard breathing.

"So, what now?" she asked.

Seemingly in reply the corridor illuminated. There was no source of light, torch or lantern, just a dim green glow that came out of nowhere. A narrow hallway stretched out ten feet before going down a flight of stairs.

Balien stood and extended his hand to Eldoth. "Greetings. I am Balien, son of Britheon."

"I am Eldoth the Red." Sephana's brow rose. *The Red?* It was better than 'the accountant,' she supposed.

"A star shines upon our meeting," Balien replied.

" 'You want to know about Tsrinn? Don't believe what you hear in the stories: there is nothing funny about them. Normal Hrallar are scary enough, but the Tsrindos are terrifying. The strongest Hrallar are chosen at hatching and learn to fight before they can learn how to walk. The first word a Tsrinn learns is 'loyalty'. Nothing, and I mean nothing, comes between one of them and their master. They'd kill their family or cut off their own limbs for them. They have these tattoos all over their body, magic ones given to them by the Djido. It makes them faster, gives them harder skin, and makes them immune to pain. Even unarmed, they have six weapons they can kill you with and they're death with those hook-swords they carry. Oh, and Eldoth says they sound like ducks. I never really got that part. ' "

—Sephana, Lord Mayor of Daranduil, recalling days long past

Chapter Eight

The stones at the base of the stairs slid apart to reveal a dark room that stank of rotting meat. Eldoth made another mark against the wall and the haunting green lights went out. "Hopefully, we can steal some horses to escape on," she whispered.

Eldoth caught her shoulder. "There are no horses in here. Draxul had them all killed."

"But...why?"

His face was grim. "They were used as fodder, for the other mounts."

"Other mounts? Fodder? What...oh." She understood, although she wished she didn't. A'Cha wouldn't need horses. They couldn't ride them, and she had already seen the creatures that they *did* ride. "Dragon-lizards."

He nodded. "This is where they are kept."

"Goddess's Strength. We can't fight those." She looked back at Balien. "What do we do?"

"We can't go back and we can't stay here," his silhouette replied. "That lizardman will have this entire keep searched. We'll be found out in minutes."

"We don't need to fight the thunder lizards," Eldoth told them. "We can ride them."

Sephana just stared. "Are you crazy?"

"Definitely not. Listen: the wizard who put this on me," He pointed to the leather headband he still wore. "He used a controlling spell on them. They have to obey the instructions of anyone who sits on them and uses the reins. They have no choice."

"They eat their riders!" she protested.

"The one Illyria saw only did that once the rider had fallen off," Balien pointed out. "Not when it was on the saddle."

Eldoth grimaced. "They resist the spell when they can, that is true, but they cannot directly disobey it."

Balien pushed Sephana into the dark room in front of him. "We don't have a choice."

Eldoth led them to a pair of stalls where two of the dragon-lizards squatted on the ground like scaly balls of malevolence. They wore saddles and had reins wrapped around their mouths like muzzles. Both lizards were awake and eyed them hungrily.

"They cannot perform any action as long as their heads are wrapped," Eldoth said. Despite the confident tone in his voice, he still looked reluctant to go near them. "We cannot move their reins until we are securely saddled or they'll consume us."

Sephana stared in horror at the creatures before her. She hadn't actually seen a whole one, just its head. *It's so…big. Its teeth are as long as my fingers. I can't ride on this.* She swallowed and motioned with her chin. "Go ahead. I'll follow."

He looked at her nervously.

"We don't have time to delay." Balien walked up to one of the dragon-lizards and, hesitating for only the briefest of moments, clambered onto its back. "You next. You'll have to share it."

"I, well, I don't do well on animals," Eldoth told her quietly, his feet rooted.

In his lack of courage, somehow she found her own. "Don't worry, I'll do everything." She gave him her biggest smirk. "It will be just like our wedding night."

As she had hoped, the gibe cut through his fear. "Witch," he muttered.

She made a show of walking casually towards the tethered monster and hoped that her legs wouldn't give out before she got to it. They were even larger close up. While the width and length of its chest was comparable to a horse's, its long neck, tail and massive hind-legs made it much larger. Knowing Eldoth's eyes were on her she steeled herself to approach it just like it was a kitten. The five steps it took to reach it were some of the longest in her life but she didn't let herself stop. Without breaking stride, she used its hind-leg as a step and settled herself across its broad back. If not for the heat coming from its body and the swell of its chest as it breathed she would have thought she was sitting upon stone.

She slid forward in the saddle and patted the leather pad behind her. "Come on. You're the one who said it was safe."

His face was stony as he advanced, but he did come forward and soon was sitting behind her on the lizard's back. Then and only then did she reach forward and carefully unwrap the reins from around its massive, toothy muzzle. She could not help but shiver as her hands passed right next to its huge, bared teeth.

It surged violently to its feet. It was only Eldoth's crushing grip around her middle and stealing her breath that prevented her from crying out. She and Eldoth may as well have been gnats for how much it seemed to feel their weight.

The lizard pawed the ground impatiently and gave a loud, blood-chilling growl. She saw the strong muscles of its neck and jaw flexing. If she fell off the saddle, those same muscles would shear through her body like a scythe through grass. *Don't think about that. Picture anything else. Think of Alwyn, naked.*

That did it.

Beside her, Balien's lizard chafed similarly. He met her eyes, his face grim. "Once we start moving, we can't stop for anything."

Face ashen and heart pounding in her ears, Sephana nodded. She nudged her heels into its sides like she would if it was a horse but nothing happened. "It's the reins," Eldoth murmured in her ear. "It only responds to the reins." She nodded, snapped the reins in her hands and then held on for dear life as the lizard surged forward like a summer flood.

I can't believe I'm doing this!

The door opened on the far side of the stable. An A'Cha looked into the darkened interior of the chamber, but is eyes were accustomed to the bright sunlight behind it and didn't see Balien and his lizard until they were almost upon him. It was barely able to cry out as a toothy jaw as long as her arm closed around its head and neck. There was a bloody squelching and snapping noise as the creature gripped the A'Cha's body with its forelimbs and pulled the head free.

Her own lizard paused at the fresh kill and bent over to examine it, but Sephana snapped her reins and it reluctantly moved past. Behind her, Balien urged his own mount forward. She shielded her eyes against the bright sun.

There was a yell from somewhere in front of them. She could barely make out the keep's courtyard piled high with furniture from Eldoth's efforts. There were people—men, she thought, not A'Cha—scattering before her.

"Make for the gate!" Balien and his savage mount thundered past her. A'Cha were yelling unintelligibly in their beastish language. She snapped her reins again, functioning somehow despite being terrified, and directed her dragon-lizard to follow Balien.

A pair of A'Cha guarded the open gate and their ears wilted when they saw what approached them. They dropped their spears and tried to flee, but only one succeeded. The second fell prey to the titan-like jaws of Sephana's mount. She cringed as she felt more than heard her victim's bones snapping. She urged her mount to leave the mutilated body but it resisted. She had to snap her reins three times before, finally, it moved on.

Balien was already ten yards ahead of her and sprinting towards the bridge. She snapped her reins once more and her dragon-lizard ran off after him. They flew off like a malevolent wind

"What in Emuranna's name?" Illyria said in confusion.

Theramus looked down at the bridge and stared. They were riding dragon-lizards. He had never seen such a thing, not in one hundred and fifty years. "Is that Balien?"

"Yes, with Sephana and someone else, too. We need to make ready." Illyria gathered her gear and readied her bow.

Theramus nodded. He was glad for the opportunity to do something. The past few hours had been torturous.

"Go to Illyria! I'll get our gear!" the warrior named Balien ordered. Any opposition they may have faced on the bridge had rightfully fled before them. Eldoth could see Sephana nodding as Balien turned his thunder lizard and ran off. The town of Durnston lay before them.

"Wait!" Eldoth yelled in her ear. "Go to that group of soldiers over there." The soldiers in question had formerly belonged to the local garrison but were now loyal only to Veeshar. They still wore the colours of their lord and were manning an improvised barricade that barred the main road into town.

She looked over her shoulder, her expression alarmed. "We can't attack them! They're being mind controlled!"

"I am well aware of that, and we don't need to attack them, just get close enough for them to see me."

"Why?"

Why did everything with her have to be an argument? "Because I can control them. They are spelled to obey my orders."

"What are you going to order them to do?" she asked suspiciously. "Will it be dangerous?"

"We don't have time for you to question my every action, you suspicious, vengeful little witch," he snapped before he could stop himself. "I am trying to save both our lives."

He could feel her body tense and knew that this was going to devolve into a bitter argument. She was stubborn and wilful, as much as he enjoyed remembering her otherwise. The giggling, doe-eyed girl who had listened to his many thoughts and theories with fascination had only ever been a fabrication.

He had to defuse it before they were both killed, and he knew from bitter experience the only way to accomplish that. "I'm sorry, I was wrong." He hated that he had to use these particular words yet again. "Please, Sephana, I will apologize later, but you need to do this. Trust me, please." He had vowed to never beg to this woman or any other ever again, and yet here he was doing exactly that.

She just sat stiffly for a moment and then, miraculously, steered the thunder lizard towards the town. Their savage mount growled and snarled as they approached the soldier's position but remained, thankfully, under the effect of the controlling spell.

Eldoth addressed the closest man, whose uniform was soiled and dirty. His wording of their orders, he recalled, had been for them to man their position 'at all times'. "Do you recognize me?"

The soldier stiffened to attention. "Yes, my lord."

"I have new orders for you. You and your men need to advance to the bridge and defend it. Don't let anyone past."

The soldier saluted. "Yes, my lord." He turned to the other soldiers. "We have new orders from the master: defend the bridge, don't let anyone past."

The others snapped to attention. "Yes, sir!"

Sephana backed their lizard away so that it wouldn't attack the soldiers as they ran past. She turned and glared. "You said that they wouldn't be hurt!"

"I said no such thing, but they will not be harmed." *Possibly.* "Draxul will countermand me before any serious fighting happens, but it should give us some time."

She looked at him appraisingly. He had learned long ago not to trust that look. "All the soldiers will obey you?"

"Yes. They all bear the mark of control."

She snapped her reins and steered the lizard towards the town's main street. "I have an idea, come on."

"It's not like I have any choice in this matter," he grumbled.

People scattered before the running dragon-lizard as they ran through the market place square. "Flee the town!" Sephana yelled at the top of her lungs. "When the soldiers leave their positions, flee south and take word that the keep has been taken!"

She had no idea if anyone heard her or not. Moments later—these dragon-lizards were faster than quicklings—they were past the square and approaching the second fortification. "Tell them to reinforce the others at the bridge," she told Eldoth and, to her surprise, he did so.

She steered her growling, unhappy mount past the abandoned barricade. It smelled prey near—which was to say: people—and wanted to feed. She turned to the right and saw Balien, gear in hand, coming up behind her. They were too far apart to speak and made their way to Illyria's position in silence.

There was a roaring cry in front of her and Sephana reined to a halt. Two dragon-lizards with A'Cha on top were facing them. The lizards were snarling and pawing at the ground.

"Will these lizards attack each other?" she asked Eldoth.

"Definitely." His grip around her waist tightened. "Without an established leader, they constantly fight for dominance."

"That's great." Her own mounted shuffled and growled beneath her and Balien's was doing the same. The A'Cha facing them looked terrified.

The one opposite Balien cried out as a white feathered arrow suddenly appeared in its chest. It dropped its reins and fell from its saddle. The second A'Cha snapped turned to run but an arrow struck it in the back of its head. It dropped its reins and sagged but did not fall.

To Sephana's surprise, the now masterless mounts did not attack the fallen A'Cha. Instead, their mouths open impossibly wide, they charged towards Sephana, Balien and Eldoth.

"Run! Let them fight!" Balien called, tossing his reins and sliding down his mount's back. It paid him no attention and instead ran towards its brethren with a savage cry. Moving as fast as she ever had, Sephana scrambled free of the massive creature. Behind her, Eldoth did the same.

Please, please, please: don't eat me. I'm too small for a meal and wouldn't taste very good, anyway.

The three riderless lizards merged into a snarling, slashing melee and the fourth ran towards it.

Sephana ran, not checking to see if Eldoth followed.

"Over here!" Theramus called, standing and waving his hammer. Sephana turned and ran towards him, followed by Balien and the stranger in a red silk coat.

A group of soldiers in tight formation held a group of A'Cha at bay at the edge of the bridge while the Hrallar stood between them, all yelling angrily. It was most confusing. Suddenly the soldiers raised their weapons, saluted, and joined ranks with the others. The now large group began to march towards Theramus's position.

Illyria looked down at the advancing enemy group and nocked an arrow. "They're all mixed in together. It will be difficult for me to target the A'Cha."

"Best not to attack then," he counselled. "Flight is our best option."

Sephana ran up to them on swift feet. "Wegottagowegottagowegottago!!" She leaned against Theramus to catch her breath.

"Who is that man with you?" Illyria asked. The man in question, obviously spent, was being aided by Balien.

"He's my..." She looked away. Theramus and Illyria looked at her oddly. "I mean, he's the wizard from the keep, but don't worry. He's on our side, I promise."

The 'wizard' arrived and collapsed to the ground. "This exertion is beyond me."

Balien handed him a water skin. "Drink, quickly. We must move."

"Can't you just whip up some spell and fly us out of here?" Sephana asked him.

The man glowered at her in a manner that Theramus did not approve of. "I told you before that my magic does not work that way. Besides, I cannot cast while I wear this accursed headband."

"Easy enough." She gripped the edge of the leather strip across his forehead and pulled. He clutched his head and fell to the ground, but the strip of leather didn't move.

He slapped her hands away. "Don't you think I haven't tried that already, you stupid, impulsive cow? It was scribed onto me in runes of my own blood. There are no mundane solutions to my predicament."

Balien sighed in tired exasperation. "Stop it, both of you. We have to go."

Theramus cast a final glance at the group of men and A'Cha coming towards them. They were closer, but not so much that they could not be evaded.

Out of the corner of his eye, he barely saw it: a scratched and bloody dragon-lizard. A survivor of the battle below, it had followed them into the hills. Its mouth was open, its claws extended, and it charged with a roar. Illyria's back was turned to it as she watched the advancing soldiers. She was its target.

Theramus hurled his body between her and oncoming dragon-lizard. Holding his mallet's handle with both hands, he forced it crossways into the creature's mouth in a vain attempt to hold it at bay.

Illyria whirled in time to have Theramus slam into her. Her bow and arrow were thrown by the impact, and there wasn't time to try and reclaim them. She scrambled to her feet and drew her sword, Maiden's Fang. *I'm beginning to really hate these creatures.*

Theramus was on his back, his hammer still jammed into the rear of the lizard's mouth like a horse's bit. The thick wood handle was already splintering against its massive teeth. She had to free him now.

She thrust her sword two-handedly into its eye. Her blade, which should have penetrated its skull and pierced its brain, instead jammed against the thick bone of its eye socket. Screaming in pain, it wrenched its head away and butted her with its massive jaw. Her sword remained jammed in its skull.

There was another roar and she saw a second dragon-lizard stomping towards them. Balien had his sword drawn and was facing it. The first one was raking at Theramus with its foreclaws while he held its mouth at bay with his hammer. The approaching soldiers were still coming closer.

We don't have time for this.

Her eyes fixed upon her sword, still protruding from the dragon-lizard's eye. Illyria ran towards the creature's head, leapt into the air and kicked out with both of her feet at the sword's hilt. The steel blade was thrust violently past the thick bone into its skull.

The dragon-lizard didn't even cry out. Its brain pierced, it simply collapsed upon Theramus like an abandoned puppet.

She had no time for self congratulation. Pulling a fresh arrow from her quiver, she ran to her bow and spun to face Balien. He was dancing around his opponent, harrying it with his sword but had given it no significant injuries.

Her first arrow struck the creature in its neck, her second in its chest but her third stuck its thick skull and embedded itself in the bone. Her brother took advantage of its distraction and cleaved into its neck. Theramus scrambled out from under first lizard's dead weight and surged towards the second with an angry bellow. Blinded with pain, it scrambled to escape and did not see Theramus' hammer come down squarely upon the top of its head.

The blow, which would have killed an ox outright, only stunned the dragon-lizard, but it still allowed Balien the opportunity to plunge his blade into its heart.

There was no time to celebrate their victory. The fight had delayed them too much and now the group of soldiers and A'Cha were here.

Illyria readied an arrow and squared her shoulders. "We can no longer afford to be merciful," she said reluctantly. "Attack the human soldiers to kill."

There was a roar and flash of heat from in front of her. Hungry tongues of flame erupted from the ground as if Emuranna herself had reached down from Alalaree and struck flint to tinder. As Illyria watched the flames stretched into a fiery wall that completely blocked off the enemy advance.

"We should leave quickly. I cannot maintain this for long." Illyria turned. Leather headband gone and red jacket flapping in the heated air, the stranger stood boldly upright and held his hands out in front of him.

Beside him, Sephana gaped. Somewhere along the way she had lost her head scarf and her hair billowed freely. "You really are a wizard!"

"The Guardians of the Wellspring of Souls are the Imvir, more commonly called 'quicklings'. It is they who watch over the passage of new souls from Imusasus into the bodies of unborn children. Quicklings are eternally happy, child-like and mischievous. When two people who hate each other suddenly fall in love or a tree begins to grow in a place that seems impossible, it is said that, somewhere, a quickling is laughing."

—Source Unknown

CHAPTER NINE

Eldoth had never run so long or hard in his life. He deplored it. Anyone could perform feats of physicality if given time and practice. It did not matter how stupid or witless they were, if they repeated the task enough times they became better at it. That was how Emuranna had made the human body. Physical proficiency proved nothing, and Eldoth had never felt the need to spend his valuable time developing it. Any idiot could swing a hammer, but true intelligence was much rarer.

A person was either intelligent or he was not. Less than one man per thousand had Eldoth's facility with numbers, and even fewer his ability to recall information or master the skills of reason or logic. Simple math, then, said that a person of Eldoth's mental acuity was exceedingly rare. It was not an exaggeration to state that he was the only person with his mental capacity in Karalon and, perhaps, all of Anshara. It did not behove him to waste his time on physical tedium, not when his intelligence was unique, or close enough to it.

That maxim had guided him his entire life. Other than the simpleminded japings of thick minded buffoons unable to comprehend his mental processes, none had complained at this division of labour. Most were content to leave the complicated mental work to him while they mindlessly flexed and lifted. Eldoth, in return, left the sweaty, tedious acts of labour to those more suited to it. In all the worlds there were masters and there were followers. It was natural. Right.

He realized, now, that he would have to make an exception for instances in which he had to run for his life.

Unlike the task-oriented labour of slave camps, flight was not benefited by intelligence. He could not use reason or logic against the brainless beastmen that pursued him. He doubted they would comprehend him if he were to try. He would be disembowelled and his body left for scavengers, or perhaps they would consume his flesh. There was a small possibility that they would take him alive back to Durnshold and give the pleasure of his painful execution to Draxul.

The unfortunate conclusion remained that, in this particular circumstance, intellectual superiority was secondary to physical conditioning. There was nothing for him to do other than continue running until he dropped dead from exhaustion.

What was more frustrating was the fact that everyone else in the small group, from the tall, blue giant to Eldoth's hated ex-wife, were so damned *good* at it. While he gasped for breath and sweat out every drop of water he had ever consumed, the others jogged blithely along as if this kind of activity was the most mundane task in the world.

It probably was. They were soldiers, after all. Soldiery was an even more of a waste of skills and abilities than physical labour. Engaging in hours of training and conditioning in order to engage in a task that had a very good chance of getting you killed? It was wasteful, illogical, and insane.

Insane or not, at the moment his safety depended on them. The one with the sword, Balien, was at least somewhat effective with his metal club. The giant was sensible enough to maximize the use of his physical might to end combat quickly if it occurred, and the blond female's choice of a bow was logical and efficient. As for Sephana, foul temptress that she was: little about her logical or intelligent, and never had been. She was sensible enough to run away when the situation demanded and, he admitted grudgingly, had possessed the courage to ride and direct the terrifying thunder lizard when he himself had not.

"Come on, we're almost there. Just over that next hill." It was Sephana, of course. Her words may have been comforting by their context, but she said them with the condescending tone he had always hated and did so while running backwards and smiling mockingly.

"I hope…" he managed to gasp, "…that you trip…on something… and sprain something…quite painfully."

"Ha! Like that's ever going to happen." She turned around. "Seriously, though, we're almost there."

"You…said that…three hills…ago."

"I'm sorry about that." She sounded sincere, but he knew better. "Illyria spotted something and changed her mind. This time we can rest and watch for pursuit at the same time." She glanced over at him. "Are you going to make it?"

"Your concern…is touching." He gasped. "I shall persevere."

She looked like she was going to reply, but said nothing. He could not be certain, but when she moved off he thought she was frowning.

Cresting the next hill was perhaps one of the most difficult things Eldoth had ever done, but somehow he managed it. The image of Sephana and her mocking smile spurred him onward.

Illyria and Balien crouched behind the crest of the hill and watched for signs of pursuit. So far, after a half hour of watching, they'd seen nothing. Balien had done his best to erase any signs of their passage, but they were moving too quickly and their numbers were too large to fool a skilled tracker. If the Hrallar, who Eldoth named

Draxul, had wanted them pursued, then she would have seen sign of it by now. While she was not letting down her guard, it was most likely that they were safe, for now.

"Do you think he's sincere?" She asked her brother, referring to Eldoth.

"Sephana trusts him," he answered after a moment's thought. "She doesn't like him, but she trusts him."

She shook her head in disbelief. "They were *married*?"

"They argue like they're married." He shrugged. "We wouldn't have gotten out of the keep without him. He knows more than he's telling us, for certain, but I don't think he's lied."

She made no reply.

"You're marriage won't be like that," he said.

She looked at him, confused. "What?"

"Your marriage to Turius. It won't be so acrimonious."

"I wasn't thinking about that." Balien said nothing, just kept looking at her and, finally, she looked away. "Maybe I was."

"You've known him since you were young." His voice was gentle. "You've always gotten along well."

"Yes," she replied with only a touch of bitterness. "I'm sure we'll be very *polite* together." She wasn't thinking about Gennald. She wasn't.

"Not every marriage can be like our parents' was."

She glanced over at him. "Is that supposed to be a warning to me or a comfort?"

"Neither. Both. There are worse things than being in a relationship that is polite. Your children will grow up safe and healthy."

He was right about that. There was nothing about life in the Petty Kingdoms that bothered her more than the rampant poverty and squalor that pervaded the lives of its common-folk. Her nightmares were filled with hollow-eyed children that had never eaten three meals in a day. "No, they'll just be insulated, ignorant of the true state of the world while they drink wine in marble halls."

"Most parents would give their lives for to see their children raised safe and worry free. Will it really be so bad?"

"I don't know." She bit her lip. "It feels petty to want to have been born someone else, considering the gift's we've received." She looked over at him. "Do you think less of me for thinking so?"

"Would you think less of me for thinking less of you?" He asked, his eyes twinkling in humour.

She had to laugh. It was so...Balien.

"You should go talk to our new friend and see what answers he has," he told her. "I'll keep watch."

She nodded. He was right. She crawled backwards from the hill crest, ensuring that, on the off chance there was someone below, didn't see her movement. It was an old ranger's trick, as natural to her as breathing. "I'd like to move out again in an hour. We should be able to get a few more hours of travel before nightfall."

He nodded his understanding, his eyes still on their trail. "Which way will we be going?"

"I'll know when once I've heard what Eldoth has to say."

"Tell us about how you ended up in Durnshold," Illyria requested. Eldoth had bathed, drunk two whole skins of water and changed into one of Balien's spare sets of clothing. The young human was marginally taller than the Nemoran prince but slighter. Without his striking, oddly cut coat, he didn't look exotic, only tired.

Theramus was no judge of human appearance but he thought that the wizard's short dark hair, dark eyes, and a roughly trimmed beard looked quite average. He judged the man to be older than the others in the group by several years. In the prime of his life but not beyond it.

"I was there because I was captured by a Djido named Veeshar."

That was bad news indeed. "A Djido. Are you certain?"

"I have seen their faces in every historical text I have read. In Akkilon, we burned them every year in effigy. I know a Djido when I see one."

"Why did he capture you?"

He smiled smugly. "Because I am a wizard and the only other being who could discover the secrets of the keep. He is obsessed with finding them."

"What secrets are in the keep?" Illyria asked at the same time that Sephana asked "How did you become a wizard?"

He sighed. "This process will take significantly longer if I must answer random questions in a random order. If would be far more efficient if I were to explain what happened to me and allowed you to ask clarifying questions afterwards. Is that acceptable to you?"

Illyria's expression remained calm and polite but Sephana, being less restrained, snorted loudly.

"Tell your tale in whatever manner you think is best," Illyria replied smoothly.

"But include the part where you became a wizard," Sephana added.

"Yes," Theramus said. "I am most intrigued by that myself. There have been no credible acts of wizardry in centuries."

"Very well," Eldoth replied. He looked at Sephana and smiled wryly. "Ironically, my path to wizardry began with you."

"Me?"

"Oh, yes. During our *courtship*." He smiled cruelly. "You gave me a book. It was very old and written in a language that I had never seen before. You said that you found it and thought that it might interest me."

Sephana examined the tips of her boots. "I remember."

"We were engaged and married soon thereafter and you kept me too distracted to do more than leaf through it and write down a few notes, but then you *left me.*" He stared at her with open hostility. Sephana was looking anywhere but at him, her face stony.

"Is this relevant to your story, Eldoth?" Illyria asked with a hint of iron. Theramus was glad that she had spoken and kept him from doing so. He would not have been so diplomatic.

"What? Oh, yes. Well, once I was alone I found I had a great deal of free time. My job was beneath me, of course. Tallying rice totals and calculating wages took only a fraction of my intellect. I found that I could do that and study the book that Sephana had given me at the same time. The book was...fascinating."

He gave a smile of genuine happiness—the first that Theramus had seen him use—and took on a nostalgic expression. "It took me months to decipher it. I relished it. It was the first truly challenging problem I had encountered. I would forget to eat for days, sleep only when my body collapsed. That book took over my life. I lost my job and my place to live. I lived under a tree on the river bank for a month, scratching my theories into its bark because I had no paper. Finally I had it." He blinked and looked around him. His customary sneer returned. "The book was a manual for basic wizardry. I won't get into the technical aspects of it; you wouldn't be able to comprehend them anyway. It's too advanced."

Sephana snorted.

"So you taught yourself magic," Illyria prompted. "When did you meet this 'Veeshar'?"

"Oh, not for years," he answered blithely. "It took me six months before I could even light a candle using my power. The book was only meant to teach the most rudimentary of skills. I wanted to know more, but to do that I had to find more information. I searched all across the land."

"And did you find anything?" Sephana asked.

Despite his dislike of the man, Theramus found Eldoth's story fascinating. "The Djido destroyed all of the towers of wizardry during the War of Blood and Tears," Theramus told them all. "It is thought that their knowledge was lost forever."

Eldoth shrugged dismissively. "And it was, for the most part. They were very thorough, but even they could not destroy an entire culture. I was actually fortunate that their works were written in their own tongue. People just saw relics of a bygone age, souvenirs, not anything of value. I could recognize the symbols, being the only speaker of this language—"

"Renfel," Theramus found himself saying. "It is called Renfel."

Eldoth looked at him shrewdly. "Is it now? Yes, that makes a great deal of sense. There are many references to an ancient caster named 'Renthalin'. In fact…" Sephana cleared her throat loudly. "Oh, sorry. Well, as the only person capable of recognizing…*Renfel*…I was able to acquire more knowledge from people who did not know the value of what they had. It took a great deal of time, but slowly my knowledge and skill increased to what it is today."

"And when in your journey of knowledge did you meet this Djido, Veeshar?" Illyria asked.

He scowled. "Last month. I have taken to investigating the sites of wizard's towers. Most things of value were destroyed or taken, but there are remnants. I have had some success searching through the ruins. I was doing that when I sensed the gatestone open."

"But the gatestones can't open. They're blocked shut," Sephana protested. "*You* taught me that."

He sneered at her. "You told me that you never listened when I—what was it? Oh yes—'blathered on and on like a myna bird'."

Theramus's fists tightened.

She looked away and scowled. "I listened sometimes, when you weren't being too boring."

"Sephana, Eldoth," Illyria said sternly. "I understand that you have a history with each other and you should talk about your differences, but this is not the time." She looked at the two of them severely, her eyes violet with anger. "Right now there are more important things to discuss. Eldoth, you said that you sensed the opening of a gatestone?"

"My *darling* wife is correct, which I suppose is the same as saying that *I* was correct." He looked very self satisfied. Theramus cleared his throat. "Sorry. The gates *are* sealed. The last High King created the Shieldstone and blocked them all during the Great War. I've been to dozens of gatestones in three different kingdoms and each them has felt as magically dead as this rock that I am sitting on now. That was why I was so surprised to sense this one opening."

"That was when you first met the Djido?" Theramus asked.

"Yes. I was investigating when one of those lizard warriors ambushed me."

"*One of* the lizard warriors?" Sephana repeated. "You mean there are more?"

"Yes. Three of them, all siblings. 'Clutch-mates', as they call themselves. Draxul, Thraxul and another whose name I didn't learn. They're Veeshar's bodyguards."

Eldoth's words sparked Theramus's memory. "I have heard of these," he said. "They are called Tsrinn. They are trained to their task from birth. They are highly trained and fanatically loyal."

"So you were ambushed by one of these…Tsrinn?" Illyria prompted.

Eldoth looked embarrassed. "They are very fast and quite skilled. It knocked me unconscious and brought me before Veeshar. He tried to dominate me but I was able to resist him. Instead, he bound my magic and took me prisoner." He shrugged. "I've been his captive ever since."

"Then you know everything he's been doing," Illyria said. "You were privy to his plans."

"I was his prisoner, not his confidant," Eldoth protested. "It's not like he *told* me anything. However, as I am not a moron and since neither he nor his minions speak Anduili very well, I was able to glean a great deal."

Sephana listened as Eldoth began answering specific questions about what they faced. How many dragon-lizards were there? Fifty, including the ones at the keep. How many A'Cha and Vaulen? About ten thousand and five hundred, respectively, all led by a Vaulen warlord that they all called 'Olamm'.

She chewed her lip, thinking. Something was missing. It came to her. "The slave-marks!"

He looked at her in that condescending way she had always hated.

"What do you mean, Sephana?" Illyria asked.

"That dragon-lizard you killed on the way to Northhaven, it had that mark on its head like a tattoo. It wasn't 'scribed' into them—not like your headband was." She said this last part to Eldoth. "It was like a wax seal had been pressed into their heads. Was that all part of the mind-controlling spell?"

"Uhh, yes. That is exactly what it is," He said after a moment's hesitation.

"You're lying," she crowed. "You're terrible at it; you always have been. Like that time when you said you'd been robbed, but you'd really been docked a week's pay because you called the overseer a—"

"Sephana, that's enough." Illyria warned. "What aren't you telling us, Eldoth?"

He sighed and shot Sephana an annoyed look. "You're right: it's not a rune. That college of magic, mentalism, is unknown to Veeshar. I was quite surprised to find how much he *didn't* know." His face brightened. "I have this theory, you see, about race and magical aptitude…that I won't get into right now," he amended at Sephana's angry expression. "I believe that Veeshar is only expert in two colleges of magic. He may dabble in some of the others, but not enough to be effective in them. Mentalism, as I said, is completely beyond him."

"Then how did he ensorcel the guards at the keep, or the dragon-lizards?" Illyria asked.

His expression became pained.

She knew that look. "Eldoth, what did you do?"

"I didn't do anything!" he hissed. "None of this is my fault."

"Eldoth…"

He sighed. "Fine. It was with a device, an artefact, which he stole off me. The 'Controlling Seal of Perceptus'. I didn't call it that," he added hastily. "It was written on its side in Renfel. Perceptus is the wizard whose tower I was searching. Veeshar stole it off of me when he captured me."

"And why didn't you tell us this?" Illyria asked.

"Because he wants it back and thought we'd take it away from him," Sephana said with disgust. "He's right, too. *I* don't want him coming near my forehead with that."

"I want to study it, not make an army of mind-controlled slaves," he protested, aghast. "It's an incredibly powerful artefact. I can't imagine how much I could learn from it."

He sounded convincing, but Sephana remained suspicious. She'd known him too long.

"You are not the only one who thought so," Eldoth said tiredly. "Perceptus was also concerned about his device being misused. In the box where I found the seal there was also a warning, that those who abused it would find their work undone by the Medallion of Negation."

"What is the Medallion of Negation?" Illyria asked.

"It is another artefact that I suspect it was in the same room in which I found the Seal, but Veeshar arrived before I could complete my investigation."

Theramus sat up straighter. "And you could use this to undo the Seal's spell?"

"I can say nothing for certain, not on this subject," he warned, "but I believe so, yes."

"Can't you just use that pen of yours, your stele, to undo the spell?" Sephana asked.

"No. The Seal cannot be countered by simple runework. That is its power."

"Where are these ruins?" Illyria asked.

Eldoth looked at the land around him and frowned. "I do not know how to get there exactly, not from here, but it is east of us and within a day's travel."

Illyria stood. "Then that is what we will do next. Perhaps we can locate this medallion and perhaps not, but it would be foolish not to try." She stopped. "Eldoth, will you help us in this endeavour? Your assistance will be invaluable."

"I have no more love of the Djido than you do, and am petty enough to want revenge." he growled. "Yes, by all means. I will help you."

" 'The Great War was fought over wizardry, you see. The Djido never had the power of the Arch-mages. They had no High Wizards. Oh, they were just as skilled as us in the fields they excelled in but where the Djido were masters of two colleges, we were masters of all of them. That was what they wanted and what we never gave them. That was why in the final stages of the war, in what history calls the 'War of Blood and Tears', they made such an effort to destroy all of the Towers of Wizardry. If they couldn't have it, then no one could. The Djido are just sore losers.' "

—A rather inebriated Eldoth, talking to an unappreciative audience

CHAPTER TEN

Alwyn yawned as he walked up the final flight of stairs to the manor's watchtower. Eight stories above the ground on the tallest hill in the region, only the view from the top of the Urdom Pass rivalled it. It was early—the morning sun was just even with the top of the tower—but the boy Davin was already there, watching the land around him for signs of the insurrection that he swore was coming.

It was Alwyn's second morning in Northhaven. The morning and afternoon yesterday had been spent offloading the cargo from the wagons and haggling for its value with Davin's factor, Addison. Alwyn may only have been a middling warrior, but he knew the value of what he carried and was sure that he had done his father proud. In the evening there had been a city-wide feast in which he and his men had been the guests of honour. The Karalinian maids had been pretty and welcoming to their northern neighbours, and a good time had been had by all. Their songs and dances were different from those that he knew but pleasant nonetheless.

With every dance he felt Illyria's absence keenly, and not just for the missed opportunity to see her wearing something prettier than travelling leathers. She and her friends should have been celebrated as much as he and his men, if not more so. With every toast of courage and bravery (and there had been several) his thoughts invariably shifted to the four people actually off doing something courageous. None of them had even been mentioned. Illyria and her companions were still a very sore spot with Davin and their names had been passed over in the name of diplomacy.

He stepped up behind the young lord to whom every man, woman and child in Northhaven gave their unswerving obedience. "Good morning, my lord. You are up early."

Davin gave an absent nod without taking his eye off the horizon. "I await word from the capital. The Bears will make their move soon and I must be ready."

Alwyn rolled his eyes. He was more than tired of the boy's obsession and he had only been here a day. He had no idea how his sister, Elorin, coped. The word that Davin awaited so eagerly was not coming, not with Durnshold in the hands of the beastmen and those wretched dragon-lizards. Davin refused to believe it, and insisted instead that it was a hoax created by the king's loyalists to strip him of his men. It was within the boy's power to eject Alwyn, his men, and his cargo from the city so he didn't press him on the subject.

"I had hoped to begin negotiations for your Karalinian goods after breakfast. Will you be joining me?"

Davin shook his head. "I have other matters to attend to. Addison will represent me."

That suited Alwyn just fine. He doubted he could get through an entire day of the boy's company without doing anything...undiplomatic. "As you wish, my lord. I will leave you to your business." Giving the surrounding countryside one final, appreciative glance, Alwyn turned and made his way down the long stairway.

He met Elorin in the Great Hall. She was wearing a light green summer gown and looked quite pretty. She curtsied deeply and smiled. "Good morning, prince. Thank you again for the dance last night."

He returned her smile and bowed to her in the Karalinian style. "The pleasure was mine."

Despite their rocky start the evening of Illyria's departure, Elorin had proved to be quite engaging company. She had taken him on a tour of the city and had been quite shrewd in her evaluation of Alwyn's imported goods. While he still lamented Illyria's absence at the feast and dance, Elorin had proved to be an acceptable substitute.

She offered him her arm and he took it, accompanying her out of the manor to the marshalling ground where the city's wares were on display.

"You are still intent on leaving tomorrow, Prince Alwyn?" she asked.

"Yes. Once negotiations are complete, we will spend the afternoon and evening getting ready for our departure." Tomorrow, whether Illyria returned or not.

Illyria. What hazards does she face now?

Elorin frowned. "I was hoping for more time. There are several dances still to teach you."

"The world seems to have other plans, my lady," He answered absently, his mind elsewhere.

"There is no need for you to accompany me," Eldoth repeated for what had to be the fourth time. "Wizards dislike thieves, and their towers are riddled with traps invisible to those who cannot wield magic. It will take more effort for me to protect you than any benefit I would gain from your presence."

"What kind of traps?" Sephana asked cautiously. They were standing around a square hole in the middle of a grass covered mound. She had expected the ruins of an ancient wizard's tower to be more impressive, but, other than a small section of stone blocks, all she saw was rubble.

"It depends on the wizard and their college of specialty. Very few are fatal. Some give poxes, or unbearable pain." He chuckled. "One transformed the victim's clothing into constricting nettles. Perceptus was a mentalist, so I imagine his would deal with illusion or emotion control. As a wizard with a stele I can bypass them without difficulty. You cannot."

Illyria peered down the hole. "How large is it down there?"

Eldoth brushed some dust off his coat. "I cannot account for its complete volume, but the room where I found the Seal was on the third level."

"How many levels can it have?" Sephana protested.

He rolled his eyes. "This was constructed by magic, not excavated with picks and shovels. One level, five levels, or ten; there is no difference to a wizard."

"You're not going down alone," Illyria told him.

He opened his mouth to protest, but Sephana cut him off. "It's not that we don't trust you Eldoth it's just that…" Her smile was cruel. "Oh, wait: we don't trust you."

Eldoth glared at her. "And what would I do that you don't trust? Abandon you? Betray you? Find some magical item and withhold it?"

"It's not that." Illyria looked at Sephana crossly. "I don't think we should separate more than we need to."

Balien and Theramus came jogging towards them. "I found tracks. A'Cha, and something else I don't recognize Hrallar, maybe."

"One of the Tsrinn, Thraxul, went off on a secret mission shortly after the keep was taken," Eldoth said. "It must have been to here."

"What forces did he take with him?" Balien asked.

"Some beastmen—I don't know how many—and two thunder lizards. I wasn't really paying attention."

"Then you're definitely not going down alone," Illyria said firmly.

Sephana was almost deafened by the sound of his eyes rolling. "Do what you must, but I will not be held responsible for anything that happens to you."

She stared down into the dark pit. "Who's going down there with him?"

"Balien and I will," Illyria said, glancing at her brother for confirmation.

"I will stay and guard the entrance," Theramus stated. "It is unlikely that I will fit comfortably down there, anyway. You may stay with me if you wish."

She almost agreed. She really didn't want to climb down into the darkness, but Eldoth looked so very smug and condescending.

"No," she found herself saying. "I'll come."

Illyria held the glowing branch that Eldoth had given her and advanced cautiously down the corridor. It was wide, but not tall—Theramus would have had to stoop—and was made from masoned stone. It was in quite good repair considering its age. A layer of dust covered everything.

A series of white statues wearing blue robes lined the walls. "They're pretty," Sephana commented, holding her own glowing stick near the face of the closest and reaching out to stroke it.

"I told you not to touch anything," Eldoth snapped. "Those statues still have active spell-traps on them."

She quickly pulled her hand back and retreated. Eldoth, holding something in his hand that emitted a focused beam of light, set off down the corridor. They followed cautiously.

"The dust has been disturbed recently," Balien said, kneeling. "They're the same tracks as above." No one else spoke and their steps echoed loudly against the silence.

It was foolish, but Illyria wished that she had not given Heartseeker to Theramus. It would do her little good down here but she still missed the comfort of the spell-wrought wood. She wore Maiden's Fang at her hip but it did not assure her in the same way. She was a skilled fencer and had honed her skill against her brother—a master of the blade—but she was an archer foremost. When she saw something in the distance, her eyes automatically judged distance, lead and trajectory. Any time she saw a new person or creature, she instinctively examined it to find where she could sink an arrow to best punch through its skin or armour.

Heartseeker had been made for one of Illyria's ancestors, Illystil Exiprion, a princess during the Great War. When the rest of the Nemoran royal family had fled to the Ilthwood to safeguard their heritage, Illystil had refused. She, and a group of those loyal to her, had ventured out to fight the Djido. For seven years she had made war and even served as a general in the army of the Anduili Remnant before finally returning home at the age of twenty five. She had then married and her daughter had been the next queen of Nemora.

When Illyria had asked for the right to bear arms alongside her father she had used the example of Illystil. What was good enough for one Nemoran princess surely had to be good enough for another. When she asked for permission to see the world beyond the borders of the forest, once again Illystil's precedent had formed the basis of her argument. Her uncle, while unhappy, had been unable to deny her, but he had used Illystil's history to guarantee her return. As Illystil had returned at twenty five to marry, so too did Illyria.

Had Illystil also chafed against her return to the sanctuary of Ilthanara? Had her matrimonial obligation also felt like chains that anchored her to a rock where her freedom was the sacrifice? The histories did not reveal such things. In this, sadly, Illyria had no precedent to guide her.

The hallway turned after forty very long paces. Sephana froze. The floor ahead of her just wasn't there. Heart beating loudly, she crept up and looked over the edge. Balien joined her. Even holding her magical torch as far down as she could she could barely see the bottom. It looked flat and featureless except for a suspicious, shaggy lump.

"Can you make another one of these?" Balien asked Eldoth, pointing to his own torch. When Eldoth nodded he broke off the glowing end and dropped it down the pit. The ghostly, bluish light fell to the bottom and told them what Sephana had already expected. "It's an A'Cha."

"That is why you don't touch things that look pretty when you are in a wizard's tower," Eldoth said unnecessarily. "The stairway to the lower level is ahead."

They skirted the edge of the pit and continued. Sephana may not have been able to touch any of the statues that continued to line the hallway, but she could still appreciate them. Each one was different and all were incredibly detailed. Some were men, some were women and all of them wore embroidered, one shouldered robes. The outer layer of the robes was all a bright, vivid shade of cobalt. She didn't know if the colour was the result of paint, glazing, or the use of a different type of stone. As much as she wanted to know, she didn't want to plunge to her doom in some pit or have her clothes turned into shrubbery.

After more tedious walking, Eldoth finally turned the last corner. There was a short adjoining hall in front of him, beyond which lay a wide antechamber and then the stairs heading down. Statues, spelled like the rest, lined its walls.

He flashed his stele's beam ahead of him and froze. There was another body, a beastman to guess by its fur, sprawled on the ground at the top of the stairway. He examined the room ahead with his wizard's senses. There was active magic going on here.

These tunnels were dead. Either before or during the tower's razing, the magic that permeated the walls and floors of Perceptus's tower had—for lack of a better word—*died*. Individual spells, like the simple triggers on the statues, remained, but the rest of the sophisticated spellwork had deteriorated beyond the point for Eldoth even to tell what they had been.

He understood little of what was around him. During his first exploration he had dismissed the spellwork in this room as beyond his ability to comprehend. He had not thought that it was possible to activate the spells, but someone or something obviously had. The body before him also bespoke the lie about magical traps not being fatal.

His pride did not allow him to admit any of that, especially not with Sephana in the room. He could easily imagine the razor sharp lash of her mockery if he were to say such a thing aloud. He kept his silence and, mindful of the people waiting impatiently behind him, cautiously stepped forward.

"Move slowly and touch nothing."

He realized his mistake half way to the stairs. He knew that the room's magic had been activated by the presence of the dead body on the floor, but he had been looking for an activation rune: something stepped on or touched. This magic did not rely on such things. Just being in the room was enough.

"Get Out!" he shouted. "Run!" but it was too late.

Illyria's third pregnancy had been her hardest. Hestus must have had Noss blood in him, for he'd been born half again as large as his older brother and sister. Walking any distance more than the length of her suite had become more and more painful, made worse by the fact she needed to use the chamber pot fifteen times per day. Her figure had never fully recovered from the birth of her eldest, and her lack of mobility after Hestus had been its death knell. She couldn't bring herself to even look at the clothing she had worn during her brief tour of Nemora five years ago, let alone think of wearing it. The duenna brought in to assist her with Hestus was young, slender, and pretty; too pretty. Illyria disliked the looks that her husband shared with the girl.

Only her eldest, Euthalia, bore the crownmark, but there were already six ahead of her in her generation. She'd never wear the Crown of the Hawk. She was an unneeded placeholder, just as her mother had been.

Illyria had never seen Balien again, or Theramus and Sephana. They'd returned to Karalon after Illyria's wedding. Nintarans from across Anshara had harkened to the call of a Vaulen kingdom and there had been no word from anyone in Karalon for two years. They were raiding across the Karnems now, she heard. Derwyn had been sacked last spring and its king, Gwyn, slain by a dragon-lizard. Djido had been sighted in Nemora twice, and, just last month, an unnaturally merged creature—some kind of armour-plated giant boar—had been killed in the Ilthwood. Ten warriors had been mauled by it before it had finally been slain.

A sound came from somewhere inside the apartment. Illyria rose with difficulty, cursing the ever present pain in her hip. Cinching her day-robe around her ever-

burgeoning hips, she limped across the sun room. The sound came again: a muffled gasp.

She found them together in the bedroom.

"How dare you!" she shouted. "In our own bed, Turius?"

Her husband, handsome and fit, rolled off of the spread, naked woman lying beneath him. She was young and perfect. Neither made any motion to cover their nakedness.

"Why shouldn't I?" he said with a shrug, sweat gleaming on his body. "You haven't shared it with me in more than a year."

She couldn't say anything beyond indignant splutters.

"We've already produced a crownmarked heir. What does it matter?" He ran one hand down the duenna's bare leg. "It was fun enough while you were pretty, but look at you now. You're disgusting."

"I gave you three children!"

"Yes, and now that you've done that I have no use for you." He turned and began to kiss his young, perfect, bed-mate. "Close the door behind you when you leave."

The last thing Illyria saw as she left the room was the look of triumph on the girls face before it was eclipsed by passion. On the far side of the closed door, Illyria fell to the ground and wept.

"Theramus, help me!" Sephana cried out from the post she'd been chained to. She had given the angry mob more than she had received, but in the end there had been too many. "Theramus, where are you?"

"Snake-spawn!" someone hissed as they passed by.

Her clothes were in tatters and all of the scales on her body were clearly displayed for everyone to see. A child ran up to her and ran a small hand along the scales on her hip before running back to his giggling friends.

A pair of Reshai, free in the way of the western clans and swaddled in white cloth as was their custom, stopped and looked at her in disgust. "Look at her tail. It's hideous."

"Disgusting," the other one agreed. He looked Sephana in the eyes. "Why did you never sever it, as the rest of us do?"

"Tails are reminders of the abominations that spawned us," the first one scolded. "Scales can be forgiven, but tails cannot."

"It was too late!" Sephana cried. "I wasn't raised in the clans. I didn't know until I was eight. Severing my tail would have crippled me."

"You should have done it anyway," the first Reshai said. "Better to live as an invalid than to be a living reminder of the Djido that spawned you."

"Today is your punishment for your lack of courage. You will die here today because you could not do then what needed to be done." Shaking their heads in disgust they left.

"I was eight years old!" she protested.

A villager hurled a ball of dung at her. It struck messily on the side of Sephana's head and the crowd cheered. More followed, along with rotten pieces of food and small rocks. Soon she was filthy and bruised.

"Theramus!" she called out with relief. "There you are. Please, get me out here. Save me!"

The Noss stood head and shoulders above the gathered crowd. He held a rock the size of her head in one large, blue hand. "Why would I save you?" His voice was dark with hate. "You manipulated an innocent man into marrying you and then abandoned him. You were unworthy even to associate with other slaves. You disgust me, Sephana."

"Noooooo!!" He raised the stone in his hand and hurled it straight towards her head.

A fear sigil. It's making us live out our nightmares. I have to find the trigger.

Eldoth reached down to get his stele but the magically induced hallucinations took over his mind.

Eldoth sprawled on his hands and knees. His head throbbed in pain but physical agony paled against the burn of humiliation. He had failed. His first wizard's duel, his first chance to show the world that there were still mighty human wizards in the cosmos, and he had failed. Badly.

Every spell he had cast had been countered. Every trick he attempted had been seen through and foiled. Near the end, when he had almost thought that he might win, he realized that the Djido had merely been drawing out the conflict. During the duel one of Veeshar's minions had been making his way behind him. One moment Eldoth had been casting fire and the next it had been over.

This is a dream. The sigil is creating this image in my head. I must fight it.

"You are not good enough," the Djido taunted him in its thin, reedy voice. "Human magic will always fail against the magic of the Djido."

"No!"

Something swept out his hands from underneath him and he fell to the ground.

"You are too pathetic for me take as a slave," the Djido hissed, "and your body is too weak to use for labour. You are good to me only as food."

Eldoth looked up to see a thunder lizard approaching him, saliva pouring from its huge, toothy maw.

I must succeed, or everyone will be trapped in their nightmares until their minds fail.

"You die now, monkey."

Eldoth cried out as the creature bit into his flesh.

Illyria lay on the dusty floor and wept. For just this moment she knew where she was. Everyone lay on the ground, immobilized. *I have to stop this.* She looked around her with eyes that could barely focus, trying to find an answer.

She could feel the next nightmare coming. Looking around her, she saw a statue with its blue robe against the wall and she knew what she had to do. She forced herself to her hands and knees and began to crawl. Visions consumed her before she even made it three feet.

She was brought before her uncle in chains. She wore only rags, her old finery taken from her long ago. She blinked at the bright lights and looked around her. She was in the Ilthanaran throne room, surrounded by her peers and family.

"How do you plead, Illyria?" a harsh voice to her right demanded.

"Plead?" She looked at the person, uncomprehending, and then realized who it was: Turius, the man she was supposed to marry.

"You have been named an oath breaker by the king of Nemora and stand accused of treason against the Nemoran people. How do you plead, Illyria?"

Crawl. You have to crawl.

Where had that thought come from? She was standing, not crawling.

"How do you plead, Illyria?" Turius repeated.

She shook her head, putting the strange thought behind her. "I did break my oath, but I never betrayed my people."

"You denied the Nemoran people a crownmarked heir. You put the royal bloodline in jeopardy, and through them all the people of Nemora," Turius thundered. "You had a duty to your people, a duty you that only you could perform, and you reneged on it."

One leg forward and then one arm. Again. Do it again.

"But I couldn't," she protested. "There was a war. Karalon was being invaded...." She saw the lack of sympathy on her peer's faces.

"And did your presence turn the tide of that war?" her uncle asked from his throne.

Illyria's face fell. "No. We were too few. Armies of Vaulen and A'Cha took the Karalinian throne anyway."

"They were outlanders! Strangers! Why would you choose to aid them when your own family had need of you?"

She bowed her head. "I wanted to help them."

"Do you think that you are so special, Illyria?" he asked her. "Do you think that you have special powers that would make could single-handedly turn the tide of a war?"

"No," she whispered.

I can't crawl. I can't even move. How can I when everyone I loved is dead?

"Where is your brother, Illyria?" came a voice from the side. Illyria turned and saw her mother, elegant and beautiful despite the angry tears that fell down her cheeks. "Where is my son?"

"He's dead," Illyria whispered. "He followed me and he died. They're all dead."

Kyria stepped forward and slapped Illyria across the face. "You killed my son. You are dead to me."

'Mother, no! Please!"

"You are no longer my daughter." With long, proud strides she left the court.

"Your family is dead to you. Your friends are dead and those you failed to help are also dead," intoned King Kefeus. "I ask you again: are you innocent or guilty?"

"Guilty," Illyria sobbed. "I'm guilty of everything."

Someone was crawling, but Sephana couldn't tell who or why. Sobs wracked her body. She pulled her knees up to her chest, wrapped her arms around them, and rocked.

"Let me up, please!" Sephana implored. She stood in a pool of human filth and waste up to her knees. The smell made her want to retch and the fumes made her eyes water. She looked up the length of the pit to the small square of light where the overseer looked down at her. "I need to get out of here!"

"You'll get out of this pit when it's empty and its walls are scrubbed clean," he called down. "There's no point crying about it. You're the midden girl and this is your place."

"But I have friends!" Sephana argued. "They won't let me stay down here. They'll come for me."

He laughed. "You don't have any friends, not with that great scaly thing hanging down your backside. You're a slave and always will be." Something blocked out the light and a moment later something landed in the muck beside her. Squinting, Sephana saw that is was a bucket and brush. "Now get to work, and get comfortable. You're going to be here until you die."

Crying, Sephana pulled out the brush and began to work.

A hand grabbed Eldoth's wrist. "Eldoth, you need to shut it off."

"I can't." Eldoth knelt on the ground. His eyes were clenched shut and his wrists pressed against his cheek. Another nightmare swept him away.

"No! This can't be happening!" Eldoth stared down at the book in horror. Yesterday there had been words and letters there—he'd seen them—but now it was gibberish. "It was here. I saw it!"

A sea of faces surrounded him. Some were sympathetic, others disbelieving. "You said you had all the answers."

"I did! I do!" He gestured to the book frantically. "They're right here!"

Eldoth. Come on.

"What? What did you say?" He blinked and looked at the kings and scholars surrounding him. They stared back expressionlessly.

We have to leave the room, Eldoth.

He looked frantically around the room. He was surrounded by books, but none of the symbols made any sense. "Who are you?"

You have to come with me.

"I can't," Eldoth wailed. "I can't read anymore. All I see is gibberish."

That's the nightmare, Eldoth. You have to get up.

"I-I can't. I don't know how!"

You have to.

Crawling towards the statue was one of the hardest things Illyria had ever done. She was weaker now than she had been after the first nightmare. She had to reach the statue while she still could, before the next one weakened her too much to move.

Balien lay dead on the ground before her. An arrow—her arrow—jutted from his chest. She dropped her bow and stared at her brother's body in horror.

Sephana couldn't take it anymore. It hurt too much. She just wanted it to stop. Rolling over onto her hands and knees, she pounded her forehead into the hard stone. The flare of pain wasn't enough to keep stop the visions from flooding her mind.

Sephana stood in the house of her noble father, as she had her entire life. Her mother, first among his courtesans, had her every whim indulged. She looked in the mirror. Under the scraps of diaphanous silks she wore, her body was lush and her scales iridescent. Among the Akkilinian elite who secretly lusted after all things Djido, her Reshai features were highly sought after.

Her father came into the room and looked her over at length. "You're perfect, my dear. I've negotiated an excellent price for your virgin night. You're going to make me a fortune."

Pain flared in her forehead. She pressed a hand against her brow, expecting to see blood, but found nothing.

Her father pressed a lotus cube between her lips. "Shh, my jewel. Eat this. All your pain, all your questions will go away."

Fighting the increasing pain in her head, Sephana opened her mouth and let the expensive drug fall to the floor. "I don't want to be your whore."

He hissed in anger, retrieved the cube and pressed it between her lips, this time holding her mouth shut. "Of course you're my whore. You're a whore's get. What other use could you possibly be to me? What other skills do you possess?"

"Not a whore," she mumbled, even though her mouth was closed. Already she could feel the lotus numbing her tongue. Her mind, she hoped, would soon follow.

The last five feet were the worst. Illyria had watched her brother die, her father reject her, and watched her friends be killed due to her failure. Sephana was eight feet behind her, smashing her bloody forehead repeatedly into the stone floor.

I hope she's close enough. I don't have the strength to back and help her.

She raised her hand and laid it on the foot of the white marble statue. *Emuranna, please let me be right.*

The floor gave way beneath her and they both fell into darkness.

" 'Rise, wizard of Anduilon, and tell this assembly what name you choose to be known as. The name of your birth is no more, replaced by this, a symbol of your power.' "

—The words of Renthalin

" 'Every wizard in history must have been a huge jerk.' "

—Sephana

CHAPTER ELEVEN

Sephana groaned and rolled over. She hurt everywhere, especially her head. She reached up and touched her brow. Unsurprisingly, she found blood. With a moan, she dropped her hand to her side and tried to remember where she was.

Abruptly, she sat up and winced. *The magic trap! The nightmares!* She looked around her but could see very little. There was some light shining down from above, but it was no brighter than moonlight.

She heard two rocks strike together. Turning, she saw sparks striking in time with the sounds and then a small yellow spark. Illyria's face, tinted orange, materialized out of the darkness as she leaned close to blow on it. When the small flame caught, she hooked the burning strip of cloth on her knife blade and held it over her head.

The small room, illuminated by the flickering light, was maybe fifteen feet to a side. There was a closed door against one side and a relief statue of a man opposite it. The other walls were featureless. Sephana craned her neck up (which really hurt) to see that they went up twenty five feet before ending.

"Are you all right?" Illyria asked.

"I think so." She daubed her forehead with her sleeve. "I don't think anything's broken. You?"

Illyria grimaced and rolled her shoulder. "The same."

"Where are the others?"

"I saw Balien trying to talk to Eldoth before I triggered the pit," Illyria said, "but I don't know if they were able to escape."

Sephana couldn't see Illyria's eyes but she was sure that they were pale blue. They always were when she was frightened. "I'm sure Balien found a way out," she assured her. "Hopefully he left Eldoth there to rot."

"You don't mean that," Illyria chided.

Sephana sighed and sat against the base of the statue. "I do, sort of. He's really annoying."

Illyria hobbled towards the door and held the improvised torch next to it. "You bring half of it on yourself. You provoke him."

"He does the rest all by himself." She scowled. "You've only known him for a few days. I was married to him. He deserves being trapped inside his nightmares, believe me."

"No one deserves that," Illyria replied, flicking the remains of her improvised torch to the floor. Only the ghostly light from above remained. It was one of Eldoth's 'torches' hanging over the edge of the pit.

"I was trying to kill myself," Sephana said quietly. "It was too much. I couldn't take it." She didn't know why she said it out loud. She and Illyria had never been close.

Illyria sat down next to her. "I know."

Having begun, she found herself unable to stop. "It's stupid. It kept showing me the past, but it was a different past, if things had gone differently than they did. It wasn't real, and part of me knew that, but…"

"I know," Illyria whispered. "I saw the future."

They were both silent, reeling from false memories.

"We probably need a stele to get that door open," Sephana said finally. "Wizard's don't seem to like door handles."

"There's a gap above the door," Illyria said, "but it's higher than I can reach. Feel like standing on my shoulders?"

They tried. Sephana was light enough and Illyria strong enough, but even their combined height wasn't enough to reach the narrow gap set high into the wall. Dejected, Sephana sat back down against the wall. "I think we're stuck."

Illyria may have glared at her, but Sephana couldn't tell in the darkness. Only her blonde hair, lit from above by the torch, was visible. It looked like she was wearing a crown. "There are too many lives depending on our success. We can't give in to despair."

"I'm not despairing, I'm being realistic," Sephana argued. "We can't open the door and it's too thick to break down. There's no lock we can pick or hinges to remove. Even if we could climb the walls we'd probably just get affected by that nightmare spell again. All we can do is wait and hope that Eldoth and Balien escaped and open the door for us. I want to get out of here, too." She sighed. "The worst part isn't dying here, its knowing that we didn't get that stupid Medallion of Negation. I saw how crazy those soldiers are under the Seal's control. They'll do *anything* they're told. What if someone like Davin was controlled by it, or the king? He could command his people to do anything and they'd do it. Veeshar could control the whole kingdom with it. *That* is scary."

Before Illyria could reply there a sound of something metal hitting stone. It came from Sephana's left.

"What was that?"

She and Illyria both looked up to the edge of the pit but saw nothing. Illyria called up but no one replied.

The floor was draped in shadow, but after a little searching her hands found something. It felt like cloth, but also metallic, and there was something beneath it, something harder. Illyria made another improvised torch (made from Sephana's pant leg this time) and they both looked at the object (no: *objects;* there were two of them) that had been dropped into the pit with them.

The first item was a glove. It was made from a series of tiny, interconnecting metal links, like Karalinian mail but much finer. A metal plate was set into the palm and there was a strap around the wrist. The second item was a dagger with a long narrow blade and large, mushroom shaped pommel. It was in a glossy black sheath made of some sort of enamel and was chased with metal filigree.

"How did this get here?" She picked up the glove, which was made for a much larger hand than hers. It was light, and felt both supple and strong. Not knowing why, she slipped the glove onto her right hand and tightened the strap.

"It fits me perfectly," she mused, alternately stretching and squeezing her fingers. It felt like calfskin on her hand, neither too long, too short, too loose, or too tight. It felt good in her hand. Right.

She picked up the knife sheath with her bare hand and drew the dagger. It was very balanced. Experimentally she switched it from a forward grip to a reverse and then back again. It felt solid and sure in her hand. "Where did this come from?" She looked around the pit again but didn't see anything. *No, wait.* She stood and turned until she was facing the statue carved into the wall.

She hadn't paid any attention to it. Between the pain from her fall and the memories from her nightmares, one more statue seemed unimportant. It was a relief, not a true statue, but still quite realistic. Unlike the others it wasn't a civilized person in robes but a warrior in armour. It held one arm against its chest, but where its hand would be and the dagger it would have held there was only a hole. She held the dagger against the statue, fitting it into the hole that had obviously been created to hold it, but it wouldn't stay.

"Thanks," she told the statue.

"May I see it?" Illyria asked.

Sephana handed the weapon over reluctantly. Illyria examined it and made some practice swings before handing it back. "It's very well made, but it's just a dagger. I'm not sure how it's going to help us."

Sephana tried using the dagger to pry the door open but met with no success. Its tip was sharp enough to chip the wall, but couldn't dig deep enough to act as a step or a piton. She couldn't stand on the statue to gain any height.

In the dim light from the room above (the second torch had gone the way of the first and she was reluctant to sacrifice any more of her clothing) she held the dagger in her hand, shifting through several of the knife fighting grips that Balien had taught her, when the pommel fell off.

"What by the goddess is…?" She picked up the pommel, which now resembled a large mushroom, and saw that it remained attached to the dagger by a thin string. No, it wasn't a string but a very small chain like what the glove was made of. She shifted the dagger in her hand and drew the pommel away from the dagger. She extended it the width of her shoulders when it abruptly snapped back into the weapon. Once again complete, the dagger looked just as it had before.

She held the dagger close to her face, twisting it to try and catch the limited light available. It was only two inches from her face when blades suddenly extended from the sides of the pommel and a wicked spike protruded from its bottom.

Sephana dropped it, startled. "What kind of dagger is this?"

Illyria watched as Sephana experimented with her newly found weapon, extending and retracting the spikes in the pommel as well as detaching and reattaching the pommel from the rest of the weapon. After a few minutes she looked at Illyria with a wide smile. "I think I know how to get out of here."

She detached the pommel from the dagger and pulled it as far away from the weapon as she could. When she had five feet of the connecting string drawn out she reached back and pulled out another. The amount of string that she could pull from the hilt seemed impossible, but she didn't stop until she held three large coils of it. "Step back."

The blades in the pommel extended with a slight 'snikt' sound. Holding it by its string she swung the pommel underhand and threw it upward as if it were a grappling hook—which, in a way, it was. The 'hook' flew through the air and vanished into the narrow gap over top of the door. Sephana pulled back cautiously until she was satisfied that it had could bear her weight.

"I hope this works," Illyria heard her mutter. A moment later she gave a startled cry as her arm was jerked violently upward towards the doorway. "Too fast," she said to herself and a moment later was drawn slowly up the wall by her new-found weapon.

Illyria watched as she wriggled into the dark gap. "I see a tunnel. I'll be back as soon as I can."

Sighing, Illyria settled against the wall to wait. The last thing she wanted now was to be alone with her thoughts. Her mother's accusation kept echoing in her mind: *'You are no longer my daughter'*. She knew that it had not really happened, but it made her shudder nonetheless.

I won't let that happen. I'll convince Davin that the threat at Durnshold is real. I'll see Alwyn back to his home successfully and I will fulfil my obligations to my family and my people. I will. She continued to repeat it, trying harder each time to believe it.

Eldoth limped down the hallway in silence, unwilling to attempt another conversation with Balien. The man was completely unreasonable. The sword wielding brute refused to perform any course of action other than searching for Sephana and Illyria, despite Eldoth's every logical entreaty. No matter that the second under-level of Perceptus's tower was a bewildering maze. Never mind also that Eldoth had twisted his ankle and that his whole side was sore from when he had been pushed down the stairs. No, the others were in jeopardy and so Eldoth had to proceed, despite the pain he was in.

He grudgingly had to admit that Balien had saved his life. It galled him to admit it, but Perceptus's fear sigil had proved too strong for him to endure. If Balien had not bullied and forced him out of the spell's influence, he would have remained until it destroyed his mind. The experience was a haze of pain and misery. He had no recollection of seeing either of the women escape the spelled area, though Balien assured him that it had happened.

The second level was much more utilitarian than the first. There were no blue garbed statues or ostentatious decorations, merely dull rock and an unending number of twisting, interconnecting corridors. On the positive side, nothing seemed to be trapped. Eldoth had only seen one active sigil in the entire (silent, painful, and tedious) time he had been down here.

He set his foot down wrong and gasped. His ankle flared in pain and he half fell, half lowered himself down the nearest wall. "Enough," he barked. "I must rest. This meaningless wandering will only serve to cripple me further. Your sister is in no more jeopardy now than she will be later."

Balien remained impassive and knelt opposite him. He looked perfect, damn him, neither tired, injured or even scuffed by the events that had transpired. Learning that his sister was lost somewhere inside the labyrinth of tunnels was the only thing that had broken the man's infuriating aura of calm, and even then only for a moment.

"We can rest for a few minutes," he said with his typical placidity. "How is your ankle?"

"In pain." He held the offending joint with both of his hands and closed his eyes. It took a moment to focus beyond his pain but he was eventually able to sense the inflamed tissue within his body and use what little magic he had to reduce the swelling. He hissed at the brief flare of *wrongness*—something like pain, something like what the sensation of having someone's fingers comb *through* your body—as his body protested the unnatural way it was being forced to heal before the magic took effect and the pain in his ankle slowly began to recede. He had become somewhat inured to the sensation, but not fully.

Eldoth knew only the rudiments of the college of body magic. He could close a shallow wound, or perform trivial tasks like regulating the growth of his beard, but that was all. Veeshar, in comparison, was able to *merge bodies*. His mastery of yellow magic, like all Djido, was so thorough he could take two separate creatures with complementary features—such as a cougar and a scorpion—and make them into one. When done properly, it resulted in something with the grace and cunning of a hunting cat and the lethal stinging tail of a scorpion. The results were messy when done improperly, as Eldoth had seen firsthand, but was still amazing. It was beyond Eldoth's means to duplicate now, but there would come a time when he mastered all colours of magic.

That day, unfortunately, had not yet come. Today he had to settle for incomplete healings and repeated abuse of a wounded joint. He pulled himself awkwardly to his feet and gingerly put his weight onto his ankle. It was sore, but tolerable.

"We should search that corridor to the right," Balien said. "We haven't gone there yet."

There was no point arguing with him. Eldoth just nodded.

"Hello?" someone called faintly. "Eldoth? Balien? Are you there?"

"Yes we are," Balien called out, already moving in the direction of her voice. "Keep talking, we'll come to you. Are you all right? Is Illyria with you?"

Eldoth hobbled in pursuit.

"We're fine, but she's stuck behind a door and I can't get it open."

"We're both coming. Hang on."

They found her a moment later. There was blood on her face and her pants were uneven for some reason, but she looked hale enough otherwise. It both relieved and annoyed him, though he couldn't say why.

She looked at Eldoth with narrow eyes. "Are you all right?"

"Your concern is touching," he replied dryly. "I am well enough."

From nowhere, her hand flashed out and slapped him across the cheek. He staggered as much from surprise as much as pain. "You're lucky I don't bury my foot between your legs, you Djido-loving bastard. You said that you'd been down here before. 'The traps were only activated if you touch something.' I didn't touch anything, so it must have been you. *Do you have any idea what I had to live through because of what you did?"*

Balien caught her hand before she could hit him again. "That's enough. It was a mistake. The trap affected all of us." She struggled to free her hand but Balien's grip was unyielding. "Sephana, stop." Anger still plain on her face, she stilled reluctantly. Balien turned to Eldoth. "Can you release my sister now, please?"

More than happy to move away from Sephana's wrath, Eldoth moved to the door. Luckily it was of the normal variety and only runesealed. It took only a single motion with his stele to open it and reveal the blonde-haired princess inside.

She smiled and accepted her brother's hand. "I'm glad to see that you're all well. Come, we must continue our search."

Sephana couldn't decide if she should remain angry with Eldoth or be thrilled with the discoveries she had made with the dagger she had found—or had it been given to her? The pain Eldoth was obviously in as he limped down the corridor was enough to assuage her for now, but she still wanted to punch him in his crotch.

Instead, she thought about the dagger. She didn't really know how she knew how use it; she just *did*. The glove was a part of it. The different things the pommel could do: release itself from the handle, extend its blades or retract the fine metal chain that connected the two, were controlled by the glove. It all depended on how she pressed her fingers against its sides or tips. It had all seemed so natural to her, like putting the glove on had been. In fact, it was like the more she thought about it, the harder it became.

They made it to the staircase without difficulty and from there went down. There were no disturbances in the dust less than a month old. None of the A'Cha inside the tunnels had penetrated farther than the nightmare trap, at least according to the tracks. Eldoth said that there were no more magical traps this far down but his assurances meant nothing to her.

The hall on the third level formed a single square ring around the landing with doors evenly spaced along its perimeter. Most were open and the rooms beyond empty. Eldoth ignored them and went directly to a room to the right of the stairs. Unlike the rest, this one still contained some furniture: a desk, some shelves and a trunk.

"I am assuming that the tower and its under-levels were evacuated during the Great War," Eldoth told them. "This room—a study, by my estimation—was overlooked for some reason." He touched his stele to a globe on the desk and it began to glow with a warm, yellow light. There was an empty box next to it. "The rod was in this box. Here is the inscription about the Medallion." He surveyed the room. "I went to investigate Veeshar's arrival before I could search for it, but I believe it is here somewhere."

"You don't know?" Sephana protested. "We went through all of that for *nothing?*"

"I never claimed with any certainty that it was here," he rebutted. "It was only ever a possibility."

Kicking him in the crotch was sounding better by the minute. "That's just great."

"Would the Medallion be magically trapped, Eldoth?" Illyria asked with her typical diplomacy.

"I don't believe so. The seal was simply in a box on the shelf."

"Then there is nothing preventing us from searching for it?"

"Nothing at all."

They rummaged through the detritus in the bowels of Perceptus' tower for an hour. It surprised Illyria that so many of the items the found—cutlery, cups, boot horns—were exactly the same as contemporary versions that she had grown up with. All the tales said that the High Wizards lived in a level of luxury that those without could not even imagine. It was comforting that, even for a wizard, a fork was still a fork.

There were also items that no one could make any sense out of: small crystalline cubes two inches on a side, multi-faceted black stones the size of a fist, or some sort of thin, hollow metal cylinder with a ring in one end. If Eldoth had his way he would have stopped to investigate each strange object found, but finding the Medallion of Negation—if it was, in fact, here—remained their priority.

Balien found it at last, inside a nondescript box at the back of a shelf tucked behind a corner. It was not the first piece of jewellery they had discovered, but Eldoth had not even needed to examine it before he declared that the green, pentagonal object the size of Illyria's palm was what they were looking for.

"I have no doubt: this is the Medallion of Negation." He laced it through a leather string and hung it around his neck.

Illyria felt giddy with relief. Finally, after all of the trials of the last two days, something had gone right. The seemingly impossible task of liberating Durnshold Keep now seemed close enough to grasp. This was why she had followed her ancestor's example and ventured beyond the protective borders of the Ilthwood. It wasn't about exploring, and it wasn't about youthful rebellion. She wanted her life to mean something beyond the dubious distinction of being a Child of the Mark. Knowing that one of her children might one day sit on the throne of Ilthanara wasn't enough. She wanted her life to make a difference. Helping to thwart a foreign invasion of Djido, Vaulen and A'Cha? That was something that she could take pride in, no matter how uneventful the rest of her life ended up becoming.

The journey back through the tunnels was uneventful. Eldoth was able to deactivate the nightmare sigil from the stairs and they were easily able to navigate around the extra pit and through the long hallway to the stairway that led to open ground and sunlight.

Lost in daydreams and exultant in her success, she did not notice until too late that the mound that marked the location of the Tower of Perceptus was surrounded.

"Give magic now," a flat, quacking voice commanded and Eldoth's blood ran cold. It wasn't Draxul, the Tsrinn who had terrorized him for days on end, but one of his tattooed clutch-mates. They all looked and acted like each other and he hated all three equally.

"You go down cave, not come dead. Have magic. Give."

Eldoth looked around him. Besides the damned Tsrinn, (was it Thraxul? Yes, it had to be) there were a dozen beastmen with spears and two more mounted on thunder lizards. It should have been possible for him to use the Medallion to free the lizards, but Eldoth had yet to determine how the device operated.

The Noss, Theramus, was being held at bay by one of the lizard riders. He looked bloody and bruised and Eldoth also noted the presence of three furry bodies behind him.

"Give magic now, or blue one die."

No one moved, each waiting for another to make the first move. Illyria didn't have her bow. Eldoth was the only one who, logically, could strike first. They were outnumbered by a factor of four to one. If Theramus could be freed, that ratio would be reduced to three. Eldoth's first act, therefore, had to involve his liberation.

Yesterday, making a single wall of fire had been the limit of Eldoth's power. Today, after a night's rest and proper nourishment, he was not so limited. He quietly summoned the power of the college of Energy within him. Depending on a wizard's level of mastery, words were sometimes used as memory aids to enable the proper formation of thought needed to cast spells. Eldoth, using the red magic that he had named himself after, did not require them.

He did not attack the thunder lizard. Any spell lethal enough to slay the massive beast would prove equally lethal to the Noss. All that was required was the elimination of the rider.

The ball of fire that burst forth was the brightest, loudest, noisiest one that he could create. Using his hands as guides for his magic was easier and more accurate, but not necessary. He made no motion, simply looked at the A'Cha he meant to attack, and the fireball leapt from his body towards it.

His target screeched in terror and held its hands before his face, dropping its reins. His lizard mount, freed from the magic that controlled it, acted as animals did when confronted with fire: it turned and ran.

The appearance of Eldoth's fireball triggered everyone on the field into action. Theramus surged to his feet and grappled with the nearest beastman while Balien and Illyria drew their weapons and advanced. The A'Cha rushed to meet them. Thraxul sprinted towards Eldoth with superhuman speed, brandishing its hook weapons.

Eldoth cringed. This is really going to hurt.

There was no point wishing she had her bow. She didn't and that was that, but she did have her sword and her brother by her side. She could take on an entire army.

The A'Cha had spears, which was odd, and they held them clumsily. "My right," Balien called, stepping that way and engaging the two A'Cha at the end of their ragged line. Illyria stayed on his left and protected him against any who might try to encircle him. He knocked the first's weapon aside and slammed into it with his shoulder. As it fell sprawling he attacked the second, cutting through its weapon into its leg. The A'Cha near him tried to attack but received a severed hand and a slash across its torso from Illyria.

After that first exchange it became butchery. Using spears the A'Cha were poor warriors and had no defence. They did not have the heart for open battle and, even bolstered by greater numbers, fell before the might and skill of Britheon's children.

If they had only faced A'Cha, their victory would have been assured.

Theramus had no time to be embarrassed. He had been outmatched. If he had wanted to fight to the end he could have, but it was not time for such a sacrifice. His friends would need him in the days ahead as he needed them now.

There was no shame in running from a dragon-lizard. It dwarfed him physically and possessed an arsenal of deadly teeth and claws. He wrestled a spear free from an A'Cha and stabbed at the creature, but the spear proved unequal to the task. What should have been a fatal strike through the beast's heart splintered harmlessly against its scaled hide. He jammed the broken shaft into its wide-open mouth and scrambled free of its clutches.

The dragon-lizard bit through the spear shaft like it was a blade of grass and roared angrily. Theramus ran.

Sephana watched helplessly as the Tsrinn sprinted towards Eldoth. She'd never seen anything move so quickly. The wizard hurled a panicked ball of fire towards it, but it tumbled gracefully beneath it. It regained its feet without slowing, slammed one blunt hook into Eldoth's face and swept his feet out with the other. Reversing the weapon in its hand so that it became like an axe, it raised its arm for what Sephana knew would be a fatal blow.

"Hey!" She moved without thinking. One touch against the proper ridge inside her glove and the dagger in her hand became a flail with a ten foot chain. She swung it once around her head to gain speed and, whirling her whole body to make the blow even harder, smashed the metal weight between the Tsrinn's shoulder blades. Only after her blow struck did she realize that she had forgotten to extend the blades in the pommel. She had caused it to stagger and not kill Eldoth, but that was all.

Did I really just save Eldoth's life? Why did I do that?

It rolled forward and came to its feet facing her. Inhuman yellow eyes appraised her coldly. It made a motion and both of its weapons interjoined, becoming a single flail-like axe more than six feet long. Swinging its new weapon over its head like a giant scythe, it darted towards her.

A circle of bodies surrounded them.

"I have to help Sephana," Balien said as he fended off three A'Cha. "Are you all right?"

Illyria, her back to him, deflected a spear, lunged and caught an A'Cha in its throat. "I'm fine. Go."

"My left on two."

She deflected two spears and stabbed an A'Cha in the leg. "One," she called out.

"Two!" he answered.

She turned to her right, slashing with Maiden's Fang so that her brother would have a gap to run through. He ran through the A'Cha she had wounded and sprinted away, confident in his sister's ability to protect him. She whirled around again to see that five A'Cha still faced her. They liked those odds and gave sharp-toothed grins as they advanced.

"Illyria!" Theramus's booming voice called. Moving at a dead run, he caught the group of five A'Cha in a huge flying tackle and all six bodies became caught up in a blue and orange tangle.

A dragon-lizard charged right behind him.

Sephana had the choice of being frightened to death or attacking. Before she could think of any reasons not to, she attacked. With both swords committed to its swing, she had a brief opening. She ducked under the linked swords and lunged forward with her dagger extended. *Chest. Go for the chest.*

Eldoth held his throbbing jaw and tried to push himself upright. Surveying the battle scene he blinked. *Sephana is attacking Thraxul?* She ducked under its attack and stabbed at it with her dagger but it lashed out with its tail and she fell to the side. Balien appeared from nowhere, slammed into it and interposed himself between them.

Theramus and Illyria were engaged in a melee with a group of beastmen. In the distance Eldoth saw the last dragon-lizard, its rider dispatched, surveying the battle with angry malevolence. There was no one near it now and no reason for him to hold back. He pushed himself to his feet and summoned fire.

Illyria dove to one side of the charging dragon-lizard. She could feel its hot breath on the back of her neck and its huge teeth clashed inches from her. She slashed Maiden's Fang along its jaw and forelimb as she came to her feet. While both blows drew blood, the massive creature showed no signs of even feeling them.

It snapped at her again and this time Illyria dove under its body and between its legs. It felt like living stone when she brushed against it. It scrambled backwards and turned but she kept herself away from its teeth and claws. The A'Cha's eyes widened as it caught sight of her but could do nothing as she scrambled up behind it and drove her sword into its back.

Pushing it to the ground, Illyria grabbed the reins from its dying hands. The dragon-lizard, momentarily free from the spell that controlled it, roared in indignation and tried to throw her. As she struggled to keep her place on its back, she thought about the giant bear four days before and could not decide which was a less pleasant mount. Finally settling into the saddle, she grabbed the reins and pulled them until the creature stilled. When she swung them around its jaw it had no choice but to obey and crouch on the ground.

It could do nothing except glare when she climbed off of its back and drove her sword into its jugular.

Theramus broke the neck of the fifth and final A'Cha. Only one pair of combatants remained standing: Balien and the Tsrinn. The lizardman was remarkably agile. It leapt about and attacked with its feet and tail as well as the hooks and guards of its weapons. Balien was more economical with his movements but nevertheless met it stroke for stroke and step for step.

The Tsrinn's odd swords were meant for capturing the weapons of unwary opponents, which Balien definitely was not. His blade was constantly in motion and darted in and out too quickly for the hooks to gain purchase, but doing so denied him the chance to strike a fatal blow. The two fighters were stalemated.

This was not an honour duel, and Theramus had no compunction against aiding his ward. Picking up a fallen spear, he advanced towards the combatants.

Balien did not require his assistance. He swung his sword from sky to ground in a powerful blow that the Tsrinn easily parried and redirected. It twisted its body and swung with its tail but Balien, keeping one hand on his sword, dropped to one knee and caught the swinging limb in the crook of his arm. Before it could wriggle free he surged to his feet, upending the creature and sending it sprawling. He kicked it twice, hard, before it rolled away and regained its feet.

"Hey, Big Blue," said Sephana as she got to her feet. She held her side tenderly and carried a large dagger in her free hand that Theramus had not seen before. As he watched she flicked her wrist and its spiked pommel fell to the ground, connected by a fine chain. "Guess we'll find out how all that fancy spinning does against three of us, huh?"

She looked nervous but not frightened and showed no signs of retreating. Theramus's heart swelled with pride.

The change in numbers was not lost on the Tsrinn. It cast assessing eyes over the three of them, snarled, turned, and ran. It was even faster on its feet than Sephana, and Theramus knew that there was no way they could chase it down before it reached the tree line.

An arrow drove into its skull before it could run even fifty yards and it fell to the ground, dead.

Illyria stepped up to them, bow in hand. "We've wasted too much time," she said coolly. "Bind your wounds and gather your things. We must return to Northhaven at once."

"People always spoke of our bravery in battle and how fearless we were against daunting odds, but few ever mentioned how hard it was to endure the constant fatigue, hunger and pain of fast-marching. Our skill at arms was important, of course, but I think our perseverance against the more mundane travails of campaigning ultimately aided us more."

—The Private Journals of Illyria Exiprion

Chapter Twelve

"You promised me control of the fortress, Djido," Ta growled. "I withheld my army by a week because you assured me that you would not fail. Now, I hear that half of the town has escaped and likely bear word of our presence. I should bury my axe in your skull!"

The Djido's lizardman nursemaid hissed and raised its weapons, but Ta was unmoved. His band-mates stood behind him. If he fell he would be avenged and Veeshar knew it.

The snakeman dropped its gaze and motioned for its minion to lower its weapons. "I have failed you, Olamm, yes, and for that I beg forgiveness. I was betrayed, but the situation is not as dire as you say. We still hold the keep and the bridge, and the southmen will not be able to rally their forces in time. You will still be able to cross the river, great Olamm, and on the open field your thunder lizard cavalry will devour their horses."

Ta looked down at the Djido in disgust. Perhaps it was right. The townspeople had only escaped a day ago. This change of fortune forced Ta's hand. If he had attacked earlier, before Veeshar's plan to use magic to take the keep, it would have been on Ta's initiative. It would have been riskier, but surprise would have been on his side. Now that he held it, however tenuously, and word of its occupation had gotten out he had no choice but to act.

'There is more, Great Olamm," Veeshar slimed.

"What?"

"My man who betrayed me, he had allies. The one who slew your mate, the dark haired human, was among them."

"Was he?" Ta raised his axe to his lips, kissed it and murmured a chant of avenging. "Perhaps there is a gem hidden in all of this offal. Send word to the Lemm," he ordered. "We march at once."

His band-mates slapped their axes to their chests. "Death and honour," they intoned.

"Death and honour," he replied solemnly. They were the only two certainties in the cosmos and the boar who slew Navoi represented both.

I will hold his heart in my hand.

"I should have you arrested as spies for the Golden Bears," Davin said crossly. "My orders were quite clear: no one is to leave the city." His hair was sleep-tousled and he wore his cloak of office over his night shirt. A pair of servants scrambled to prepare sweet meats and oat tea.

Illyria did her best not to let her irritation show. She and the others had marched hard and dared another difficult river crossing to get back to Northhaven by nightfall. She was tired, hungry and dirty, but, while the others had sought out baths, provisions and food, Illyria had instead met with Lord Davin.

She tilted her head and smiled with as much warmth as she could muster. "We're not spies, my lord," her words laced with sugary sweetness. "You aren't really going to arrest us, are you?"

His eyes widened. "I…uhh…no." He flushed and squirmed in his seat. "But, you, ah, you still left. You shouldn't have. I'm the lord."

"I had to, my lord." She let her smile fall away but kept her tone gentle. "What I said before is true. Durnshold Keep has been taken, and I have risked my life to discover more information. Don't you want to hear what I learned?"

Elorin swept into the dining room, wearing a clean dress and her hair tied back hastily. "Yes, he would be most interested." Alwyn entered behind her.

Davin's face lost its vacant expression. He glared at his sister. "Yes," he said reluctantly. "Tell us all what has happened to you."

Illyria told her tale without omission or exaggeration. There was a moment of silence.

"I…that's…I mean, it's hard to believe," Davin said, sipping his tea.

"I give you my word as a Child of the Mark to the crown of Nemora that I speak the truth," Illyria said solemnly. "My lord, I understand your hesitation, but now is the time for action. Their hold on the keep is fragile. You must give the word to attack now before they reinforce it."

"She's right, Davin," Elorin said into the silence. "You have to."

"I…" The boy licked his lips nervously. "I mean, it's…" He set his jaw. "No. This is just another lie being told to me by the Golden Bears." He snorted. "Dragons? Djido? Wizards? Do you really expect me to believe that?"

"My lord, no one is trying to trick you," Alwyn said. "I have seen these dragon-lizards. They *are* real. As for the rest," he glanced at Illyria, his face unreadable. "I have learned to trust Illyria. She has yet to lead me astray."

Illyria had never liked Alwyn as much as she did right now.

"Brother, believe them," urged Elorin. "It is not a trick."

"You must agree that a foreign invasion is a greater danger than civil war," Illyria urged.

"I-I can't leave the city defenceless," he protested. "What if there are more of them? What if they attack here?"

"They will not," Illyria insisted. "Every dogman within one hundred leagues is readying to attack Durnshold and cross the Lyssal River."

He looked panicked. "I can't take that chance. The dogmen don't organize like that. There could still be more."

Alwyn took a deep breath. "My lord, my force is not great, but I will swear my fifty men to the defence of this city if it will aid in your decision."

Illyria looked at Alwyn in surprise and respect. His expression said that he was as surprised as she.

Elorin gave Alwyn a look of adoration. "It's the right thing to do, Davin. Let Sir Gennald out. He'll lead the men to victory."

It was the wrong thing to say. At the mention of the knight's name Davin's expression closed like an iron gate. "I knew it! This was all a plot to get him released. You're conspiring with him, aren't you?" He looked at Illyria and Alwyn. "All of you are. You're trying to depose me!"

Elorin's eyes widened in horror. "Davin, no, please. I'm sorry I mentioned him. This has nothing to do with Gennald. Please, don't change your mind."

His jaw tightened and he glared at all three of him.

"My lord, do not let your animus against Sir Gennald prejudice your actions." Illyria channelled all of her calm into her words. "I will swear by anything you wish me to that there is no conspiracy. I will perform any act of penance you desire in order to gain your trust but, please, heed my words and council. For the sake of your countrymen you *must* do this. Please, my lord, I beg you.

He looked at her sharply. "You said that half of the town escaped during your flight."

She blinked. "I'm sorry?"

"I have just caught you in your lie." He smiled triumphantly. "You just said that 'there was no one else' that could stop this horrible thing, but earlier you claimed that many townsmen from Durnston escaped. Surely if that many people were freed they could bring word to another city and they could send men."

"I do not lie, my lord." She reined in her anger with difficulty. " 'Half the town' may be an exaggeration, but while people some did escape, I do not know if they escaped the forces occupying the keep. Even if word did get out, there is no city closer than Northhaven. You remain the best hope for retaking the keep."

He glared at her. "I will not fall prey to trickery. I am acting lord of this city and as you have pointed out, you do not belong to me." His adolescent face stormy, he turned to Alwyn. "Are your wagons ready to leave in the morning?"

He was surprised by the question. "Yes, but—"

"Then you may leave with my thanks and blessings and you can take your guide and her friends with you."

"My lord, you are acting hastily…"

"I am not your lord!" the boy's voice echoed in the small room. "If I was we would not be having this discussion because you would *be doing what you are told!"*

Alwyn's face became blank. "I see. Well, goodnight then."

Davin made no reply before sweeping angrily from the room. Elorin, calling his name, followed.

"He called you a liar to your face," Alwyn growled. "He should be beaten. He's been bad enough to deal with the last two days, but this insult is too much."

Illyria gave him a weak smile. "Thank you, but there are greater concerns now than my honour." She rested her forehead against her palm. "How can one person's foolishness condemn a whole kingdom?"

He sat down across from her. "Is it that bad?"

She nodded. "It is. Don't ask me how. I just know."

He looked confused, but nodded. "I meant what I said before: I trust you, no matter how crazy your story sounds." He brightened. "However, Davin has made it abundantly clear that it is no longer our concern. We can be free of this kingdom and its foolish lords by the end of the week." He cleared his throat. "You believe in this, I see it in your eyes, but, Illyria, I cannot help but feel relieved. This path you want to follow is dangerous. This way, you will be safe."

Illyria stood. "None of us are safe anymore, Alwyn." She left him before she could say anything she would regret.

Sephana eyed the platters of food hungrily. Their feast had been hastily assembled and consisted mainly of leftovers, but neither she nor her stomach gave a damn. If she'd had her way she'd already be on her third bowl of stew, but Balien had insisted that they wait for Illyria.

She had changed into clean clothing—of the concealing variety, unfortunately— and gazed longingly at the feather-stuffed bed before returning to the private dining room where the others waited. Eldoth sat at the far side of the table, studying the Medallion, making scribbled notes, and muttering to himself.

Idly, she flicked the pommel of her new dagger outward and retracted it back into the handle before it could strike the table. The trick, she had discovered, was in how fast she released the chain and reeled it back in. Both rates were variable. She didn't know how she knew that—or anything else she had discovered about the weapon— she just *did*.

"That is most impressive," Theramus said. "You are mastering the use of that weapon very quickly. You've had it less than a day."

She shrugged self consciously. "It just came to me."

"Can I see it?" Balien asked. She gave him the knife with just a bit of reluctance, but not the glove.

"I believe blade is made of Ansharite," Theramus said, watching Balien test the blade's balance and sharpness.

Beneath her head scarf, her brow furrowed. "Made of what?"

"Ansharite is a magical metal, something like heartstone. If I am not mistaken, it is razor sharp and harder than any metal. It will keep its edge forever."

Balien took out his own dagger and used Sephana's to cut off a thin part of the blade "This is made from the finest Ilthanaran steel and your dagger peels it like a fruit rind." He handed it back to Sephana.

"You're not going to take it from me are you?" she asked worriedly.

The two exchanged curious looks. "Why would we do that?"

She suddenly felt foolish. "It's just that this is really rare and valuable. This is the kind of thing you give kings."

"It's not ours to give away," Balien explained. "You found it. Besides, I think you'd use it the best of any of us."

She flushed at the unexpected compliment.

"Yes," Theramus said. "All of us are equal inheritors to the legacy of Anduilon."

"You should name it," Balien suggested. "All great weapons should be named."

"Really?"

"Yes," he answered. "Illyria's bow is an heirloom from before the Great War and it has a name. Your dagger is at least that old."

"I never knew that," Sephana mused. "What about your sword? Does it have a name?"

He smiled. "I call it 'Britheon's Gift'. My father gave it to me, but it's just a sword, made by men. It's not like your dagger."

Sephana thought a moment and swept the blade in front of her, watching it move. It was silver with just a hint of green, like a berry just coming to into ripeness.

"Dawn's First Crescent," she announced. "When I swing it like this it reminds me of the first sliver of sunlight in the morning."

"I like it," Balien told her. "I thought you might call it 'entrail sticker.'"

She grimaced. "That's how men name things. There are too many things in the world with ugly names. The world needs to have more pretty things." She shrugged, suddenly self-conscious. "So I gave it a pretty name."

"It is perfect," Theramus said.

Heavy footsteps came from down the hall. Sephana glanced up in time to see Illyria stomping past the dining room. Balien gave everyone a worried look before hurrying out the door. Sephana and Theramus rushed after him.

"Lyri?" Balien called through her closed door. "Is everything all right?"

His only answer was the sound of objects being slammed around. He reached for the door handle but it opened before he could touch it. Illyria stood in the doorway without her tunic or boots and holding a bag of toiletries. Her eyes blazed violet with anger. "I'm having a bath," she snarled before sweeping past everyone.

"I should talk to her." Balien said.

Sephana, surprising herself, put her hand on his shoulder. "She's going to the *women's* bath. Let me."

He hesitated, then nodded. "We'll be waiting."

Sephana acknowledged him and followed Illyria. Her stomach growled fiercely, but she ignored it. She knocked on the door to the women's bath as she entered. Illyria, partially undressed, looked over with undisguised irritation.

"It's just me." Sephana smiled disarmingly. "Would you like some help with your hair?" The two women weren't close, but their gender occasionally united them against the stupidities of men and a mutual protection of modesty. They often bathed together and helped each other with grooming, but their conversations seldom passed beyond idle chatter. The cultural gulfs between a former slave and a princess were too great for anything more.

Illyria stared, her jaw clenched, before nodding. "Thank you."

The women's bath in the manor was one of the nicest Sephana had been in, though that wasn't saying too much. A warm fire burned merrily on one side, there were fresh flowers in vases along the wall, and soft furs protected bare feet from the cold stone floor. The bath itself—small by Akkilinian standards—could fit ten comfortably.

Sephana looked at the clear well-fed water and shivered. She knew that servants had added hot stones, but that didn't make it warm. Akkilon was a jungle, and in Nemora the cool pools had been a relief from the heat, but Karalon was neither of those. It didn't seem to bother Illyria, who stepped into the tub without hesitation.

Sephana debated whether to risk undressing. It was seldom safe for her to risk bathing anywhere her scales, tail and earpits might be seen. Shunned as she had been in Akkilon, she had almost never had the chance before getting married to Eldoth.

Illyria glanced at her and sympathy softened her angry features. "It's all right, you don't have to. I'll be fine." Free of clothing, her otherwise flawless (and scaleless) skin was marred by a number of painful bruises and scrapes. Sephana winced.

She jammed her new dagger under the door and began to undress. The water was cool but still felt good. She took care cleaning Illyria's various wounds and washed her golden hair with delicate thoroughness. She purposely limited the conversation to trivialities until finally Illyria's tension started to melt. "Do you want to talk about it?"

"I've seen everything that's going to happen and I can't do anything about it." Illyria told her bitterly.

They sat on benches near the fire. Illyria had her back turned while Sephana slowly combed her hair. "What do you mean?"

Illyria told Sephana about the nightmares that Perceptus's tower had conjured for her. Sephana shuddered. "I thought that I could change them. I thought that those were what would happen if I didn't do anything; if I chose not to get involved. But I am involved," she insisted. "I want to be. I can change this, I know I can." She turned, her eyes wide. "I mean you. I mean us. All of us. I didn't—"

Sephana smiled. "It's all right."

"I'm sorry if it seems like I take you for granted," Illyria said quietly. "I have no right to speak for you. You're not my servant. You don't *belong* to me."

"I can't think of anywhere else I'd rather be," Sephana told her, surprised by how true the statement was. "You and the others are my only friends. I'd...do anything for you guys."

Illyria turned. "I do think of you as my friend. I'm sorry if I don't say it much."

Sephana shrugged, uncomfortable, but still felt warmed by the statement. "Those nightmares show you the absolute worst that things can be, not what's real," she said. "Just because you saw something horrible doesn't mean it's going to happen. They aren't prophesy."

"I know," Illyria sighed. "In my head, I know you're right. Even if we do leave tomorrow, it doesn't mean that Karalon will fall. Maybe Davin is right and someone in another city was warned by the people you freed. Maybe they can take the keep back without our help. In my heart though..." She took a deep breath. "In my heart all I see is war and death. If it's in my power to stop that and I don't, then I have as good as killed them myself."

There was a knock at the door. "I brought fresh clothing for you," Balien called. "It's outside the door." He paused. "We're in the next room if you want to talk."

"Thank you. We'll be out soon," Illyria turned. Her eyes were as blue as the sky. "I don't know what to do," she whispered.

Sephana tried to think of something to say. She had never thought that she would be reassuring *Illyria*, the bravest, most confident woman she'd ever met. "You don't have to figure it out yourself," she managed to say. "I mean, there's your brother and Theramus and Eldoth, too, I guess. Just…explain everything that happened and we can all come up with an answer together."

Did I really say that? That sounded good!

Illyria nodded, stood and gave Sephana's shoulder a comforting squeeze. "You're right. Thank you."

When the two women finally emerged from the bathing room Theramus was waiting patiently. Balien tried to appear unconcerned, but had spent much of the last half hour glancing anxiously at the hallway. Illyria was clean and relaxed. With her hair combed back, face scrubbed clean and wearing a simple white shirt, she looked close to Elorin's age.

"What happened?" Balien asked her bluntly.

Her ill-fated conversation with lord Davin had unfolded how Theramus had expected.

"I am neither one of you or sworn to the lord of Northhaven, whoever he may be," Eldoth said. "Am I also to be expelled from here?"

"This isn't about you, Eldoth," Sephana scolded.

"I disagree. I am the only one that can use the Medallion of Negation. Any attempt to retake the keep is going to involve me. Also, my acts while Veeshar's prisoner in the keep could be considered criminal."

"What do you want to do, Eldoth?" Illyria asked quietly. "You're right; you are not one of us and we shouldn't assume that our intentions are the same. You are welcome to join us, no matter what we do, and I will do what I can to help you avoid arrest."

"Thank you for the offer." He looked at Theramus shrewdly. "At the moment it benefits me to stay in your company, so I accept."

"The important question is then: what we intend to do about Durnshold if aid from Northhaven is not forthcoming?" Balien said.

"What *can* we do about Durnshold?" Sephana asked around a mouthful of food. She swallowed before continuing. "There's only four—sorry, five—of us. I'm not being an ass," she added hastily. "I'm not questioning whether or not it's the right thing to do. I'm with everyone else here saying that letting this Olamm guy and his army across the bridge is a bad thing, but, really, what can we do?"

"We cannot retake the keep with five people," Theramus reluctantly agreed.

"If we did get inside, we would have access to the keep's defences," Eldoth said.

Everyone stared at him. "Do you know where they are?" Illyria asked.

He made a face. "Of course I do."

"But, before you said you couldn't find them," Sephana protested.

The wizard smiled smugly. "I said that to Draxul. Obviously, I was lying."

Illyria stroked her lip thoughtfully. "This changes everything." She looked at the others. Her features brightened and her eyes slowly turned brown. "Is there a way we can sneak into the keep?"

"Maybe, but we won't be able to hold it, not with five people," Balien answered. "The walls are going to be defended. Getting over them will be difficult."

An old memory surfaced. "There may be another way," Theramus said. "I did not say it on our previous mission because we did not have a runecaster, but it is likely there is another path into the keep."

They all turned to him. "Many Anduili fortifications of this era had secondary entrances," he explained. "But they were secret and only accessible by wizards."

Illyria's eyes glowed. "Do you know where we'd find this secret entrance?"

Eldoth snapped his finger. "The waterfall. There is a hidden door in the lower level. It referenced a waterfall, but it made no sense to me. I dismissed it as a bad translation, but in light of this new information it is likely that it refers to this entrance."

"Why didn't you escape through it?" Sephana asked.

"I did not have my stele, but even if I had, Draxul was watching me too closely," he answered. "As I said, I thought it was a bad translation. For all I knew it led to a broom closet."

"Is there a waterfall near the keep?" Theramus asked.

"Three Maiden Falls is about two miles downstream, according to the map I studied," Illyria told them.

"Two miles?" asked Sephana with wide eyes. "Is that even possible?"

"Were you not with us beneath Perceptus's tower?" Eldoth asked Sephana with the tone of derision that he used only with her. "These tunnels were constructed by the High Wizards. Such distances would be trivial."

"Sorry, I was too busy living magical nightmares that *you* didn't warn me about," she snapped. She turned to Theramus. "Do you think that weird path we found by the river is part of this?"

"I would think it likely."

"Lyri," Balien said gently. "I'm sorry to ask about this, but what about your wedding? The date is getting fairly close."

Her face hardened. "There are far more important things at stake than my loveless marriage of political obligation. If immanent war and death make me late for my wedding, then that is simply how it will be."

He nodded.

"There is still the matter of holding the keep," Theramus reminded her. "We are still only five, and none of the men within this city can aid us."

"Not everyone," Illyria said.

Alwyn stared at her incredulously. "Illyria, do you know what you are asking?"

"Yes, I do. You're their only hope, Alwyn."

When she had come to him during the caravan's final preparations, looking grim, tired, but still oh-so-beautiful, and asking to speak to him privately, he had been expecting an entirely different subject of discussion. Knowing her as he did, a plea for aid should not have surprised him.

"It's not that I don't feel for their plight, Illyria, it isn't. Derwyn has had more than its share of raiders and these Karalmen are good people, despite their idiot lord and their stupid politics. It's just that, well, there is a great deal resting on my returning this caravan back to Nemora." He lowered his voice. "My inheritance is at stake. My father will name the son he feels is most worthy to be his successor and so far, well, I have not impressed him. My brother, Emrys, is quicker and more decisive whereas I have always been more reasoned in my actions." He snorted. "Never mind that his knee-jerk decisions get him into trouble as often as they don't and that I have succeeded in every task I have set my mind to. He sees Emrys as 'more kingly'. I had to beg for this mission, did you know that? I know that it is irrelevant to your dilemma, but do you see why I cannot do this for you?"

"Your situation is a difficult one, yes. I sympathize." She smiled wryly. "I am not unfamiliar with the familial obligations of royalty, but this has nothing to do with that. This is more than a trade mission, Alwyn. This is a reconnection between two lands that have been strangers for centuries. You may not see it, but you are taking the first step towards rebuilding the High Kingdom." Her eyes were brilliant in their intensity. "Nemora and Karalon are stronger together than each of them apart. Together you can share resources, knowledge, and manpower. Perhaps not this year or even the next, but if the two kingdoms were to marshal their strength there is no telling what they could do. Drive the A'Cha from the mountains, or fight off the coastal raiders."

"But that's all the more reason to take the caravan back across the mountains!" he protested.

Illyria shook her head. "No. The caravan is a means to an end. We are *building peace*. You asked before why I'm helping you. This is why. It's not for you or your father; it's for everyone. It's for Anduilon. How can you have peace with Karalon if their capital has been sacked, and even if they do survive this why would they trade with the people who abandoned them? Alwyn, what would forge a stronger peace: trading goods, or coming to their aid in their hour of greatest need?"

Her passion assailed him like a battering ram and he felt himself yielding. "Illyria, I only have fifty men."

"It will be enough," she assured him. "We have a plan for getting inside the keep. Once within we can hold it against thousands."

"Thousands," he wheezed. "Illyria, why do you ask this of me?"

"'To see evil done and do nothing is to be party to it,'" she replied without hesitation. "That's not who you are, Alwyn. You're a good man."

His heart beat faster just to hear her say it. *If only she could look at me with such passion when she was* not *asking to me to risk everything I am.* "Illyria, when this is over, is there any chance…"

Her smile was gentle and sad. "No, Alwyn, not even if things were different. I don't think of you that way, I'm sorry."

She'd never loved him. The knowledge pierced him like a flaming brand. He barely registered that she was still talking.

"If you do seek a marriage to solidify your claim, there are other, closer women, who might be open to your proposal."

He looked at her curiously. "Really? Who?" She just raised her eyebrows. He blinked. "Really?"

She chuckled. "If we succeed at this, I guarantee it, and there would be no better way to cement peace between your two kingdoms." Her expression turned serious. "Will you do this Alwyn, not because of what you feel for me, or because you think it will impress me, but because it is right?"

He wanted to say yes to prove to her the kind of man he was. He wanted to say no to spite her for the pain she had caused him. He wanted to laugh in her face. He wanted to run crying from the room because this hard decision fallen to him, a glorified merchant from a petty kingdom (he was aware of what the elves called his people) but then he thought about Illyria's words and what she had already faced in the name of peace. He thought about Elorin—did she really feel that way about him?—and what would befall her if he did nothing.

When viewed that way the decision was easy. "I will do it," he said finally. "This is not for glory or a marriage alliance with Northhaven." Relief and anxiety warred within him. *I can't believe I'm doing this.* "When do we leave?"

Her smile was radiant. "As soon as you can gather your men. We travel light. No more than they can carry."

"Two hours?"

She nodded. "Two hours at the front gate." She gripped his wrist. "This is the right thing, Alwyn."

Goddess, I hope so.

" 'I don't trust those Noss. All blue, as big as houses and answerable only to the High King? What can any of us do if they take the law into their own hands? How would we stop them?' "

—anonymous

CHAPTER THIRTEEN

"I haven't had a full night's sleep since before that fight in the mountains with the giant bear," Sephana grumbled, even though no one was really near enough to hear her. "Since then it's been all late watches, secret missions and forced marches. I think I've had two hot meals." *And one of them wasn't very hot, either.*

"Do you always complain so incessantly?" Eldoth asked from behind her, breathless. "Does it benefit you in any way, other than annoying me?"

She smiled sweetly. "No, but I consider annoying you a benefit."

His eyes narrowed. "I may not yet possess the magic required to seal your lips shut on your face, but I will, and on that day the whole world shall thank me. Until that time comes, I will endure your mindless prattle as I do every other tribulation forced upon me."

Sephana frowned. Somehow she'd come out on the losing side of that exchange. She forced a smile onto her face. "Suffer away, but remember that when you're laying on the ground moaning about all the pain you're in that I feel *just fine.*"

He didn't reply.

It was early afternoon. The five of them, along with Alwyn and his men, had been marching since just before midnight. Durnshold keep sparkled like a jewel off in the distance. It was all so unreal. The very last thing she thought she'd ever do when she stole her freedom four years ago was help break a siege in Karalon against an army of Nintarans aided by a Djido wizard and his stolen mind controlling rod.

Balien waved to her from the head of the column. She gave Eldoth a parting smirk, left the line of marching soldiers, and jogged up to him. As she arrived, Owain, one of Alwyn's eorlmen, made the signal for the marching men to stop and rest. There was a collective groan of relief as everyone flopped down onto the hard-packed trail and dug out their provisions.

Well, everyone except her. Balien waved her over to the sheer edge if the river valley. "Are you sure about this?" he asked quietly. "We can find another way down."

"Not faster than this." She looked over the edge of the cliff and saw only roiling rapids. If the invisible path she had found before was there, she couldn't see it. *Of course, if I could see it, then it wouldn't be invisible...* "I hope Theramus was right. If this doesn't take us to the waterfall it's a huge waste of time."

He just shrugged. "Are you ready?"

"Hang on." Looking around the cliff edge it took her a moment to find what she was looking for: a crack in the stone about the half of the length of her finger. She looked up and grinned. "Watch this." Separating the mushroom pommel from Dawn's First Crescent, she jammed it into the hole in the rock. The blades extended with a 'snikt'. As she hoped, it didn't budge when she pulled on it.

"I'll be right back," she said with a cockiness she didn't feel and swung herself over the edge.

She tried to clear her mind. Before, in the pit/cell with Illyria and later in the fight against Thraxul, she'd been able to use Dawn's First Crescent by not thinking and letting her strange new instinct take over. In spite of her every effort that wasn't working now, not with the only thing between herself and a watery death being a chain no thicker than a piece of yarn.

Whatever you do, don't look down! She could do this. She had practised how to release the chain slowly, but her life hadn't depended on it before. As long as she gripped the knife handle with the controlling glove, her grip on the handle wouldn't falter or weaken...or so she hoped. Slowly—at about half of her walking pace—she lowered herself down the sheer cliff wall.

The chain in Dawn's First Crescent was, fully extended, about ten yards long. That was only a third of the way down the cliff. Somehow she had to re-anchor the pommel to something without falling to her death. To do that, she needed to grab the cliff. She swung herself outward and then in, managing on the second try to grab an outjutting rock. *All right, now what?*

She couldn't quit. She'd die before she climbed back up looking like an idiot in front of almost sixty people—especially Eldoth and Theramus, although for very different reasons.

She kicked off from the cliff, looked around and, when she saw what she was looking for, swung back to the face and 'ran' along it. The small fissure ran vertically and she was able to find grips for both of her feet and one hand as well. Once she was sure it would bear her weight, she triggered the parts of the glove that retracted the pommel blades and the chain.

There was no longer an easy way back up. Like it or not, she was ten yards down the side of a sheer cliff face. Sephana jammed the pommel into the fissure and— making sure her fingers were nowhere near it—extended the pommel blades. She lowered herself down another eight yards before she saw it: a stone line invisible from above sticking out of the cliff face. She had to swing out and in again before she could catch the cliff and step onto the path, but once she had done so she could stand on it freely.

"That was impressively acrobatic, but pointless."

She whirled around and raised her dagger, but it was only Eldoth. Down here. On the secret, invisible path that she had just rappelled down to.

"How did you get down here?"

He snorted. "Did you ask me? Did you consult the one person in your company who not only has studied magic, but has successfully navigated through wizard-made structures? Did it occur to you that I might have an informed opinion on how to access this hidden *magical* pathway that doesn't involve hurling yourself over the side of a cliff?"

She was speechless. A small part of her was aware that her mouth was opening and closing like a fish, but mostly she was trying to decide just which of his many questions she wanted to sneer at. The rest of her wanted to bury her foot so far between his legs he would spend the rest of his life sounding like a ten year old boy.

"You were in the room," she said through clenched teeth. "We talked over the whole plan *right next to you,* but every time someone asked you something you made some snotty comment about research and ignored us."

"If I'd known that you were discussing something important I *would* have paid attention, but it was all tedious logistics and other mundanities."

She counted to three and tried to think of something that didn't involve stabbing him or pushing him into the river. Nothing came to mind. "How did you get down here, anyway?"

"The path joins with the cliff top a few hundred yards back. It is concealed by illusion, but perfectly visible to—"

"—to someone who can read magic runes, I know." He frowned at her interruption but she ignored him. "Well, then, let's go tell everyone that we have an easier way to access the river path. Theramus will be happy that we don't have to lower everyone down on a rope."

Theramus and Balien shared the rear of the column as their small force made their way to Three Maiden Falls and the secret entrance that they believed awaited them there. The path was smooth, even, and wide enough for two men to walk abreast. He could see the thin line of soldiers making their way along the path when the twisting channel allowed it. They were perpetually in shadow.

Soon the straight, green length of Northmarch Bridge appeared above them. Balien touched Theramus' shoulder and pointed to the rapids beneath it. Unlike the rest of the river, which was mostly clear, rocks beneath the bridge jutted from the surface like daggers.

"Unpleasant," Theramus yelled over the water's roar.

No mundane architect, no matter how skilled, would have been able to build this bridge. It had no arch. Its length spanned the chasm like a plank with no support columns anywhere along its eighty yard length. It was made entirely of heartstone, as no other substance could withstand those stresses and not shatter. Viewing it left him both saddened and renewed.

Something else grabbed his attention. At first he thought that the bridge was merely thicker on its ends, but that was not the case. Underneath the bridge—a place that no man had seen in hundreds of years—great cylinders rested between the bridge and the cliff, like huge rows of barrels laid end to end. Taken in conjunction with the dagger-like stones below, he understood exactly what at least one of the keep's magical defences was and marvelled anew at the power and might of the High Wizards of Anduilon.

The waterfall was deafening. Eldoth had been trudging along this magically shaped pathway for what felt like hours. Being second in the column behind Illyria and followed by two and a half score of burly soldiers meant that he could not stop for fear of being trampled, no matter how much his feet ached or he needed to void his bladder.

Physical discomfort aside, he was being denied the chance to examine the spells that made this hidden pathway. The shaping of the stone was inconsequential; it was rudimentary orange magic, although the scale of its construction was impressive in its own right. He was much more interested in the invisibility spell cast upon the path. The runework etched into the stone contained symbols from at least three colleges. Some of it was orange—he could recognize those symbols, at least—but the other two were beyond him. Perhaps he would have time later.

Later.

Like so much else since he had gotten ensnared in this disgusting affair, it would have to wait until he was free. Had freedom ever really benefited him? Yes, freedom meant not being enslaved by Djido sorcerers, but it also meant wandering without direction and scrambling for food and shelter. On previous occasions, such as with Veeshar, it had been taken from him, but at other times he had given it willingly. The bittersweet experience of his marriage had definitely been a surrender of his freedom. In the beginning, when Sephana had still bothered pretending, he had given it to her most willingly. His current association with her—and, by extension, her friends—was no less a sacrifice. Certainly it was less onerous than being threatened with death, but there was no way, had he been free, that Eldoth would ever have *chosen* to infiltrate an occupied castle.

It was worth it. The potential rewards gained from the examination of Sephana's fascinating new weapon and the possibility of access to royal archives *had* to be worth his present discomfort and potential upcoming danger. If it wasn't, then he was being a fool. Eldoth was many things, but a fool was not among them.

The river fell away abruptly. Incalculable volumes of water plunged over the edge, creating the mist that pervaded the air and the rumble that he could feel through his boots. The Lyssal River, while narrow, was fast and deep. If he were to be caught by it, not only would he be crushed to death, but his body would never be released from its watery grip.

The thought of such an unpleasant end was why what lay before him caused such alarm. The path he stood on ended abruptly just before the waterfall's leading edge. There were no runes or other evidence of magic on the water-slicked cliff so he knew that the entrance to the keep did not begin here. He was beginning to doubt that it existed. The runes he had read within the keep had said 'water' and 'pouring'—easily interpreted as 'waterfall'—but his mastery of Renfel was incomplete. There had been no indicator as to whether the passage let out at the top of the 'pouring water' or at its base. He had hoped for the former, but, like everything else that had happened in his current ordeal, it did not seem to be the case.

Illyria waited for him at the edge of the cascade. The river at this point was roughly sixty feet across. She said something and pointed below her but verbal communication was impossible. He gestured his incomprehension and she nodded, waiting until he arrived at her side.

The channel tripled in width beyond the waterfall. The word 'waterfall' was also a misnomer, for there were at least two of them. The initial cascade fell five yards into a huge, churning vortex of thunder and foam. Fifty yards beyond that it fell again, this time a much longer distance based on the size of the mist plume that hung above it. The river fell once more in the distance, though by that point it spanned the entire channel and fell into a broad, richly coloured lake.

Illyria pointed down the channel wall and Eldoth immediately saw the problem: the there was a large gap in the path. It ended at the top of the falls and was seen to continue down at the waterfall's base, but there was nothing visible between those two points. Empty space.

He knelt and laid his hand on the path. It was dry despite the heavy mist—one more piece of runework he needed to investigate—and did not end despite what his eyes told him. He examined the runework and saw that a fine crack in the stone, originating somewhere high above them, had run through one of the symbols and destroyed it.

Even the greatest works of magic are not immune to time and entropy. He wasn't sure if he found that reassuring or saddening.

Illyria looked puzzled. He sighed, stood and placed his mouth next to her ear. He had thought that she possessed a modicum of intelligence, but apparently could not grasp the plainly obvious. "The invisibility spell has malfunctioned. The path exists, we simply cannot see it."

"Can you fix it somehow?" she yelled and, after a moment's pause, he nodded. He was unable to restore the original spell—he thought that it required knowledge of the college of spirit—but repair was not necessary. The path needed to be made visible and that could be accomplished through a simple application of red magic. He was Eldoth the Red, was he not, named for his college of mastery?

He could only illuminate what he could perceive and that was limited to what he stood upon. He had to modify and recast his spell several times as he slowly felt his way down the path. It was time consuming but ultimately effective and by the time he was done, the invisible section emitted an easily seen reddish glow.

The men behind Illyria watched nervously. She closed her eyes briefly before calmly walking along the glowing path. Once past it she paused for a moment, stepped past Eldoth and retook the lead position. The line of soldiers followed her cautiously.

The path levelled out less than a yard above the churning froth and led behind the waterfall. The wall of falling water was so thick and turbulent that it blocked all of the light from beyond save the path's narrow gap.

Behind the waterfall, the stone path widened as it rose. A shallow cave, obviously created by the force of the moving water, stretched the width of the cascade and extended backwards. The floor of the cave had been raised by the use of magic and bore the same drying enchantment. There was more than enough room for their entire force to gather. *Good.* Finally Eldoth could sit and allow himself to release the tension tightening within him.

Sephana's breath caught as she came to the edge of the waterfall. *Goddess's Grace, what a beautiful colour.* The panorama of the multiple waterfalls, framed as they were by the cliffs with the gorgeous deep turquoise of the lake beyond made her want to weep. For a brief moment she was able to forget who she was, the sins she had committed and the injustices that had been done to her. None of that mattered here, not in view of the splendour of Emuranna's finest work.

This is what I was meant for.

She ran her hands through her hair and closed her eyes, lost to sensation. She could feel a sliver of the evening sun strike her face and cool waves of boiling mist waft against her skin. The roar of the falls made her bones tremble

A pair of hands pushed her from behind and the spell was disrupted. Blinking, remembering where she was and that Alwyn was behind her, she made her way down the glowing red path. The magic of her situation partly returned and she could not help but smile at the poetry of their route being in a secret passage behind a waterfall. It made everything even more perfect.

She was completely unprepared when a hand grabbed her by her shirt and threw her against the stone wall. All she could see was the tip of a broadsword at her throat and Alwyn's furious face behind it. She couldn't hear him over the roar of the waterfall, but she could read his lips: 'Djido spy'.

She was abruptly reminded of who, what, and where she was.

Alwyn's uneasiness peaked when he saw that he was required to walk along red tinted nothingness. What in the Goddess's name had he committed himself and best of his father's soldiers to? Illyria and her rhetoric about peace suddenly sounded very, very hollow. He must have gone insane. There was no other reason for him to be doing this.

In front of him, Sephana stopped to admire the view of the falls and the lake beyond. Perhaps if he had not just made the greatest mistake of his life, he might have been more impressed with it. Frightened and impatient to be off this treacherous path, he pushed at her to continue.

That was when the cloth that she covered her hair with fell away.

At first he thought it was a trick of the light. Her hair was thick enough that seeing anything underneath was difficult but by the time he reached the bottom of the path he was sure. She had *scales*. More than that, she bore a pit on the side of her head where her ear was supposed to be. He had seen those features before.

He waited until the path widened. Until it did, he could do nothing but wait and grip his sword with a hand suddenly covered in nervous sweat.

He should have run her through. It was what he meant to do, but instead found himself grabbing her shoulder and holding his blade to her throat. Her hazel eyes were wide with fear. It was a shade, he realized now, very close to the yellow of a snake.

"Djido spy!" he spat. It was difficult to hear anything but his men could see that something was happening. "To arms!" he yelled. "We've been betrayed." They were confused and tired but obeyed. There were soon fifty swords drawn, though no one seemed to know where to point them. Several men guarded Alwyn while others pointed their blades at Illyria and the snobbish man in the red jacket.

The man just looked worried and confused, but Illyria's hands were held out in a gesture of peace. She was too far away for Alwyn to hear her and it was just as well. She was the one who had bewitched him. His heart wanted to believe that she had done so for honest reasons and that the snake girl had deceived her as well, but he could take no chances.

"Disarm them," he ordered.

Something was missing. In his fear he had forgotten something. With a sick feeling he realized what. *Where are Balien and the giant?*

He was about to turn and give another order when he heard a loud bellow, clearly audible even over the roar of the waterfall. A hand as strong as Anshar himself grabbed his jacket and Alwyn found himself hanging in the air.

"You will not harm her!" Theramus thundered, his eyes ablaze with fury. He held Alwyn aloft with one hand and his mallet in the other. "Sephana is far greater and braver a person than you will ever be, 'prince'. There is no shame to be attached to her heritage. That her forebears were abused by Djido means nothing. That she still bears the blood of her oppressors is not a source of shame, but a badge of courage. She has done more with her meagre beginnings than any of you so called 'petty kings' and princes." With each shouted statement he shook Alwyn like a dog would a toy, and with the same effort. Alwyn's boots were dangling five feet above the ground.

The giant Noss turned his tremendous rage to the rest of Alwyn's men, who watched with slack jaws and wide eyes. "You modern men disgust me!" he yelled. "You watch your world rot and do nothing while other people, truer people, fight and die for you. Sephana is worth a hundred of you!! Would any of you worthless dogs have come on this mission if this one—" he gave Alwyn an especially strong shake "—had not doubled your pay? Did not one of you volunteer to do this because it was *right?*"

A group of men raised their swords and approached him.

"You raise weapons against me," Theramus spat. "You think to threaten me with your numbers. Do you think that that I still could not kill every one of you?" He raised his hammer menacingly. "Hundreds of men have been slain by my hand, those who were too blind to see the light or followed the orders of fools. In days past, before you were born, I was called the 'Steel Colossus' and I slaughtered *armies*. Come: test your fate, sons of cowards. Face me with steel, though I bear only wood, and see who is sent to their graves!"

Alwyn was certain that he was going to die. If Theramus made good on his threat his first action would be to crush his prisoner before he waded into the others. Here, in the narrow confines of this cave, Alwyn had no doubt that the enraged Noss could live up to his boasting.

"Big Blue, put him down." Alwyn barely heard the words. Twisting, he saw Sephana lay her hands on Theramus's chest. Her scales were plainly visible on her forehead. "You have to stop this."

"He threatened you with a sword. He would have slain you!"

"He was scared. He's tired and he's out of his depth." She looked up at Alwyn and gave him a pointed, angry look. "I'm sure he's very sorry. Let him down."

"An apology is not enough!" the giant protested. "He should grovel before you and beg your forgiveness. All of them should."

"This is wrong, Theramus." It was Balien, barely audible over the waterfall. "It's not what we came here for."

Theramus growled and turned Alwyn to face him. His broad, blue-skinned face was twisted with anger. "It is only because of the wishes of better men that I return your life to you. You will beg for Sephana's forgiveness and *never* disrespect her again. Do you understand me, petty prince?"

Alwyn nodded frantically. "Yes. Yes, I understand."

"Good. Do not forget it." Instead of lowering Alwyn to the ground, Theramus simply dropped him.

Balien helped him to his feet. "Don't grovel and don't show weakness in front of your men," he said as he dusted Alwyn off. "Apologize to Sephana so that everyone can see you do it, then tell your men sheathe their weapons."

"But you've seen her," Alwyn hissed. "She's a—"

Balien put a comradely hand on his shoulder and squeezed. Hard. "Your thoughts are your own, Alwyn, no matter what I may think of them, but do not say that in my presence, or, if you value your life, anywhere near Theramus. I trust Sephana with my life, and she has risked hers on your behalf. That should tell you enough of her character. Every man chooses his own path, Alwyn, regardless of his ancestors."

Alwyn nodded stiffly, picked up his sword and sheathed it. He walked over to the curly haired snakegirl, who eyed him cautiously. "If by my words or actions I have given you offence, Sephana, then I apologize for myself and on behalf of my men."

She smiled graciously, but her eyes spat fire. "I may not want Theramus to kill you, but I still think you're a pathetic toad. Zulum take you, Alwyn."

He kept his expression flat. He turned to Owain, who hovered nearby. "Get the men to put away their weapons. This was a misunderstanding."

"We're a long way from home, prince," the older man replied over the roar of falling water. "Another of these 'misunderstandings' and we might not make it back there."

Alwyn nodded and walked over to Illyria. She did not look pleased.

"To His Royal Highness Altus Whitecrown, High King of Anduilon, from his Most Loyal Champion, Odom 'The Dauntless':

"It is with a horrified heart, sire, that I report on the latest tactic of the Djido enemy. Not only is it true that they have native Akkilmen fighting with them, but they have begun using their magic in horrible new ways. They have been taking the bodies of different beings—sometimes animals, sometimes Nintarans, sometimes captive prisoners—and merging *them. It is hideous, sire. The Djido have no control over these beings, but control is not needed. They need only be unleashed. You see, not only do these creatures combine the most horrific aspects of their hosts, they are also huge, immensely strong, bloodthirsty, and completely mad with rage. All the Djido need to is release these...feral giants...near friendly forces, watch them wreak havoc and exploit the weaknesses in our lines that they create.*

"I beg you, sire, to send aid here as soon as you read this letter. The Nemoran royal families have fled with their army and cannot be found. I rally what peasants and remaining soldiers I can, when I can, but our hope and our resources grow thin. Without additional forces, battle-wizards especially, I fear that this kingdom will not last the summer.

"I remain yours until the end, sire, though I hope that is later rather than sooner."

—undelivered letter found on the body of royal courier, three months after the fall of Nemora

CHAPTER FOURTEEN

Olamm-Ta jogged alongside his fellow Vaulen. His people had become horsemen soon after arriving in Anshara but they had not forgotten the ways of their ancestors. Before the Bleakness had driven them away, Ta's ancestors had ruled Nintara carried only by their feet. In the ancient stories, tribes ran for days on end before fighting. The Bekkit-Ta were not up to those standards but they remained hardy enough to cross between their secret camp and the human fortress called 'Durnsuld'.

If Veeshar's claim held true then Ta's army would take their rest inside its walls, and if not they would conquer it before moving on. These southlanders did not know war, not like the Vaulen. From what Veeshar had told him, the humans placed their faith in their horsemen and their fortresses. They had not faced anything greater than isolated packs of A'Cha dogs in more than a century.

Ta smiled as he ran. He would show them real war.

Eldoth had found the entrance right where they had hoped it would be. If everyone hadn't been so tired from twelve hours of marching, Illyria would have started them walking down the passage right away. Keeping the tired men focused on an activity— any activity—would have distracted them from the unfortunate events that had transpired between Alwyn and Theramus. As necessary as it was, this rest break was toxic to morale.

It was very easy to dismiss Theramus as harmless. Illyria was just as guilty of it as everyone else. Yes, he was eight feet tall and, yes, his body bulged with rock-hard muscle, but with his soft voice and gentle manner it was easy to see him as a gentle and wise—albeit blue—grandfather.

No longer. All of Alwyn's men were casting distrustful looks towards him and, by extension, the company he kept. The revelation of Sephana's ancestry had been poorly timed and did nothing to improve their current situation. Hatred of the Djido ran long and deep throughout the Petty Kingdoms—something that Illyria, raised in isolation, often forgot. It was that deep-seated hatred, combined with ignorance and incorrect folk knowledge, that had made Alwyn act so rashly.

Sephana had told them repeatedly about the importance of her remaining disguised, but Illyria had dismissed her fears as paranoia. She had refused to believe that people would react so foolishly and condemn someone for sins committed by their parents (not that they had committed any sin worse than surviving) but that exact thing had happened before her eyes and from the last person she had expected.

It doesn't matter how badly the roast is burned, you still have to serve the meal. They still had a mission and, because of Davin Jannery's juvenile paranoia, there was no one else to do it. Illyria nodded to the others and got to her feet.

Alwyn wouldn't meet her eyes as she walked over to him. "Illyria, I—"

She held up her hand. "Mistakes were made on both sides, Alwyn. We need to get moving." She lowered her voice. "I need to know if you and your men are still with me."

"I am. We are." He stepped in until his lips were almost at her ear. "Illyria, she has snake blood. She's a spy. You can't trust her."

She bit back the answer she wanted to give. There simply wasn't time. "You're wrong, Alwyn. She's my friend and I know exactly who she is. Get your men ready."

He opened his mouth to speak, hesitated, and nodded.

Illyria cursed under her breath, hoping that this mission wasn't doomed before it began.

Sephana wasn't sure if she was hiding behind Theramus or if he was acting as a shield between her and the men of Derwyn. Certainly, she hadn't seen him move more than five feet from her side since Alwyn had held her at sword point and he'd threatened to battle an entire room on her behalf.

Part of her wanted to Alwyn to die. At that moment he had been every person who had ever spat, shunned, or threatened her because of what she was. Unlike all those other times (and there had been a lot), at that moment she had possessed the ability to strike back. Allowing Alwyn to be killed wouldn't have made her childhood any less hellish, or her time before she met Theramus less frightening, but it would have balanced the scale just one small bit. After a life filled with running, begging, hiding, and grovelling because she had scales and a tail, even one small act of turnabout would have been nice.

She couldn't let it happen. She couldn't let Theramus become a murderer because of her. If he had entered a pitched battle against the men of Derwyn, she knew that Balien and maybe Illyria would have as well. All of her friends might have been killed because of her. Not only would that have been horrible, but then the keep could never be retaken and the army of A'Cha, Vaulen, Djido, Tsrinn and dragon-lizards would enter into Karalon unopposed. Hundreds—no, *thousands*—of deaths would be her fault, and Sephana could not allow that.

She wanted to cry. After everything that had happened it seemed impossible for her *not* to but she refused to give Alwyn and his men the satisfaction. Maybe her eyes did water a bit, but no one could see it in the dark and the occasional sniffle was lost in the roar of the waterfall.

Or, at least, it had. After the longest, most awkward rest break in history, they had left the waterfall cave and now the only sound was the stomp of booted feet. It was tall enough for Theramus to walk easily and was lit in the same mysterious way as the secret passage in the keep. While the cellar underneath Perceptus's tower had been made from brick, these walls were smooth, seamless stone.

No one was talking. At the end of this tunnel and another secret door was Durnshold keep and however many A'Cha and ensorcelled soldiers were defending it. Once everyone passed through the door at the other end of tunnel, it would be time to fight and die. Sephana, even though she had an eight foot, blue shield to hide behind, was marching *towards* a pitched battle.

At the end of the tunnel was a square shaft that went two hundred feet straight up. That shaft was lined with stairs and at the top of the stairway was a landing that ended in a door. The landing was large enough for all of them to gather and now fifty six pairs of eyes were fixed on Illyria. She turned to Eldoth, all too aware of everyone's scrutiny. "Where does this door open into?"

He looked green. "The cellar beneath the main keep. There shouldn't be anything in there. At least, there wasn't before."

"The cellar opens into both the courtyard and the kitchens in the main keep?" she asked. He nodded. "Alwyn, you and your men take the main doors into the courtyard and get to the two corner towers. Once you secure them the walls are yours." He nodded, but didn't meet her eyes. Illyria raised her voice and looked at the gathered men of Derwyn. "You may see townspeople and guardsmen. They may fight you. Spare them if you can; their minds are not their own."

Illyria continued. "My companions and I will be making our way through the kitchen into the keep itself. That is where the keep's magical defences are controlled and our mission. We'll render you what aid we can, but the securing of the courtyard and the walls is your responsibility."

The air of unease and nervousness in the room was palpable. *This isn't what they need to hear. They need inspiration, not directives.*

The words came with surprising ease. "What I am asking you today is hard. You are risking your lives for people you don't know in a kingdom not your own, but I need you to remember that long ago, before there were places we called Derwyn or Ilthanara, we were one people. We weren't Nemormen or Karolmen, we were Anduilmen. Elf, Human, Noss, or even Reshai: we are one people. What we are about to do is for peace and the future. Every blow we strike brings Nemora and Karalon closer and that means a land where it's safe for us to raise our families without fear. What we are doing is right. I believe this with all of my heart and I thank all of you for helping me make it reality."

She could feel every eye and ear follow her words. More importantly, she could feel hope.

Alwyn, his eyes glowing, raised his fist. "For peace and for Derwyn."

"For peace and for Derwyn!" echoed fifty voices.

Illyria raised her hand and within seconds there was silence. "You all know your duties. Follow Alwyn and your eorlmen. They'll be singing songs of your courage for generations, I swear it." They cheered but hushed when she held her finger to her lips. "We maintain silence for as long as we can." She nodded to Eldoth, who used his stele to scribe a symbol in the wall next to the door.

Emuranna willing, this might just work.

The cellar was dark except for the focused light emitting from Eldoth's stele. Simple light spells were elementary applications of red magic; even first ring novices could perform them. Keeping twenty lit was more of a challenge but well within Eldoth's abilities. It took a portion of his concentration to keep so many spells active—it was akin to constantly keeping your fist clenched—but wasn't taxing.

Balien held up his hand and barred anyone else from entering the room. "Something is wrong. Stay here."

Wrong? What is he talking about? Eldoth directed his stele into the room's darkened corners but saw nothing beyond barrels and crates ransacked by a week of beastman occupation. There were four others in the cellar besides Balien and himself: Illyria, Sephana, Theramus (although the massive Noss really should have counted for two) and one of the small-brained idiots from Nemora.

"I think I found something," Sephana called out. "I think something big is living here."

"Be careful," Illyria cautioned, holding her curved sword. "There are many places for something to hide."

"There's fur here, and…scales?" She sifted through the debris at her feet. "That doesn't make any sense."

"Fur and scales?" Eldoth echoed. Memories of twisted flesh and indescribable suffering assailed him. "It can't be. It died!"

Balien turned to him. "What died, Eldoth?"

A strange roar came from the corner: a sick blending of two sounds. The idiotic Nemorman that had had joined them emitted a scream than ended abruptly. The sudden, pregnant silence was filled by awful sounds of ripping and crunching. Eldoth, panic rising in his chest, turned his stele towards the noise and found his worst fears confirmed.

It looked just as hideous as the last time he'd seen it. Its saurian legs and tail merged at the chest level with the fur and heavy upper body of an A'Cha warrior. Its face, like its body, contained elements of both original creatures. Its jaw and teeth were still huge and terrifying—made worse by the glistening blood and flesh from its most recent kill—but only slightly less than the gleam of intelligence that shone behind its fierce and deadly eyes.

"Before Veeshar mastered the use of the Seal," Eldoth explained, "he tried to control the thunder lizards in the Djido way. He took the lizard's pack-leader and merged it with a beastman. It didn't work well." When last he had seen the creature it had been in so much agony that even moving was too much for it. Apparently it had gotten better.

The creature stared at Eldoth with feral hate and sprang towards him, claws extended and mouth wide. Rational thought fled. Eldoth raised his hands, summoned all of his magical power and encased his body within a shield of fire.

The light spelled onto Illyria's sword went dark. In fact, all of the lights that Eldoth had created winked out of existence at the same time while, simultaneously, the wizard's body wreathed itself in angry red flame. A large, dark silhouette rushed towards him, but screamed when they came into contact. There was a sudden, intense smell of burning flesh as it fled into the darkness.

A strange, ghostly, red image, like hundreds of fireflies moving in concert, darted behind a shelf. There was a flash of steel as Balien pursued it, followed by a roar and the smash of a shelf collapsing.

"Eldoth, put it out!" Sephana yelled at him. "You're going to burn the whole room down!" The wizard was lost to his panic and did not hear her.

Illyria left him to Sephana and ventured towards where the creature had last been. A snarl and flash of movement was her only warning of danger. She dove to the side and lashed out with her sword. Its claws missed her by inches. Theramus came up on her right, mallet swinging. It stumbled and fell into a stack of barrels.

A ball of fire streaked towards it, but it rolled to its feet and leapt out of the way. The barrels must have contained some kind of oil, because they immediately burst into flames.

"Eldoth!" Sephana wanted to slap him, but the red sheathe of flames around his body was ridiculously hot. Even five feet away her hair was starting to singe and she didn't dare get any closer. "There has to some way to get to him," she muttered. Everything in the room would burn to ash before it reached him. She needed something strong enough to resist his flame.

She looked down at Dawn's First Crescent, and Theramus's words echoed in her mind. *'It is razor sharp and harder than any metal. It will keep its edge forever.'* "I bet it's fireproof, too." As much as she wanted to stab him, she knew she shouldn't. *Yet.* She flicked out the weighted pommel, whirled it over her head and sent the mushroom shaped weight (blades retracted, sadly) through the angry, red flames into the centre of Eldoth's forehead.

The nimbus of fire around him winked out as he stumbled backward, tripped, and fell.

He clutched his forehead. "What do you think you're doing, you ill-mannered cow?"

Oh, I am going to get you for that later! "No time!" she snapped, running over and pulling him to his feet. "We need light now and then you need to put out that fire."

He looked around, confused, as a trickle of blood dripped down the bridge of his nose. "What? Light? Fire? Oh." He waved his hand sharply and a dozen brightly glowing globes burst into existence. The room was flooded with bluish light.

It became impossible for anything to hide. Sephana squinted and tried to shade her eyes with her hand. Everyone else reacted similarly but none as much as the A'Cha/dragon-lizard/monster/*thing* which screamed and covered its face.

Eldoth gestured towards the burning barrels, and the bright yellow flame *leapt into his hand* as if it were an eager puppy. His face now bearing a fierce grimace, he struck the creature with the ball of flame in his hands, causing it to scream and writhe on the floor.

Sephana was too stunned to resist when Eldoth grabbed her by both shoulders. "Strike me like that again and I will burn your body into a cinder!"

She broke out of his grip. "If you didn't get all hysterical on me then I wouldn't have to!" She took a deep breath, ready and willing to unleash another furious tirade on her ass-faced, thick-headed turd of an ex-husband when she saw something hurtling towards them. She pushed Eldoth away without thinking.

The claw swipe that would have ripped open his throat instead opened four shallow, bloody cuts in the front of his coat. Sephana, standing in its way, was hurled across the room.

Theramus held up his hands in a vain attempt to protect his eyes from the sudden light. He could barely make out the feral giant as it slashed at Eldoth and hurled Sephana away from it. Half-blind, he lunged towards the creature and grabbed the nearest part he could—its large, dragon-lizard's tail. He could barely see as it snapped at him. If Illyria had not struck with her sword at that moment he would have been its meal. It raised one arm to protect its face and swung its tail in a large arc that Theramus could not see to avoid. It struck him with the force of a falling log and knocked him the length of the room.

It surveyed its situation with intelligent, angry eyes. Eldoth lay on the ground, Illyria stood with her sword bared while Balien, Sephana and Theramus all crawled to their feet. Presented with odds so unfavourable it listened to its A'Cha nature and chose to run.

Wooden doors shattered before its strength and it ran into the open courtyard, yelling aloud in a voice that was part A'Cha and part lizard's scream.

Still on the floor, Eldoth clutched his chest. "It has the medallion!"

"What did you say?" Illyria looked down at him with disapproval.

Eldoth felt his chest and winced as he pressed his newest wounds. *I am a wizard, not a pugilist.* It was entirely inappropriate for a man of his abilities.

"Eldoth, I swear I'll whack you in the head again," Sephana warned.

He glared at her and envisioned painful death. "The medallion is gone," he repeated. "It must have taken it."

Balien stood at the door and watched the courtyard. "They know we're here." On the other side of the room, the mass of Derwyn soldiers poured in from the tunnel passage.

"Emuranna protect us," Illyria muttered. "All right. Sephana, Balien and Theramus, go after the creature and get that amulet. Alwyn, you and your men need to take those walls before they can assemble a defence. Eldoth and I will support you."

Eldoth stared at her. "We will?"

"They're coming!" At the door, Balien slew an approaching beastman and Theramus joined him there. Together, the two of them protected the width of the door.

"You keep telling us how tough a wizard you are," Sephana chided, "but all we've seen you do is attack some barrels."

"I am the greatest wizard in five hundred years!"

She just shrugged, her expression indifferent. She pointed at the doorway, where both Balien and Theramus were fighting. "Prove it."

He snarled and strode towards the door angrily. Taking a breath, he pushed up the sleeve of his left arm and bared it to the sharpened point of his stele. He disliked bloodcasting. While it increased in the power of his spells tremendously, it was also draining and painful. Eldoth only ever considered it after all other options had been exhausted, but none of that mattered now.

He plunged the magical stylus into his flesh and began to scribe runes into his skin using his own blood as ink. He felt the result immediately. "Get out of my way," he growled, not really caring if anyone did or not. The power within him needed to escape and, one way or the other, it would. His tone must have alarmed everyone, for they melted before him as he advanced.

There were two beastmen before him with countless more behind. Eldoth bared his palms and pushed as if he was opening a door. Blood red lightning leapt from his hands, coursed through their bodies, and into the ones behind. The first two died immediately and the others less than a second later. There were more in various places around the courtyard. He extended his fingers into a fan and his lightning broadened to encompass them all.

Perhaps an archwizard could have slain them all outright, but it was beyond Eldoth's ability, even empowered as he was by his blood. Lightning arced from one body to another, criss-crossing the open space seemingly at random. Dozens of beastmen writhed and twisted in agony, but fight remained in all of them.

The power in his veins screamed for release and Eldoth forced as much of it into his lightning as he could. This was the danger of bloodcasting: a wizard within its rage was unaware of his body's limits. All of his life force could be pushed into his magic and he would not know that he had killed himself until too late. Eldoth tried to always know where that line was, no matter what his state of mind. He had never crossed it and always kept the feeling of power-drunkenness at bay, but he had never, ever been so angry casting a spell as he was now.

A small part of him was still able to exercise caution. *I need to stop. If I kill myself now, there is so much I will never learn.* That thought, more than any other, was enough to bring him to his senses. Releasing the blood-tainted lightening was painful, but he forced himself to let it go. He staggering in the spell's aftermath and only Theramus's large hands prevented him from falling.

"They are injured but not dead," he gasped. "You should have no difficulty dispatching them."

Sephana, like everyone else, gaped at the massive display of magical power that Eldoth unleashed. *He's really not the man I left in Akkilon, is he?*

"Sephana, you must come now." Theramus held out his hand to help her to her feet.

When did I sit down?

His face was solemn. "I am sorry that I cannot protect you from what is to come. You must be a warrior now, Sephana."

She took the proffered hand and pulled herself up. "I will be."

They stepped around the charred corpses and into the main courtyard. It stank of burning fur and something else: an acridness that burned her nostrils. There were easily a dozen A'Cha, maybe as many as twice that, in front of them. They were burned, but still alive and very angry. The hybrid/monster-thing was nowhere in sight.

"Do you see it?" she called out, readying Dawn's First Crescent.

Balien pointed to a tower across from the gate. "It went in there."

'There' was across a courtyard filled with angry, singed A'Cha. Balien was already making his way towards the tower, slaying those he could not avoid. Theramus followed, swinging his mallet and sending broken bodies flying with every strike.

"Right. I'm a warrior now." She'd said it without thinking before and now had to find a way to live up to her words. An A'Cha, looking especially tall and dangerous, lunged at her. She side-stepped and slashed like Balien had taught her. The Ansharite blade cut to the bone with frightening ease. It howled in pain and, when it fell, she thrust her red-flecked blade into its neck.

She stared at the dying, tawny-furred body before her. It wasn't the first time she'd killed someone, but it had never been so...*easy* before. She took a shuddering breath. *I don't have time to think about that now.*

" 'So this fortress, Durnshold: they call it a keep and it's on the edge of the Northmarch, right?' "

" 'Yeah, so?' "

" 'Don't you see? It's a keep. On the borderlands.' "

" 'I don't get it.' "

—*Conversation overheard between two Nemoran soldiers*

CHAPTER FIFTEEN

Olamm-Ta stared up at the imposing fortress that the southmen called 'Durnsuld'. His army had run the length of the day to get here and all looked well. The gate was open and A'Cha were patrolling the walls, but something worried him.

"Send a rider to the fort," he ordered.

A loyal Vaulan nodded and barked out an order. Moments later, a single mounted A'Cha was running up the narrow path to the fortress.

Illyria watched her brother and their companions fight their way across the occupied courtyard. "Alwyn, this is your time. You need to secure the courtyard and take those towers."

The Nemoran prince nodded. His face was white with fear, but his voice remained steady as he ordered his men forward.

Illyria knelt beside Eldoth. He was slumped against the wall, disoriented but conscious. "Eldoth, you have to get up. I need you."

The bearded wizard blinked and looked down at his arm, which was bleeding. She didn't recall seeing him take an injury there. He looked up at her, his brown eyes slowly coming into focus. "Yes, I'm fine."

The two stepped into the courtyard in the wake of Alwyn's men. The remaining A'Cha were being dispatched by one group while the rest of the Nemoran soldiers rushed the corner towers on either side of the heavy, wooden gate. The gate which was currently *open*.

A dragon-lizard and rider stood just inside it, and it hadn't come from the stable. *They're here!* Illyria loosed an arrow but it wheeled around even as her arrow left the bow and she struck its shoulder. She nocked another arrow, but it had already passed beyond sight.

She turned to Eldoth. "Can you get that gate closed?"

He shook his head. "Only with brute strength and there are others here better suited to that. It is beyond my current magic."

There was no time to curse. She called out to the closest Derwyn soldiers. "Bedwyr, Cadoc. The enemy is here. We need that gate closed."

They leapt to close the doors and bar them but the damage was already done: Olamm knew that they were here.

Two groups of A'Cha met them in the climb up the tower and were slain quickly, but any delay right now was too costly. The Medallion was too important for them to give up.

Balien and Sephana both beat Theramus to the top of the turret. The creature, burnt and bleeding, hissed at them. Its A'Cha features were just visible within the perverse monstrosity of its face, but were dominated by the dragon-lizard's savagery and power. It looked tired and frightened, but Theramus did not lower his guard. Wild creatures were their most dangerous when cornered.

Its eyes darted between the three people that confronted it. Sephana had separated the pommel of her Ansharite dagger and held it in her free hand. "Do we have a plan?" Her voice was wary but not frightened.

"Theramus, confront it directly," Balien ordered in even, non-aggressive tones. "Sephana and I will flank it. Sephana, try and get the medallion." The item in question was tangled by its cord around the creature's left claw.

Theramus nodded and firmed his grip on his weapon. For the first time in decades he wished he had his sword. He had left that path long ago, he had thought for good, but perhaps another branch lay before him. His mallet would have to do until then.

He charged and feinted towards its face before slamming the heavy wooden head into the creature's side. The mallet, damaged from days of heavy use, snapped upon impact.

The creature slashed out with an A'Cha arm that was sized for a dragon-lizard. Each was as large as one of Theramus's legs. He defended as well as he was able, using the splintered shaft of his hammer like a staff, but was forced back with every powerful strike. As focused upon him as it was, Balien able to impale it upon his sword.

It lashed at Balien, but aborted its attack when the weighted pommel of Sephana's dagger, now bristling with sharp blades, raked along the side of its face and took out its eye.

It knew that it was doomed and charged at Balien. Theramus drove the remains of his mallet into its back in the hope that his weight would slow it, but it remained unaffected. Balien drove his sword into its breast once more, but the creature was beyond pain. It grabbed both of his arms and prepared to bite its immobilized target.

"NO!" Theramus wrapped his arms around its neck, braced his legs and pulled backwards. Heaving for all his worth, he pulled the creature off of its feet. Falling onto his back, he flung it over himself and backwards.

He had not realized how close he was to the edge of the tower. The A'Cha/dragon-lizard abomination, still clutching Balien in its arms, fell right over the edge.

"Boars in the castle, and a sow," the A'Cha reported between blood flecked coughs. "Dozens. They fight us."

Ta glared at Veeshar. " 'Control the keep', do we?" he snarled. "I gave you a hundred A'Cha to hold the fortress, and you give me nothing in return."

"The scout said that there were only 'dozens' of them," it assured Ta slimily. "They cannot keep the fortress from us, not with so few."

"The gate is being shut even now," Ta growled, "and there is no time to construct war engines."

"That gate is wooden," Veeshar told him. "I can have it down in seconds. I just need to touch it."

Ta nodded. "I'll hold you to that." *Or I'll hold your head.* He turned to his band-mates. "Bring up your strongest A'Cha. Attack!"

Eldoth did not concern himself with the soldiers and their task. This keep was where he had been imprisoned and terrorized and, through the cruelties of fate, he stood once more in the place of his humiliation. *It will be different this time.*

A hissing cry came from his right. He turned and saw a line of dirty, ragged soldiers assembling in front of the hall's main entrance. Behind them, ordering them in its quacking voice, was Draxul.

"Draxul!" Rage that had nothing to do with blood-scribed runes overtook him. Spheres of angry fire appeared in his hands. "I dare you to threaten me with your claws. You will not find me so easy this time!" He hurled the burning orb towards the object of his hate.

It dodged Eldoth's magic with fluid, simple movements, but Eldoth saw something in its eyes that hadn't been there before: fear. *Good.* He grinned and summoned more fire, but Illyria grabbed his wrist before it could be hurled at his foe.

"Stop!" She stepped in front of him. "He's using the soldiers as shields. You'll kill them."

She was right. The soldiers, spelled to obey Draxul with fanatic devotion, would think nothing of laying down their lives for the protection of their 'master' but he could still accomplish his revenge. His fire and lightning could cut straight through the unfortunate, hapless men. He could spread his lightning so wide that Draxul would be unable to escape him. A loss of twenty lives was sad, but acceptable.

"No." Her voice was implacable. "It's murder, Eldoth. I won't allow it."

Allow it? He looked in her eyes and saw only resolve. Behind her, Draxul quacked out another command and the soldiers retreated inside the hall.

"Damn you, I would have had him." She opened her mouth to reply but he held up a hand to silence her. He sensed magic.

Veeshar! He turned towards the gate. Iron-banded wood over ten feet wide and twelve inches thick curled and warped like a leaf thrown into a fire. The scream of twisting, ripping lumber was deafening.

Sephana leapt onto the top of the wall and flung the pommel of her dagger. Balien pushed himself free of the monster's grip and caught it just before it reached its full length. Even bracing herself against the crenulations and aided by the strength of her glove, his weight pulled her completely over the edge of the wall.

"No!" She hadn't even fallen eight feet before her descent halted abruptly. Something—no, some*one*—was holding onto the end of her pant leg. "Do you have him?" Theramus asked from above her.

"Barely." Her whole body was hanging down the wall while she clung to Dawn's First Crescent with both hands. At the end of its unbreakable chain Balien hung in exactly the same pose, only reversed. They were like reflections in a pond. His eyes, when they met hers, were calm.

She felt her pants begin to tear. "Theramus?" A string of hysteria threaded through through her voice. Below her, Balien gathered his feet under him.

"I can't—" Theramus called out and tried to firm his grip. Her pants continued to rip. "I must—"

"Theramusssss…" She felt her pant leg split along its seams and then she was falling.

The A'Cha, led by a group of Vaulen, charged.

"Do something!" Illyria snapped at Eldoth even as she drew an arrow and loosed it against the closest attacker.

Most of the Derwyn soldiers were engaged in the towers, but there a few remaining in the courtyard. "Form lines! Don't let them through!" she called out as she loosed her second arrow. The soldiers hastily drew their swords.

A jet of flame erupted from her left and enveloped several A'Cha. Eldoth held out both of his hands and stretched out his fingers. The jet turned into a fan five yards across and the A'Cha retreated before it. They hadn't fallen back more than five yards before the Vaulen began to rally them.

Illyria targeted Vaulen when she could see them and the A'Cha began to falter. "Hold the right!" she called out to the men of Derwyn.

She could see more A'Cha marching up the twisting path beyond the narrow gate. The valley was filled with thousands of furry bodies.

They were only twelve in the courtyard. Illyria renewed her attack.

Theramus looked down in disbelief. Balien and Sephana had not fallen to their deaths. Instead they had caught a projecting stone between the chain they both clung to and were hanging midway down the wall like a cloak from a hook. If he had not seen it happen, he would never have believed it.

Surely Emuranna is watching over us.

"Are you well?"

"I think we're ok," Sephana's called up to him, her voice weak from surprise. "But I don't know how we're going to get back up."

A happy chuckle escaped his lips. "I will find you a rope."

There was a loud wrenching sound from the courtyard behind him. Theramus turned and watched with horror as Illyria, Eldoth and a handful of men stood valiantly against a sea of attackers. They would not be able to withstand such a tide on their own.

"Go. Help them," Balien called, somehow knowing Theramus's dilemma. "We can take care of ourselves."

Eldoth threw another ball of fire at a nearby beastman and smiled thinly as its fur caught fire. Fire was not only painful but visible. All beings instinctively feared it and beastmen, being little more than savage animals, feared it doubly. He was able to keep the entire left side at bay by himself simply by wielding it.

"Can you create a wall of fire across the gate?" Illyria asked. Her arms were in constant motion, drawing and loosing arrows with rapid fluidity. From what Eldoth could tell, every one struck a target. "We can handle the ones inside if you can seal them off."

He didn't want to squander his power, but her strategy was sensible. "Yes. One moment." Eldoth reached within himself to his well of magical power...and found it blocked.

Eyes wide with fear, he tried again to tap his power and was once more thwarted. A Vaulen—he had forgotten just how tall and muscular they were—rushed towards him with its axe raised and was struck in the face by an arrow. Eldoth ran to Illyria.

"I can perform no magic. Veeshar is near and blocking me." It was like his first spell duel all over again.

It was indigo magic—the college that controlled magic itself. It was this college—for which the Djido were famous—that allowed a wizard to open and manipulate gatestones, sense the etheric lines that interconnected the Titan-Worlds and, perhaps most importantly, counter another wizard's spellcasting.

Illyria began releasing arrows, if it were possible, with even more speed. Nothing living came within five yards of her. "This act of countering your magic, does it take concentration?"

"Yes, of course,"

"Then keep trying to cast spells," she instructed. "Your part of a group now, Eldoth. By occupying Veeshar you *are* countering him, for the rest of us." She loosed another shaft and another A'Cha died.

"I... that had not occurred to me." He attempted to access his magic and found himself still blocked. It wasn't as satisfying as raining fiery death upon his enemies, but it would do for now.

Sephana sat on the ground next to the wall and massaged her ankle. It was just as well that Balien had known what to do because but she wouldn't have had a clue. It had involved raising and lowering themselves like weights on a pulley and had ended with a long but survivable fall. She didn't want to do it again.

"Come on, I can see the body." Balien ran down the steep hill—thankfully, they were on the opposite side from the fighting—to where the monster lay. Sephana hobbled after him. The horrible, disgusting *thing* was definitely dead.

The medallion was, amazingly, still tangled in its claw. Balien pulled it free and gave it to Sephana. "You need to make sure that Eldoth gets it."

"Me? What about you?" The walls of the keep, behind him, shone reddish-orange in the setting sun.

He pulled his sword free of the body and inspected it for damage. "I can't get back up that wall, not in time. You have to do this yourself."

"But how are you going to get back in?"

His smile was reassuring. "Don't worry about me. Eldoth needs that medallion."

Sephana looked at the wall looming above her and swallowed. It seemed impossible.

Balien put his hands on her shoulder. "You can do this. You've already proved yourself. I've said it before, Sephana: you're brave and strong. You're not a slave like you were in Akkilon and you're not the back-stabbing monster you think you are for what you did to Eldoth. We can't win this without you, so stop wasting time talking to me and get back in there."

She smiled, her eyes watery. "That's probably the nicest thing anyone's ever said to me."

"And I meant every word, but there's no time. Go!" he turned her towards the keep and pushed her forward.

Theramus burst out of the guard tower carrying a large halberd that he had found within. The situation was dire. A'Cha and Vaulen flooded through the open gate and the few men trying to hold it back were sorely outnumbered. Illyria and Eldoth held the left side alone.

If I must walk the path of the Steel Colossus once more then so be it. Giving out a deafening battle cry, Theramus charged the line of enemy warriors.

Sephana ran up the hill towards the keep wall. It still looked impossible, but after Balien's words she was willing to try anyway. She held Dawn's First Crescent in her gloved hand and whirled the weighted pommel in the other. She threw it towards an outcropping of stone and when the pommel blades caught it she retracted the chain as fast as the dagger could. *Don't think about it, just do it.*

She found herself hurtling upward as if she'd been thrown by a titan. Less than a second later she was hanging in mid-air five feet above the anchor point. Arms and legs flailing, she threw the pommel and caught another stone jutting out across from her. Instead of falling, she swung in an arc underneath it. She retracted the chain as she swung and by the time she was underneath the stone she was flying upward.

If Reshai had been meant to fly we'd have feathers, not scales! Her fingers caught a decorative line of stonework and she took a quick moment to figure out where she was. The top of the wall was less than eight yards above her. It took one simple cast to toss the pommel blades over the edge like a grappling hook and then she was back on top of the wall.

I just scaled a sixty foot wall in less than a minute! She looked down at where she had just been—it was so far!!—and saw Balien watching. She gave him a wave and turned towards the courtyard. The gate, twisted and warped, lay on the ground next to its shattered hinges and an endless stream of A'Cha surged through the opening.

Goddess protect me, I need to find Eldoth!

Olamm-Ta watched impassively as the last of the A'Cha-occupied turrets fell to the human boars occupying the greenstone fortress—*his* fortress. They would soon be using their vantage point to bombard the forces making their way up the narrow, twisting roadway to the gate. Casualties were about to increase.

"Have Lamm-Del line the roadway with Vaulen bearing shields," he ordered one of his band-mates. "Give his A'Cha extra javelins."

The humans in the fortress were giving stiffer resistance than Ta had expected, but they could not hold out forever. He commanded overwhelming numbers of A'Cha and hundreds of brave Vaulen. He would grind them into powder eventually. To give the sorcerer his due, Veeshar had in fact destroyed the gate before disappearing inside. Ta had expected his soldiers to storm through the opening like galloping horses but they had been stopped cold. *We face strong warriors. I will honour them after they are dead.* He was civilized after all.

Before he could honour them, however, he needed to kill them first.

Sephana leapt from the top of the stairs and landed in a tumble at its bottom. She frowned, stopped, and freed her tail. Fear of discovery normally prevented her from walking around with it 'naked', but that secret had already been unmasked. Admittedly, if it were not for Theramus's intimidation and Illyria's diplomacy she would likely have been killed but for this brief moment she was free to move about without hiding who she was. It felt good.

She rounded a corner and found herself suddenly facing a wall of A'Cha. Apparently there were still some groups hidden in the wall towers. They seemed just as surprised by her appearance as she was of theirs. She thought briefly about running but realized that backtracking would add minutes to her time.

'It is time to be a warrior', Theramus had said to her. *'You are brave and strong. You are no longer the slave girl who left Akkilon'*, Balien had said.

She drew Dawn's First Crescent and let the weighted pommel fall to the ground. The blades extended with a 'snikt'. "It'll take more than the five of you to slow me down," she muttered and swung the bladed pommel into the face of the first A'Cha.

It fell howling and clutching its face as the others advanced. Catching the returning pommel in her free hand (blades now retracted) she threw the razor-sharp Ansharite blade into the throat of the next. The last three were upon her then, claws extended and seeking her flesh. Sephana ducked between the two on her left, slicing her blade through the knee of the nearest. She dove and rolled away from the others, regained her feet and swung the pommel in a large circle around her. They had seen the bite of her blade and hesitated.

She snapped it forward like a whip, catching one in the cheek. The two beastmen looked at her, hesitated, then turned and ran around the corner she had come through.

They ran! A'Cha warriors ran away from me!

Her exultation was short lived. At the bottom of the flight of stairs stood a Tsrinn and behind it, with the same scales, ear-pits, and tail as her, was a Djido. "You have an item of great magic on you, by-blow. Give it to me."

The battle was going poorly. Eldoth's magic—the one real edge they had—had been nullified. Five of the ten men aiding her had fallen and she was out of arrows.

History was replete with tales of small groups holding off vast hordes. Some were fanciful, and others exaggerated to the point of myth, but all held one common thread: the larger force had to be contained. Hallways, valleys, and narrow defiles were all examples of places that smaller forces could use to hold off armies. After today, the destroyed gate of Durnshold Keep needed to be added to that list.

Illyria's small army of loyal friends and brave Nemormen had failed in the single most important part of holding off a large army: they had given up their narrow defile. They had never really held it. By the time Illyria had realized that the gate was destroyed and Olamm's army had breached the keep, it had been too late to stand shoulder to shoulder across the ten foot gap and hold the enemy at bay. Perhaps they could have if Eldoth had been able to replicate the wall of fire he had conjured outside Durnston, but Veeshar's appearance had prevented that, and there was no value in lamenting what could not be.

What they now held was an aisle-way forty feet across just inside the narrow gate. With Eldoth nullified, five soldiers too wounded to continue, and Illyria's quiver nearly empty, they could no longer hold their attackers in such a narrow space. Soon they'd have to retreat into the hall or one of the towers and then they'd be lost. Once the A'Cha gained access to the wall it would be the beginning of the end for all of them.

Theramus's arrival had been a gift from Emuranna.

He had appeared from nowhere minutes ago, armed with a pole-arm and shouting loud enough to wake a titan. She had seen him fight before but never with such passion. Without his unstoppable presence they would never have held out as long as they had, but even now they were only moments away from retreat.

This was, after all, only a holding action. Their intention had only ever been to occupy Olamm's army until Eldoth could use the Medallion of Negation to free the ensorcelled soldiers from Veeshar's grip and access the mysterious defences of the

Keep. Their only hope lay in Sephana and her brother returning with it. Both were still missing and Theramus was too busy holding the line's centre to tell her where they had gone.

Illyria slew another pair of A'Cha before confronting the Vaulen that accompanied them. It wielded its axe and shield with skill, but not enough to save it. She jerked her blade free of its chest and immediately engaged another A'Cha that rushed at her.

Three more dead. Three fewer attackers alive to threaten them. It was meaningless. Against an army of thousands, killing three more was as useful as killing one wasp in a hive.

Where was Balien?

" 'When a warrior is put on trial he determines his own innocence.' "

—*Khalamm-Boed of the Vauls*

CHAPTER SIXTEEN

Olamm-Ta glared at the stone fortress that continued to defy him. His band-mates were aware of his ill temper and waited nearby, silent. There was nothing for anyone to say.

"Olamm!" A warrior, one of those securing the rear, approached and knelt. "Olamm, we have a prisoner. It is the one who slew Navoi."

Ta turned to him, surprised. "Is it now? Where did you find this boar?"

"He was attempting to sneak past the line and enter the keep."

Ta smiled. "Bring him to me. I would look on his face before I avenge my band-mate."

The line of corpses in the courtyard continued to grow. It was the way of the A'Cha to prey upon the weak and, even when they were armed, they were ill-equipped against opponents not frightened of them. Theramus, far larger and wielding a seven foot halberd, cut through them like grass.

Even cutting grass could be wearying if you did it long enough.

He knew that the soldiers on the wall were doing their best to stem the tide. Without their rain of arrows upon the exposed ramp the A'Cha would have been storming the gate by the hundreds. He spun and impaled an A'Cha through the chest, stepped forward, and chopped another through its arm and into its ribs. He drove the halberd's steel-shod butt into a third's leg then raised the blade high and cut down into another deeply enough to cleave into its chest.

He grunted in pain as an unseen enemy raked his back. He swung the butt between its legs then turned and drove his blade into the kneeling creature's spine, but the damage was done. Even if only one A'Cha in five managed to wound him, he would fall eventually.

I fight to give the others time. Sephana and Balien will retrieve the Medallion. Even if I do fall, I will give my charges every chance to succeed in their mission. My death will not be in vain. It is not so!

He ignored the pain, fatigue, and the ever increasing weight of the weapon he bore. Bolstered by his belief, Theramus confronted the latest wave of A'Cha attackers.

Sephana stared in horror at the source of her nightmares made flesh. A Djido. It had to be Veeshar and with it one of the two remaining Tsrinn. He'd made it inside the keep somehow and was hunting...her?

Great.

It hissed something and the lizardman (was it Draxul, or the as-yet-unnamed third clutch-mate?) and it flashed up the stairs towards her. It was just as fast as its late sibling. There was no way that she could cross the room and get though the open door before it caught her.

She didn't let herself panic. Acting just as quickly as the thoughts occurred to her she leapt off the railing over the stairs and flung out her pommel chain. It caught the hanging candelabra and she used it to slow herself enough to land without injury. After climbing the sheer wall outside, this was easy.

Of course, having escaped the unnamed Tsrinn (Braxul? Craxul?) For the moment, she was now next to Veeshar. *I don't think this is actually a better place to be.* She swung her pommel weight in a quick figure eight to keep it at bay while she backed towards the door.

The Tsrinn performed some sort of rolling cartwheel that allowed it to quickly clear the staircase and interpose itself between herself and Veeshar. If it tried to hook Dawn's First Crescent with its swords, Sephana knew who would win the tug of war. She retracted the chain back into the dagger, turned, and ran.

The Vaulen formed a circle of shields at the base of the ramp and outside of arrow range. Ta looked at Navoi's slayer. He looked...ordinary. "This is the boar?" he asked Gharda.

"Yes, Olamm."

Ta held the boar's sword to his face and examined it. It was long, yes, but just as ordinary as its owner. "And this is the weapon that he slew her with?"

Gharda nodded.

Ta entered the circle of shields. The human boar stood straight and tall. He watched Ta warily but otherwise did nothing. "I am Ta, Olamm of my people and future king of this ice kingdom," he said in the language of men. Only a fool did not learn his enemy's tongue. "Who are you, boar?"

"Who are any of us?"

Ta snorted. "A philosopher, I see. What is your name?"

"I am Balien, son of Britheon."

"Are you a chief among your people?"

The boar, Balien, shook his head. "I am no one."

"How does 'no one' slay my band-mate in single combat?" Ta growled.

His eyes lit in comprehension. "The one I killed in the pass, she was your mate?"

He did not understand the Vaul. "She was my band-mate. We shared tents and food. Like family, but not blood."

He nodded. "I understand. You will kill me now, to avenge her?"

Ta snorted and tossed the warrior his sword. "I avenge her, if the Eye wills it."

"The Eye?"

"The All Seeing Eye of Gidim, who watches the fate of all Nintarans."

The warrior raised his weapon in a two-handed high guard. "And if the Eye does not?"

Ta began circling. "Then her death was meant to be."

Balien turned to keep Ta before him. "And if I kill you, will another one of your band try to avenge you?"

"No. I am Olamm. Vengeance lies with me and no other. If the Eye wishes for my death, then you will go free."

Ta feinted: a quick thrust to Balien's chest, but the boar stepped away and the blow struck nothing. Ta probed again: a quick series of stabs and strikes to the chest and shoulders that were, again, easily deflected. The human struck quickly with his long blade: fast, testing strikes that Ta batted aside. He was indeed very skilled, as Navoi's slayer would have to be. *Good.* Ta shouted a battle cry and the battle began in earnest. Axe met sword and the air was filled with the sound of steel on steel.

Their first exchange ended with a bruised jaw for Ta and a shallow cut along Balien's shoulder. "What happens to your army and the attack on the keep if you die?" the boar asked as they manoeuvred. "Do I become their chief?"

Ta laughed. "If you want to become Olamm then you can try, but you would fail. Men are not strong enough to lead Vauls."

Their weapons clashed again. Balien changed his combat style, gripping his blade above its guard with one hand and stepping inside Ta's reach. His foot almost snagged Ta's ankle and Ta was forced to retreat.

"You say you are no one, but you fight like a Kalum prince!" Ta said with admiration.

Balien looked at him oddly. "I do?"

Ta said no more. There had been enough words.

166

The boar was an excellent fighter and no stranger to the ways of axe fighting. Ta could not recall having been challenged similarly in several years. *The Khalamm.* It had been during the contest to see who would become Khalamm that Ta had last found his skill so tested.

It was that quick recollection that undid him. Even as Ta chastised himself for letting his mind wander, the boar, Balien, seized the opening. Ta overswung, and in that one moment Balien's shoulder dug into his chest and Ta found himself sprawling backwards onto the ground.

Ta tried to bring his axe to bear but Balien kicked it from his grasp. He scrambled after it but a kick to the stomach knocked him onto his back. When Balien drove his blade through Ta's forearm and into to the hard ground beneath they both knew that the battle was over.

"Do I have to kill you for the Eye to see this was not meant to be?"

Ta shook his head. "No. You have beaten me. Navoi was slain by a greater fighter. Such is her fate."

Balien hesitated. "And if I let you live, do I get some special favour?"

"You have earned a boon from me," Ta admitted, "but it will not be enough to stop this war."

"You said I was free to go. Will you let me cross your lines and rejoin my people?"

Ta nodded. "That is within my power."

Balien jerked his blade free and extended his hand. Ignoring the pain and blood pouring from his wound, Ta took it. "You are a great warrior, Olamm-Ta, and it was my honour to fight you. I am sorry for the loss of your band-mate. She died well."

Ta nodded. "You may rejoin your people within the fortress, but you will die there. We will give no quarter. Walk away, Balien, son of Britheon, so that we might fight another day."

The boar shook his head, as Ta knew that he would. "I cannot."

"Pull back the A'Cha," Ta ordered. "Allow Balien ten minutes to enter the fortress before resuming the attack." He turned to Balien. "You will not be harmed, on my word as Olamm."

Balien nodded. "Good-bye, then."

Ta returned the gesture. "I will remember your name."

Theramus leaned against his halberd and gasped for breath. None of them knew why the A'Cha had ceased their attack, but the timing could not have been better. He would not have lasted more five minutes.

"Where are Balien and Sephana?" Illyria asked with the bluntness of the very tired.

"They were outside the keep," he answered plainly. "I do not know where they are now."

The door from one of the farther towers burst open before Illyria had a chance to reply and Sephana sprinted out. "Helphelphelp! Veeshar and a Tsrinn are right behind me!"

Theramus was thrilled to see one of his wayward charges alive, though her words sickened him. She had been forced to confront a Djido and his bodyguard alone? Unacceptable. She had not even run ten steps before a tattooed, yellow scaled Tsrinn burst out of the doorway. *She is alone no longer!* With a roar, Theramus threw his halberd like a spear.

The Tsrinn evaded the hurled weapon easily, not realizing that it had not been Theramus's intention to hit it. He had merely wanted to disrupt the creature's motion and give Sephana a greater chance to escape.

Theramus had observed Thraxul during its fight with Balien. It was very fast and quite skilled with its blades. Any opponent who fenced with it would likely get disarmed, raked, kicked or struck by its tail, but Theramus had one weapon against which it had no defence: overpowering physical force.

He approached it at a dead run and grabbed for it with both arms. It tried to flee, but Theramus had been wrestling for over a century. He only needed to get one hand on one part of it, any part, and it would be his.

Illyria ran for her bow. She only had three arrows left, but she trusted her archery over her fencing skills against a Tsrinn and a Djido.

Sephana ran up to her as she nocked an arrow. "I have it, Illyria. I have the Medallion."

Emuranna's Grace. Relief flowed through Illyria like a wave. "Give it to Eldoth. Go with him into the hall and protect him as he accesses the keep's defences. We'll make sure no one follows you." Entering the keep meant facing Draxul and its ensorcelled defenders. She didn't want to say 'keep Eldoth in check' but Sephana was one person to whom such a warning did not need to be spoken.

Theramus was occupied wrestling with the Tsrinn. She saw a slight figure covered in brown scales and yellow stripes in the open doorway beyond him. She recognized its features from illustrations in Ilthanara. It was an enemy to all free men and women on Anshara: a Djido.

She loosed her arrow, but it ducked behind the doorway. She could hear its footsteps retreating up the stone steps and hesitated. Eldoth and Sephana were taking the Medallion into the keep and Theramus was twisting the Tsrinn into a knot. Balien was...

There was no one else. As loathe as she was to pursue a Djido wizard alone through a narrow corridor, she could not allow it to wander freely through the keep.

She chased after it into the guard tower.

The Tsrinn's neck broke with a satisfying 'crack', and Theramus dropped its lifeless body to the ground. He looked around for his companions but all were missing. When he looked at the gate he saw a single person bearing a familiar weapon walk through the open gate.

Only Balien could accomplish such a miracle. "I did not expect to see you again in this manner," he called to him.

"Never question the fortunes of war," he replied.

*That phrase...*Theramus looked at him oddly. "Indeed. Where did you hear that?"

"It's something my father used to say to me."

"He was wise." Theramus's mind whirled. He had known Balien for more than a year and had never suspected. *Is it possible?* He stifled the line of thought. It was not the time or place to dwell on such things. "Have you negotiated peace or will they resume their attack?"

"Their leader gave me ten minutes. They'll come again soon."

Theramus nodded and picked up his halberd. Whatever occupied his companions, he knew what his role was to be. "It will be good to have you by my side."

Sephana and Eldoth entered the Great Hall, the same place they had met again after four years apart. It looked the same as it had two days ago: half full of jumbled furniture and fallen tapestries. "OK, I have the Medallion. What do we do now?"

"It's about time," Eldoth growled and snatched it from her hand.

It would have been very easy for her to snarl something and remind the annoying turd who had left a dent in whose forehead but she didn't. She didn't want another fight and there were more important things at stake than a four year old game of 'whose fault is it'. "We need a plan, Eldoth. What is the best way to use this?"

He looked…worn. It was more than the round bruise in the centre of his forehead, his bleeding arm and the claw marks in his chest. His skin was grey and his face was lined with fatigue. "Using the Medallion takes a great deal of focus and its area of effect is limited," he wheezed. He stared through the medallion at mysteries which non-wizards could not conceive of. He blinked and looked up at Sephana, his expression oddly earnest. "To be used most effectively, I will need to be surrounded, but I will be very vulnerable. Can…" he hesitated. "Can you help me in this? Get me close enough to use the Medallion and not let them kill me?"

His honest admission of vulnerability and barb-less request surprised her. "Yes," she replied with equal candour, "but I'm not sure what we're doing here. Are we freeing the soldiers or are we looking for the keep's magical defences, whatever they are?"

"The soldiers are with Draxul and all of them are loose somewhere in the building. It would be foolish for us not to eliminate their threat."

Sephana frowned. He had a point, but he was talking about the two of them confronting more than twenty people. "Look, let's just find the find the defences, OK? Maybe there's something in there we can use to help out everyone else."

It was comforting, in a small way, that Veeshar: the Djido sorcerer who had created the monstrosity they found in the cellar, was running from *her*. According to Eldoth's brief explanation on Veeshar's mastery of 'yellow' magic, it could do anything it wanted to her body: age it, heal it, change it into some creature or slay it outright. To administer the more fatal effects it had to touch her—there was a long winded explanation about the nature of magic that explained it—but there were many unpleasant things it could do to even if she never got close to its scaly fingers.

It had that power but it hadn't used it and, instead, had chose to run. The loss of its bodyguards might be enough, but perhaps there was another reason…

Illyria knew what she had to do.

Sephana didn't need to look into the room to know that it was where Draxul and his mind-controlled bodyguards were hiding. The stench of twenty-odd unwashed bodies in mail that hadn't been cleaned in a week was telling enough.

"That's where the defences are hidden?" she asked in a fierce whisper. "They're in the same place as all the people we're trying to avoid and you're trying to tell me it's no coincidence?"

"It's the most defensible room in the keep," Eldoth replied crossly. "The logic for Draxul hiding here is the same logic why the defences were placed here: there is only one entrance and no windows."

"Great. So now we attack them and you use the Medallion to set them free, right?"

Eldoth looked away, embarrassed. "We can't. Not yet. Veeshar is still blocking me. I cannot access my magic or use the Medallion. There is nothing we can do until he does."

At the base of the hill, Ta watched the green stone fortress with its open gate impassively. "He has had his ten minutes. Resume the attack, but do not send any more A'Cha. Send in the thunder lizards." His band-mate nodded and ran off to relay the order. "Good bye, Balien, son of Britheon. Greet Navoi when you meet her in Zulanan."

Her arrow struck the Djido in the back of its leg and it fell to the ground. Illyria had chased Veeshar to the top of the turret and along the wall away from the fighting. Here, overlooking the raging Lyssal River, she finally had a good, clear shot. Killing it outright would have been preferable but one way or another, it was ending here.

She nocked her last arrow and approached it cautiously. It was smaller than she had thought it would be. *A race that had destroyed the six kingdoms of Anshara and brought centuries of war ought to be taller.*

"You won't use magic against me, will you?" she asked as it pulled itself to its feet. "Any spell you cast will free Eldoth and end this whole war, won't it? He has the Medallion of Negation—the one thing that can counter the Seal that you stole off of him—and the moment he's free, everything you've done falls apart. Either you cast a spell against me or you die." She drew her arrow back to her ear and sighted for its heart.

She saw the fear in its eyes. It made a gesture with its claw and she loosed her arrow.

A spasm of pain coursed through her as her arrow left the bow, causing her to shoot wide. She wasn't going to give it any more chance to bewitch her. She was standing alone on a wall with nowhere to hide facing a wizard that could kill her with a touch. *If I die now, I die fighting!* She rushed towards Veeshar and drew her sword. She had already won—Eldoth's power was freed—but she would end Veeshar's life if it was within her power.

Veeshar fell to the ground and her sword sliced the air above where it had been. Reversing her grip, she stabbed down at where its slender, sinuous body writhed on the ground. Her blade struck only stone as it...*slithered* away.

Was it magic or just some strange aspect of being Djido that allowed its arms and legs to absorb into its body and slither away like...well, like a *snake*? It was a question best answered by scholars, for Illyria wasn't going to stop to ask it. She gave chase, unwilling to allow it to gather itself and cast another spell at her. She had no desire to become a newt.

It did neither. To Illyria's surprise Veeshar slithered up the wall and gave her a final, contemptuous glare. "There will be more," it spat just before leaping over the side. She looked over the wall in time to see its body get swallowed by the roiling waters of the river.

Eldoth couldn't describe the sensation, especially to a non-wizard. He could *feel* his magic. It sat inside him always, the centre of his being, he just couldn't touch it. It was like in a dream, when no matter how much you tried to catch some elusive object it remained forever out of reach or dying of thirst tied to a tree right next to a stream of water. It was torture.

The opposite of that: when you finally reached while you dreamt or took even a sip from that stream, was the most exquisite of pleasures. It was better than a cold beer on a hot day, a dry bed after a monsoon rain, or an intelligent conversation after a year of being surrounded by idiots. He could try to explain this to Sephana, but she wouldn't understand or, even if she did, would never admit to it. Thus there was no point in responding to her queer look the moment after Veeshar's barrier between him and his magic disappeared. Instead he just growled 'we can proceed now,' and said no more.

She muttered something under her breath and held up her enchanted dagger. "Let's go."

They rounded the corner and the odour of unwashed, sweaty men hit them like a wall. The men in question, eyes ablaze with ensorcelled fanaticism, raised their weapons.

"Kill!" Draxul quacked as they ran forward.

Eldoth should have been frightened. The odds were terrible: two against twenty. Yes: he had the Medallion and could nullify the controlling spell, but not quickly or easily. He had to rely on Sephana to keep him safe, and that was why he was not afraid.

"Watch out," she warned before snapping her wrist, causing the weight on the end of her chain to hurtle forward like a sling stone and strike the lead soldier in his face.

She was like a reflection on the water: lithe and graceful, everywhere and nowhere at once, dagger flashing and chain swinging like extensions of her arms. There were twenty men in the room and none could get close enough to harm him no matter how hard they tried. She was magnificent.

"Any time soon," she grunted as she jerked a man forward with her chain and tripped him with her tail. "We're as surrounded as we're going to get."

Eldoth started and remembered why he was there. He stared into the Medallion, purged all thoughts of dancing from his mind and focused his will into it. "Tosh," he intoned, using the word as a guide for his thoughts and his magic. Vocal spellcasting was a novice's crutch, but, for this particular casting, he was leaving nothing to chance.

The violence and mayhem continued around him but Eldoth didn't notice. Unaspected magical energy—without colour—entered the Medallion of Negation and turned…every colour. It exploded out of the disk, primarily blue but with tinges of red, orange and colours he didn't recognize. When the bursts of magical energy struck an ensorcelled soldier his forehead glowed momentarily before he collapsed.

When Eldoth looked around him every man in the room had fallen to the ground, unconscious. Only Sephana, himself and Draxul remained standing.

Sephana couldn't believe that she'd done that. She had never fought so hard or so desperately before. She hadn't thought about her actions, she just…done them. The impossibility of her task and her exhaustion had combined to a point where her body had simply acted and, somehow, she'd done it. She'd fought off twenty men and the worst injuries that any of them had were bruises and shallow cuts.

She had to think now, and she was frightened. They were still in a room with an angry Tsrinn and there was no Balien or Theramus here to save them this time. She'd seen Draxul's late brother match Balien sword-stroke for sword-stroke—something she'd never seen anyone else do. She wasn't in Balien's league—not even close—and Eldoth hadn't done too well against the -axul brothers the last time, either.

She eyed Draxul warily. "Any ideas?"

"One." He extended his hand and a bolt of bluish lightning leapt from his hand. Draxul proved just as nimble as its brother and evaded. Eldoth released another bolt and again it leapt clear.

"Come on, hit it!" she urged.

"I challenge you to better," he snapped. Another bolt leapt from his hand. He stopped for a moment, then smiled. "Guard my side," he said curtly. He stepped forward and pushed both of his hands away from him. Draxul was already moving, stepping out of the way of the attack when both it and Sephana realized that there was no discharge of lightning, just Eldoth's hand movements. Draxul leapt in to attack and a bolt of blue energy leapt *from Eldoth's body* instead of his hands and struck the Tsrinn in its chest.

Waves of lightning radiated outward across its body and Draxul staggered but did not stop. More lightning struck it and enveloped its body but still the creature remained upright. "Use your chain!" Eldoth ordered her. "Bind it."

She didn't stop to think about how indignant she should be that he was ordering her around. She gave the chain one whirl and wrapped it around its leading leg. Pulling it tight, she jerked the chain to the side. The creature clutched at its leg and fell, screaming.

Draxul seemed to have completely forgotten them and writhed on the ground. Its leg was bleeding badly and looked…bent. *I didn't do that, did I? All I did was tighten the chain.*

Eldoth knelt next to Draxul and placed his hands on its head. "I could be merciful and end this for you," he spat with an anger that she had never heard from him, not even at his worst. "But I would rather that it was as painful as possible. Burn!"

It began to jerk and scream hysterically. Sephana watched in horror as the skin on its face began to darken and then smoke. Soon most of its skin was smoking and spots of black char began to appear. On its head, where Eldoth had touched it, the charred skin *split* and small flames began licking through the cracks. Draxul's screams were horrific and it began to thrash wildly as its body burned from the inside out. In less than a minute Sephana's dagger was wrapped around the leg of a charred corpse.

She looked at Eldoth in disgust, horror and fear. Who was he that he could inflict such cruelty? It took three attempts to find her voice. "Defences?" she finally squeaked.

The thunder of approaching dragon-lizards echoed through the open gate of the keep. They had dealt with the creatures singly and in pairs, but never in the numbers that approached them now. Theramus and Balien shared a grim look and waited in silence.

Eldoth stepped over the charred body of his former captor and strode stiffly to the far end of the room.

It took all of his effort not to vomit. Essential Flame was difficult to create and was especially deadly. Its viciousness had repulsed him and he had sworn to never summon it, but seeing Draxul in that room had resurrected every memory of pain and torment ever inflicted upon him. In that moment he had wanted Draxul and its duck-like voice to suffer and the forbidden spell seemed appropriate. He had not thought about how the sound of its death screeches, the smell of its flesh cooking, or the sight of its smouldering skin would affect him. He would never do such a thing again. He knew now that no one, not even Veeshar, deserved such a cruel fate, and that some magic was better not learned.

He had been unable to pull his eyes from the blackened corpse until Sephana had spoken. There was fear and revulsion in her eyes but, also, wary respect. It was that last part that allowed him, somehow, to harden his resolve. Whatever else he felt, he could not allow himself to appear weak before her. He had to convince her that he was strong and he would never admit to any errors. There was no nausea and there was no regret. There was only the next task.

He walked up to the obvious rune markings on the far wall and scribed appropriately. The wall flowed open as silently and smoothly as on the day of its creation, more than seven hundred years ago. The room beyond, untouched since the end of the Great War, was equally pristine. There was no dust—a spell that surely belonged to the orange college of magic; he would have to investigate that later—and no furniture save a large glass sphere in the centre of the room. The walls were covered in runework. Eldoth forgot everything that had come before as he stared in wonder at the intricate magic surrounding him.

"You can see through the walls," Sephana said with wonder. Her words broke his reverie. He looked and saw that some of the brickwork had indeed been rendered magically transparent. It was more orange magic, or perhaps green.

She made a horrified squeak and clutched Eldoth's shoulder painfully. "Eshath's Light, look! Eldoth, do something!" Eyes widening, she dropped her hands from him as if she'd been burned.

He looked at where she was pointing and saw a column of thunder lizards charging up the narrow ramp to the keep, twenty strong. The archers on the wall were shooting at them but having little effect. Standing in the courtyard just behind the open doorway were Theramus and Balien. They looked very small.

Eldoth reached out with his stele. "It's a simple matter. I have only to close the gate."

Sephana looked at him oddly. "But the gate is broken."

He made no reply, just scribed a line between two runes. In the courtyard the heartstone walls on either side of the open gate flowed towards each other as if made of water. The thunder lizard riders, only yards from the wall, were barely able to prevent their mounts from running headfirst into the now gateless wall.

He smiled at Sephana's incredulous expression. "That wooden construction was *not* the gate created for this keep. Obviously the Karolmen constructed it after the fall of the High Wizards." He shrugged. "It is fortunate for them that the last wizard here left it open or this building would just be an ornament on the top of a hill."

Ta stared at the fortress and its now featureless wall in shock. In the distance he could hear both angry cries of the thunder lizards and happy cheering from the human boars defending the walls. His band-mates stood near him in uncomfortable silence.

"It is—it is the Eye's will," he stuttered. "The fortress is not ours to take." He tore his eyes away from the unclaimed walls. "Recall the lizard riders," he ordered hoarsely. "We cannot attack them, but they are also unable to prevent us from crossing the river. Order the Lemm to move their clans across the bridge. We will occupy the town and move out in the morning."

Sephana's relief at Theramus's reprieve from death was short lived. "Oh no. They're going to cross the river." She felt her stomach fall into her pants as she watched the army of A'Cha, Vaulen and dragon-lizards march down the road and towards the bridge. There were thousands of them and she shuddered at the thought of how much devastation they could wreak against the Karalinian countryside.

Eldoth chuckled and the sound of it made her blood freeze. It wouldn't have bothered her five minutes previously, but Draxul hadn't been burnt to a cinder then, either. "What are you laughing at?" Her voice was shrill.

"You didn't examine the underside of the bridge earlier, did you?"

She hated him when he was like this. "No. Why?"

"Wait and observe." He ran his stylus across the wall.

Ta tallied the losses he had taken thus far. A few hundred A'Cha and twenty Vaulen were acceptable. He was more concerned that Veeshar was missing. The Djido had either died in the assault on the fortress, fled, or possibly even defected. Without the sorcerer present, he did not know for how much longer he could rely on the thunder lizards. He would order them killed tonight, once they were tethered. Confronting the Karalinian cavalry without them would be more difficult, but he could not risk advancing with so sharp a dagger pointing at his back.

Without Durnsuld he had no secure means of retreat and—more importantly—a vulnerable flank. It was no longer possible to march against the ice kingdom's capital. He would have to content himself with conquering and holding some lesser territory. Perhaps their king would be open to negotiation in the spring…

It is the Eye's will. I must accept that. It was a bitter thought, but undeniable. Gidim's lessons, when given, were invariably harsh

176

There was a deep booming noise and the ground shook beneath his feet. "What is that?"

The bridge out of this accursed valley was only yards ahead of him. He saw his soldiers on the bridge deck look at their feet in confusion. There was another boom. The bridge shook so hard that those on it stumbled and fell.

With sickening certainty, Ta knew what would happen next. The Eye had yet to fully inform its servants of its will. "Get off the bridge! Now!"

He was too late. A thousand A'Cha and Vaulen—a fifth of his army—fell into the river and were crushed against the rocks below.

Eldoth nodded with satisfaction and turned towards the glass globe in the centre of the room. It was lined with runework and it radiated an unknown colour of magic. Suddenly, Eldoth understood.

"The gates and even the bridge are minor acts of magic," he mused aloud, moving around the sphere's circumference and examining it closely. "There is no reason to create this room for things that would be so easily controlled elsewhere in the building. Mage-runes are invisible to the mundane eye and do not require such secrecy. It must fulfill another purpose."

He looked around. Sephana—oddly quiet—watched him warily. He pointed to the glass sphere. "This is the reason, right here. I thought there would be weapons in here, objects like the fear sigil we encountered, only on a greater scale, but then it occurred to me: this fortress was designed to be defended by wizards. *The wizards are the weapons*." He lay both of his hands on the sphere and felt the magics within. "What is needed is something to make a wizard more effective against a large group. This," he reached into his pocket and held up the Medallion of Negation, "and this." He pointed to the globe.

He laid one hand on the sphere and focused his power into the medallion. He could feel the powerful magic passing into the sphere and then multiply somehow—something that Eldoth thought impossible. In defiance of his understanding, the magnified magic of the Medallion enveloped all of the area outside the keep. With his expanded awareness he could feel all of Perceptus's enchantments break.

He did not need to look to know that the remaining dragon-lizards, now released from the spells that bound them, were undoubtedly very unhappy.

"What do we do, Olamm?" asked one of Ta's band-mates. He, like Ta, stared down into the chasm where hundreds of their comrades lay either crushed or drowned.

"Retreat," Ta ordered. It galled him, but he could no longer deny the Eye's will. His force was decimated, there was no way to advance, and the fortress was lost to him. What else was there but to retreat to the mountains?

There was a roar and a scream from behind him. Ta turned in time to see one of his tribe fall under an attacking thunder lizard.

"Still more punishments, Great Eye?" Turning to his soldiers, he ululated and raised his axe high. "To me, Vaulen, to me! Today the Eye tests us and I call on all of you now to prove that you are worthy. Kill these accursed lizards, no matter how many A'Cha it takes. Then find me the Djido, Veeshar, and bring me his head!"

Yes, the day was lost. Perhaps he was being punished for allying with a Djido or, worse, for defying the Khalamm, but such philosophical thoughts would wait for tomorrow. Today he was a warrior and an Olamm. His people needed him and there were monsters to slay.

Olamm-Ta raised his blooding-axe, gave a great war cry, and charged.

" 'Let us now sing the praises of Alwyn Longstrider, hero of Dragonhead Keep!' "

—The Taking of Dragonhead Keep, *anonymous*

CHAPTER SEVENTEEN

"Your highness, I've found another one!" one of Alwyn's men called, holding up a severed dragon-lizard head. He, like Alwyn and the other twenty seven survivors of Durnshold Keep, were labouring in the killing ground in the front of the keep. Alwyn saw no reason to deny them their search for booty and trophies, considering how much they had risked. None of them, Alwyn included, had anticipated being besieged when they had left Derwyn forty days ago.

"Put it with the others," he ordered, gesturing behind him to a line of severed dragon heads set upon stakes along the path to the keep. It was a gruesome and imposing sight. "Humph. They should call the place 'Dragonhead Keep.'"

A runner came down from the keep. "My lord Alwyn, riders from the south. Knights. There must be a hundred of them."

Alwyn nodded and cleaned as much dirt and grime from his coat as possible. He watched as the column of armoured soldiers, resplendent in their matching colours and banners, rode along the length of Northmarch Bridge, now back into position.

The man at their head was older and bore the crest and colours of Northhaven. He reined in his horse in front of Alwyn. "Who by the Light of Eshath are you?"

Alwyn bowed. "My lord Jannery, I am Alwyn ap Gwyn, Prince of Derwyn. I am pleased to finally make your acquaintance."

Willem Jannery's face clouded in confusion. "Alwyn? From *Nemora?* By Emuranna and all the Makers, how did you come to be here? Where is Lord Hanley?"

"Lord Hanley fled the keep when it was attacked, my lord, and was injured. He rests in Northhaven." Alwyn smiled. "As for why I am here, there was no one else and my conscience demanded that I act."

The mounted lord looked shocked. "No one else? What idiocy has my son been up to?"

"A question you should ask him yourself, my lord." Alwyn owed the boy no favours, but he would not betray him to his father.

"Some idiotic conspiracy, no doubt. I'll flay his hide." He eyed Alwyn appraisingly. "You came anyway, and risked your life for my people. You are a hero, sir."

Alwyn coloured. "You are kind, my lord, but the true hero here is Illyria Exiprion."

"Illyria? The elf princess?"

"And her companions, yes. Victory would not have been possible without them."

He dismounted and walked up to Alwyn. "The keep is secure? You have routed the enemy?"

"Yes, my lord. The survivors have fled back into the mountains."

"I'll have their heads if they have not," Hanley muttered. He turned to the knight at the head of the column. "Sir Lanton, would you do me the honour of harrying any survivors and ensure that none remain in the Northmarch?"

The knight saluted. "With pleasure, my lord." He motioned to his subordinates and the column of horses proceeded out of the valley.

Lord Jannery put his arm around Alwyn and led him into the keep. "You must tell me everything that happened, prince Alwyn, starting with what manner of creature belonged to this head. Is it a dragon?"

"It is a very long story, my lord." They passed into the threshold of the keep.

Sir Berand Dasanny was the senior-most knight in Durnshold and second in command behind Harrin Hanley, Gennald's father. He had slept, bathed, changed into clean clothing, and was now overseeing his men as they began the arduous task of cleaning up.

"I remember my time under the Seal," he explained to Illyria, "but it doesn't seem real. If I hadn't woken up covered in filth and seen all the bodies, I'd have thought it a horrible dream." He looked over the wreckage of the courtyard and the shattered wooden gate. "Forgive my asking again, My Lady, but are you certain that my lord Hanley is alive and well?

"He was asleep when I last saw him two days ago," Illyria assured him, "but his fever had broken and he was recovering. I am sure he's fine now."

"Emuranna's Grace. He's a good knight. If he hadn't gotten word out, none of this would have happened, would it? You'd never have gotten your warning, the dogmen would have crossed the river and Emuranna knows how many people they'd have killed."

"I'm sure that he will get the recognition he deserves," she assured him.

There were shouts from the other end of the courtyard. Illyria turned and saw several soldiers fall to one knee as their lord, Willem Jannery, walked through the (now re-opened) gate. Alwyn and a pair of knights followed him.

Illyria bowed. "My lord. Your return is unexpected, but welcome."

"I was delayed in Sukhold and received word that Durnshold had been taken. I gathered what troops I could and returned as soon as possible." He looked around him. "I see that my return was unnecessary. I understand that I have you to thank for that?"

"In part. It would not have been possible without Prince Alwyn's bravery."

"Yes, yes. You have both been very quick to praise each other," Lord Jannery said gruffly. "I am a march-lord, my lady, a soldier sworn to keep my kingdom's border safe, not some courtier from Aukaster. I have no patience for the double-speaking games of politics. Tell me what has occurred here, plainly and from the beginning. Do not leave out any details, no matter how damning—especially if they concern my son."

Illyria hid a smile. She had forgotten how much she liked the gruff, straight-speaking noble. "Yes, my lord."

He stared across the courtyard. "Eshath's Light! What foul creature is that?"

Illyria did not need to look to know who he was referring to. "Her name is Sephana, my lord. She is my friend, not 'some creature', and she was instrumental in the retaking of the keep. You owe her your thanks, not revulsion."

He continued to stare. "She has a snake's tail. Is she…"

"She is an Anduilman, as we all are," Illyria answered evenly. "Her ancestors were enslaved by the Djido and she bears their mark, but she is honest and loyal."

"It's true, my lord," Alwyn added, flicking Illyria a guilty glance. "Sephana fought with us from the beginning. You shouldn't judge her by her race."

Lord Jannery looked between Illyria and Alwyn. "I am hardly in a position to argue with the heroes of the hour. If you name her your friend, then I will as well." By his expression he remained unconvinced.

Illyria changed the subject. "Shall I tell you about what happened now, my lord?"

"Yes. Do you have any food or wine? I have a feeling this story will take a while."

"I'm sorry, my lord. The A'Cha—pardon me, the *dogmen*—consumed everything during their occupation."

"Never mind. I brought my own. Now, start at the beginning. How did a bunch of stupid dogmen take my keep?"

Illyria's explanation lasted into the afternoon.

"I'm sorry, I did not realize how it was for you," Theramus apologized to Sephana. He had been watching how the men of the keep, now freed from Veeshar's grip, looked at her. He did not like what he saw. "I understand now why you dress as you do and hide who you are. I was wrong."

She wore a short-sleeved blouse that clearly displayed the lines of scales that ran across her arms and shoulders. Her tail hung freely. "No, you were right. I *was* ashamed of who I was, and I don't need to be anymore. I keep forgetting that I have friends who will stand beside me now." She leaned back and met his eyes. "Thank you for before, under the waterfall. What you did and said, it means a lot."

"I meant every word," he said sincerely, "but do not endanger yourself for my sake. I will respect you no matter what face you present to the world."

"You have a big opinion of yourself, don't you?" She slapped his knee lightly with the tip of her tail. "Don't worry. I'm doing this for me. I'm tired of hiding. I don't think that Alwyn's reaction to me would have been as bad if he'd known what I was from the beginning." She grimaced. "Besides, I hate wearing clothes that don't fit."

You will always have my support." He looked around. "Where is Eldoth? I have not seen him since breakfast."

"He's, uhh..." She paled and swallowed then waved a hand vaguely upward. "Still in his secret room, looking around."

Theramus grew concerned. She looked more frightened than she had been on the keep's wall. "Are you well? What happened when the two of you were alone? Did Eldoth do something to you?"

She didn't meet his eyes. "He didn't do anything to me. Nothing happened." She shrugged and continued in a lighter voice. "He's sulking because we never recovered the Seal of Perceptus. I guess Veeshar had it on him when he jumped. Do you think he's alive? I don't see how anything could have survived that river."

"I do not know. Only time shall tell."

If she wished to avoid the subject than he would humour her for the moment but he would get to the truth of what transpired between her and Eldoth. He would also watch the wizard closely. He still did not trust the man.

"I want to create an order of knights," Illyria stated abruptly.

Theramus looked at her, concerned. She had been lost in thought throughout dinner, not that any of them were speaking much after the long, laborious day. All of the draft animals in Durnshold had been consumed during its occupation, and the unpleasant task of body disposal had to be performed by hand.

"I think that you should explain yourself, Lyri," Balien said.

She blinked, as if she had just realized that she had said an unformed thought aloud. "Sir Gennald explained the idea of knighthood and fealty to me. He said that a knight swears loyalty to his lord and in turn becomes his lord's representative. It becomes his duty to uphold his lord's ideals."

"But that's stupid," Sephana protested. "What happens if your lord is an idiot? Sir Gennald marched himself right into jail and closed the door when Davin told him to."

Balien's brow furrowed. "She has a point. Who would these knights be sworn into service to?"

"The High King," Illyria answered.

Theramus fought to conceal his smile. *It is happening!*

Everyone else exchanged glances. "There is no High King," Balien said. "Not anymore, anyway."

"It was the responsibility of the High King to protect Anshara against foreign invaders," Illyria continued. "No one has done that in five hundred years, and look at the state of our world: A'Cha and Vaulen attack from the mountains with impunity, raiders maraud the coastal cities, and everyone pretends that it isn't happening. No one cares about what happens beyond their borders, and it's even worse in Nemora. Veeshar said something to me before he escaped. He said 'more are coming'. The Shieldstone is weakening, the Djido are starting to return, and nobody is doing anything about it. That's why we have to."

Balien's face was troubled. "A noble goal, but what does this have to do with knighthood?"

"A knight swears an oath to Emuranna to obey his lord and uphold his ideals. That oath cannot be overruled or countermanded by anyone. Even a king cannot command a knight to betray the loyalty of his lord."

Balien continued to press. "I would guess that becoming a knight would mean that you're breaking off your engagement. Lyri, is this just about finding a way out of your promise?"

"No!" She paused. "Maybe that was part of it at first, but it's more than that. Whether or not I get married next month is meaningless compared to the safety of the whole world. Mother and Kefius will be angry, but they'll have to accept that I can contribute more to Ilthanara's future as a knight than just continuing the royal bloodline. I believe that and I'm not going to apologize for it."

"I believe that as well," Theramus announced. His heart could not contain the pride he felt. "The path you propose to follow is one I have sought for many years. You have done great things in the short time that I have known you, Illyria, and you will do greater in the days ahead. I will walk by your side."

"Thank you." She turned to her brother. "Balien, will you stand with me?"

His face was stone. "I will swear to Emuranna and I will fight by your side, but I will not give blind service to any man," he warned her.

"That's enough," she assured him.

"Then, like in all other things, I am with you."

She smiled widely and turned to Sephana. "I know this isn't ever what you planned to do, but will you help me in this?"

She looked at Illyria pensively. "I used to be a slave. I'm a Reshai. My ancestors are our enemies and even my own people hate me. I've done…a lot of things that I'm not proud of. Are you sure you want me?"

"None of those things matter, not to me, not to her, nor to anyone here. You acted with intelligence and courage and I would be honoured to have you stand by my side."

"As would I," Theramus murmured.

Sephana brushed away a tear. "Then I'm yours."

"No, in this we are equal," Illyria corrected. "We are all Emuranna's, and the High King's. I don't demand your loyalty or your obedience."

"I'll be a knight with you," she whispered.

Illyria turned to Eldoth, who had been silent thus far. "I would be happy if you would join us, Eldoth, but I understand if you feel that this is too much to ask."

"The High Wizards swore a very similar oath," he said gruffly. "All Wizards and Arch-Wizards had to swear their loyalty to the crown. I have no objections, on the condition that you do not hinder me in my pursuit of magical knowledge. Such knowledge benefits all of us."

"I have no objection."

"Then I accept."

Illyria took a deep breath then looked at Sephana and Eldoth. "There is one condition, however, that I will impose onto the two of you." Eldoth frowned in irritation while Sephana's face tightened in worry. "I understand that the two of you have a history together and that has caused some differences. I wouldn't mention this if there was any indication that you could keep your grievances private, but you haven't." She looked at both of them sternly. "I will not have this Order founded on bitterness and acrimony. Your marriage ended years ago and both of you are different people now. Eldoth, Sephana, can you move past your differences and treat each other as adults?"

Eldoth looked offended and Sephana ashamed. They exchanged glances. She tried to hide the fear in her eyes but could not do so, not against Theramus. "It won't be a problem," she said quietly. Eldoth looked strangely sad but hid it as well.

"We need a name," Balien said after an awkward moment of silence. "All knightly orders have names, don't they?"

Illyria thought for a moment. "I don't want anything too pretentious. I think the 'Knights of Anduilon' describes us enough."

He nodded. "I like it."

"As do I." Theramus had thought this path lost, but Illyria had re-found it.

The night sky was beautiful. At rest at last, Theramus stood on the wall of Durnshold and surrendered himself to the cosmic spectacle. Alalaree, the 'Mirror of Heaven', hung above him and for the first time in months he was free to enjoy the panorama. It was all coming together, finally.

A boot scuffed behind him and he turned. It was Balien, silent as a cat as usual except for the one sound that had revealed him. They nodded in silent greeting to one another—Balien was never one for idle chatter—and observed the stars together in comfortable silence.

"Down by the waterfall," Balien began casually, "you mentioned that you were once known as the 'Steel Colossus'."

"That was many years ago, before you were born."

"You slaughtered an army?"

"I may have...exaggerated." They both laughed.

They were both silent for a while. Again, Balien spoke. "When I was fighting Olamm-Ta, he said that he'd seen my style of fighting before. He said that I fought like a prince from Kalumfar."

Theramus looked over at Balien's silhouette. "Is that so?"

"My father taught me to fight and he gave me my sword. I've never seen anyone fight like he did and he never told me where he learned. You've travelled. Do you recognize my sword style? Do you think he may have come from Kalumfar?"

Theramus thought on his reply. "I have seen the fencing style of the Kalumfari princes. There are similarities between how they conduct their honour duels and how you fight, it is so, but you have moved far beyond that. Your style of fighting is your own. As for your father, I do not know. Perhaps."

"I don't know who I am, Theramus," he admitted quietly. "I know who I'm not: I'm not just some mongrel half-blood tolerated because of his sister. I know that I am Britheon's son, but I don't know who he was and probably never will."

He had never heard Balien speak so. "That is not who you are, it is who you were. You *are* a Knight of Anduilon, and you are my friend," he said with sincerity. "The greater question is who you will be, and that answer we can discover together. It will be so."

Balien thought for a moment and nodded. "We should go back inside. I think they're ready."

"I will be along shortly."

Theramus watched him disappear into the darkness. He looked so unassuming but, if Theramus was correct, he was so very important. He had not been completely truthful. He *did* recognize Balien's fighting style. Yes, there were several aspects that were distinctly his, but its core was similar to Theramus's own. His own sword, untouched for twenty five years, was much the same as Balien's. As the Steel Colossus, his body sheathed in impenetrable steel plate, he had used it to cut a swath through the Akkilinian army and ensure the escape of his Prime. That man's name had been Baldwin, not Britheon, but Theramus had passed the fencing style of the Anduili High Kings as it had been taught to him. He that thought that line had been severed, but perhaps it did in fact live on.

Please, Mother of Wisdom, let this man and these people be enough to save our world. He did not know if Emuranna was listening, but made the prayer anyway. *Please, Great Goddess, let it be so.*

The oxen stood patiently, content to wait and chew their cud until being given the order to move out. They'd feasted on southern oats and rye for the last fourteen days and looked strong enough to easily haul the heaping wagons of Karalinian goods back to Derwyn.

Alwyn leaned down to share (yet another) good-bye kiss with his new fiancé. Elorin returned it as eagerly as decorum allowed, considering that they were being watched by her father and a hundred smiling Nemormen. "I'll be back in the spring, my love," he promised her, "and then we can be wed."

"I miss you already," she pouted cutely. "No winter will ever feel longer."

"It will be your last one surrounded by ice and snow," he promised. He took both of her hands and held them to his heart. "Next year we'll celebrate Year's End with wine and fresh flowers."

She leapt up and wrapped her arms around her neck. "Hurry back," she whispered into his ear.

"An army of dogmen couldn't keep me away," he murmured. He'd been so blind before, not to see how perfect and beautiful she was.

Lord Willem cleared his throat and they parted reluctantly. Elorin, flushed red and rejoined her father and brother in front of their manor house. Davin had been released from his room only on the condition that he say nothing more than decorum demanded. Willem had been thrilled with the offer of marriage to Elorin and had heaped Alwyn's wagons with gifts, both for the engagement and in thanks for the Nemorman's deeds.

"Farewell, my lord," he said formally to his future father-in-law. "I shall be counting the days until my return."

Willem nodded in return. "May Emuranna bless your travels. Good journey, son."

Every soldier in Northhaven, resplendent in their gleaming yellow and black tabards, lined the road to the gate. It was a pleasant contrast to the last time they had left the city. Ten horsemen and twenty footmen headed by Sir Gennald waited outside to escort them to the edge of the marchlands. Illyria and her companions waited alongside them. His horse—resplendent in its freshly tailored 'clothes'—waited for him.

He could not look on the beautiful Ilthanaran princess without a pang of regret. Did he love her still? Yes, and no, but he also knew that he could never have her. She was magnificent and perfect, but he knew that she was meant to be so much more than the wife of a petty prince.

She looked different than the last time he had seen her. Certainly her travel garb was cleaner, but there was something else about her: a contentment that hadn't been there before.

She nodded in greeting as she fell into step beside him. "Your highness."

"My lady," he replied. "You're still choosing to remain? I cannot convince you to return with me?"

She smiled. It was not the first time they had shared this conversation. "You can follow the road back to Nemora just fine on your own. Besides, we're needed here."

"So you're all knights now, sworn to defend all of Anduilon." He shook his head bemusedly. "If anyone can do it, Illyria, it's you."

The brightness of her smile was rivalled by the sparkle of her brown eyes. "Thank you. You still have the package I gave you, and you'll follow my instructions?"

It wasn't the first time they'd had this conversation, either. "Yes, I still have your ring and, yes, I will take to the edge of the Ilthwood. When the border guards confront me I'll give them the message you had me memorize. Don't worry, Illyria. I'll honour the trust you've placed in me."

"Thank you."

"No, thank you for everything you've done." He turned to look at her. "I'm engaged to a wonderful woman, I'm the heir to the richest kingdom in Nemora and I've finally earned my name. I would never have had any of that if you hadn't pushed me into it. I don't know why chose me as the target of your generosity, but you did, and for that I thank you. I hope…I hope you find happiness." He hoped that he didn't sound too bitter. "You deserve it."

She smiled and kissed his cheek. "Thank you, Alwyn. You deserve your happiness too, with Elorin."

Sephana stood with the others and watched as Alwyn and his caravan of wagons and men disappeared into the endless sea of deep green pine. People still eyed her cautiously but word of who she was, what she had done and who her friends were had spread. She still felt a little frightened but, mostly, she felt free.

"So, we said that we're going save the world, right?" she said into the silence. "What's first?"

END

Did you enjoy this novel?
There is more at www.titanheart.ca.

Read novels, download podcasts and check out exclusive on-line content including:

- *Additional and deleted scenes*
- *Previews of upcoming work*
- *The Titanheart database (The 'Library of Alashadimm')*
- *Character Profiles & More*

Why Titanheart?

- *Weekly Updates*
- *On-line content is always free*
- *Two complete novels published per year*
- *Your choice of format: Novels, PDFs, Kindle, iPad, MP3s, Podcasts*

About this book: This novel was written in Microsoft Word 2007 on a HP netbook PC running Win7 Starter. It uses the Americana BT, Stoertebeker, and Times New Roman fonts and uses a customized formatting template created by the author. All significant editing and formatting was done by the author (though he'd be happy to pawn the job off on someone else if they offered).

About the Author: Ross is an intellectual, creative geek and proud of it. He has had many jobs but in his heart he has always been a writer. It took twenty years of frustration and a world-wide recession before he finally found the courage to become a full-time novelist. His education, like his career, is widely varied. Notable among his many literary influences are Jacqueline Carey, web author Minisinoo, Andy McNabb and Suzanne Brockmann.

Ross currently resides in Edmonton, Alberta where, when not writing, he spends his free time kayaking, trying to create the perfect bottle of mead, and torturing others by means of karaoke.

www.ingramcontent.com/pod-product-compliance
Lightning Source LLC
Chambersburg PA
CBHW072131170626

46813CB00004BA/1528

* 9 7 8 0 9 8 6 6 8 7 7 0 9 *